KILLER
CONDO

KILLER CONDO

A Melanie Deming Manhattan Mystery

NANCY GOOD

LeVel
BEST BOOKS

First edition

ISBN: 978-1-68512-710-7

Cover art by Level Best Designs

This book was professionally typeset on Reedsy.
Find out more at reedsy.com

For Aimee, the best cheerleader and friend there was.

Praise for Killer Condo

"Nancy Good's *Killer Condo* sticks a sharp knife into the cutthroat world of high-end New York City real estate, and the result is a rollicking ride of a story. With wit and humor, the plot unfolds in a setting of luxury apartments, exclusive private schools, and dressed-to-kill characters. The writing is sharp, the plot engaging, and the resolution satisfying. Unlike the victim at the heart of this twisty novel, fans of The Melanie Demming Manhattan Murder mysteries run no risk of buyer's remorse."—Lori Robbins, award-winning author of the On Pointe and Master Class mystery series

"*Killer Condo* is a cool murder mystery in a luxurious, high-end building, where the price tags of condos are as lofty as the egos of the prospective buyers. At an exclusive viewing, the glamorous setting quickly turns grim when one of the guests is found dead. Enjoy the hijinks of Melanie Deming among the rich and rotten."—Sonia Pilcer, Author of *The Last Hotel*

Chapter One

I should have realized an open house for a $4.6 million Park Avenue condo was never going to be just another amusing hour spent in the company of over-privileged, underweight women being catty about dated decor.

Being fully transparent, I already knew when I was around this group that bad scenes happened. Cornelia blamed this on my annoying honesty. Rebecca said I'm just clueless. But really, nothing that took place at the open house was my fault at all. Susie Carlbach, the real estate broker, should never have invited me.

Still, looking back at the events *after* that morning's disaster, I have to admit I just possibly went looking for trouble. And found it.

* * *

It was a Tuesday morning in September when I got the invite to view an apartment with an eight-hundred-square-foot terrace and seven thousand dollar monthly maintenance. Susie, the broker, was a fellow parent at the Huntley Day School. The rumor around school was she had closed a deal for a $25 million Midtown triplex in New York City. So, in her world, a $4.6 million place was practically a dump, and Daniel and I could afford it. Wrong. My husband and I were writers, and not the John Grisham kind. $4.6 million, to us, was the GNP of a small nation.

The invitation was no chintzy postcard, but a ten-page book of glorious eye candy.

A vast living room, with charming French doors that opened onto the planted terrace. A dining room large enough to host a state dinner. So cozy. Those two rooms, placed end to end, could easily have swallowed our entire rent-controlled apartment, where nothing had changed in the forty years since Daniel's parents had moved in. We'd inherited it, along with its dirt-cheap (by Manhattan standards) rent just by moving in when they moved out.

I continued turning the pages of the slick booklet.

> *"Entering this gracious home, built by renowned architect Rosario Candela, you are greeted by a magnificent five hundred square foot gallery."*

The gallery was larger than studio apartments. Here in the Big Apple, that entryway alone would run $750,000.

The person to ask about this strange invitation was Cornelia Waterbury—Park Avenue denizen, Huntley parent, and unexpected friend who knew everything about the tribal rituals of multi-millionaires, because she was one. I called and got lucky; she answered instead of her secretary. I jumped right in.

"I got an invite to an open house on Park Avenue, and I can't figure out why Susie wasted the postage. I don't suppose you got one."

"Well, *hello* to you *too*, Melanie." Cornelia's tone implied that my telephone etiquette, like so much else about my breeding, was lacking. "Yes, I got an invitation, although I don't know why. It's a bit insulting, really, since she knows four thousand square feet is half the size of my apartment. It's a starter Park Avenue place." I could almost see her sneer. "Why *you* got one is easier. Susie thinks because you sold a screenplay, and Daniel's latest cookbook is in stores, you could be in the market for a small Park Avenue place."

I sneered back.

"Small Park Ave place? You and Susie live in some alternate universe. And by the way, a screenplay option for a first-timer like me doesn't pay for two of your Chanel suits. Royalties on books take years to earn, if the publisher ever coughs them up, and don't forget the agent takes fifteen percent." I let out a martyr's sigh. "I have a perverse interest in going though. Is there a dress code?"

"Why would you ask me that?" Cornelia laughed her familiar, tinkly, snide laugh. "You never take my advice on clothes, remember? You always 'do your own thing.'

"Well, I have to do my own thing; I certainly can't afford to do yours. Come on. Give me some ideas. Jeans are out?"

"My valuable opinion is that what you wear to an open house on Park Avenue doesn't matter. How much money you have does."

"For once, I agree with you. So, I'll see you there?"

There was a long pause.

"Only if you're willing to be the buyer, and I'm there to give you advice. Can you really pull that off, considering your past performances at Huntley affairs? Airing your views on the wretched excesses of the rich and why we should all eat tasteless macrobiotic food? I'm not sure you can handle an acting job like this."

I should have said forget it. But curiosity won over a queasy uneasiness.

"I'm not macrobiotic. And, of *course,* I can pull it off," I said, though I wasn't sure at all. "I don't want to get flooded with calls from agents. Daniel and I are never giving up our apartment unless death or divorce do us part." I heard Cornelia drum her nails on her ivory-inlaid telephone table.

"There you go again, with your annoying honesty," she said. "I know I'll regret this."

"I hope *I* don't," I laughed nervously.

"I'll meet you there tomorrow at 11:45," said Cornelia.

Click. She was gone.

Maybe I was bored. I definitely had writer's block since my screenplay, *Playground Hero,* was now in the hands of a production company, and my writing partner, Devon, was traveling again. Full disclosure: he was more than a writing partner. But I tried not to think about that. I'd sworn it would only happen once.

Then there was my column, "Aftermath," in the *Wild Westsider* online paper, where I covered police investigations on the West Side and interviewed people impacted by the crimes. It was engrossing, but not as exciting as solving a murder and working on the screenplay with Devon.

At this open house, the only crime I was likely to hear about would be insider trading from investment bankers. Maybe Harold, my editor, and upstairs neighbor would be open to that new twist.

I suddenly realized I had paced in and out of the kitchen four times. I stopped in front of my herb cabinet. Thirty bottles of remedies called to me. I pulled out six bottles and mixed twenty drops each together with spring water, including ficus carica for the stomach and California poppy and passionflower for calming. Other people take pills, I take herbs and have been known to preach just a bit, that they can fix everything from panic attacks to altitude sickness.

I sat in one of the oak chairs around the small kitchen table and drank the mixture, relieved Daniel wasn't home shaking his head at me. He was a well known restaurant reviewer and cookbook editor. Herbs were only meant to be used on large quantities of meat, according to Daniel. We were definitely the odd couple.

My pedometer said 4,672; way too low for this late in the morning considering I'd already been to fencing class. Twice around the Central Park reservoir would get me near 14,500 steps, the point where I got an endorphin buzz. A therapist once warned me not to become an exercise addict. I told her there are worse addictions.

* * *

Nine-sixty-two Park Avenue, as I gazed at it in the almost-noon sun the next day, looked like every other imposing building on Park. All were built in the 1920s and '30s. All held out the promise of elegant, oversized rooms and glass-paned French doors but on the condition that only the staid and boring would be approved. Too big a price if you asked me. But then, I couldn't afford to live here anyway.

The white-gloved doorman was trying hard not to look annoyed at having so many strangers trekking through his gleaming lobby, leaving dirt on the oriental rugs, sitting on the soft leather couches and velvet armchairs.

"Hi, Melanie. Super surprised to see you here." Buffy Clifford looked me up and down as she sat on a couch. She was a power broker among the Huntley School mothers; I had clashed with her at many a parent meeting. Buffy, and Fawn Billings, her second-in-command, took in my outfit with undisguised disdain—black jeans, a no-name blouse, and a trusty old Theory blazer. Clearly not up to their East Side standards. Buffy was in a blue sleeveless silk A-line with a matching cardigan. I don't do cardigans. Fawn wore a carbon copy in yellow.

"You Eastsiders look like you're having so much fun, I just had to come." It took effort not to laugh. "But why are you here? Looking to buy?"

Buffy dismissed my question with an annoyed shake of her perfect blonde bob. She had come to snoop, just like I had. Her townhouse could swallow up two apartments this size. I continued to the elevator. Buffy returned to huddle with Fawn.

The eighth-floor private landing was so filled with flowers, I thought I'd stumbled into a wake. The overpowering perfume of lilies made me sneeze onto the back of a woman standing in the small landing who jumped as if she'd been bitten by a python. It turned out to be Susie Carlbach, the broker who'd invited us all. She had the exclusive listing to sell this apartment. Anyone who bought it had to go through her. Other agents brought their clients to these showings. If their client bought, Susie and the agent split the commission.

"Sorry," I chirped, though really her florist should be apologizing.

Susie shook her head and muttered something. With an annoyed flick of her hand, she motioned me in. Susie was decked out in a beige linen suit, her expertly streaked Martha Stewart hair, huge gold ball earrings and heavy gold bracelets attempted to proclaim that she didn't really need this sale. I scooted past the prospective buyer she'd been fawning over—a slim, striking woman dressed in a form-fitting grey silk suit with a low-cut pink silk camisole. Long legs punctuated with three-inch patent slingback heels, impeccable skin, outrageously high cheekbones that could have been augmented, and perfectly highlighted hair completed the picture; she looked like a Russian model or a news anchor, dripping sex appeal. Did she stare down her thin, straight nose at my Banana Republic jeans, or was I just having an attack of insecurity?

Susie was clearly infatuated with her and wanted me far away. Whoever Miss Cheekbones was, she had money. I did not.

The gallery was filled with browsers—and agents with their clients. Cornelia waved from the other end of the huge space. I made my way through the crowd, nodding at Babs Bernstein, who had to be here for purely social reasons. The terrace of her Park Avenue duplex occupied the entire roof of her building. Maybe she needed a place to put her parents when they visited.

"She'll probably get a full-price offer today," I heard as I passed a striking brunette talking to a sharply dressed man with slicked-back hair, who I assumed was her husband.

"Not a chance. The market's down." Mr. Slick clearly didn't want to be pushed.

"Where have you been?" Cornelia greeted me impatiently. "You're ten minutes late."

"It took me ten minutes to get off the elevator. It's like Wall Street when the market opens." I didn't just mean the size of the crowd. Everyone was dressed like a banker. My neat but humble black jeans were not Sevens, the $300 version of the moment. Why had I ever let Daniel's mother convince me to let her pay Chloe's tuition and drag us into this ridiculous private school world?

"Melanie, I see your face. Get a grip. Nobody cares that you look like you're out for a hike." Cornelia was in a pale mint suit, which might have been Chanel.

"Well, thanks for that, Cornelia. I feel so much better. Let's get on with the tour before I'm out of here."

Cornelia gave me an imperious nod and viewed the walls of the cavernous foyer. I snapped a photo of the room and the chattering crowd.

"This gallery is badly done. That generic striped wallpaper—it'll cost a fortune to get rid of it," she announced.

"Good to know. Goes in the minus column."

We glanced briefly at the suite-sized bedrooms, each wallpapered with contrasting borders of sailboats or birds or soldiers.

"Sloppy decorator. And it's ten years old, at least." With a wave of her hand, Cornelia dismissed the giant bedrooms. We continued on into the living room.

"The fireplace would be nice, except for the wall of mirrors." I raised my eyebrows at this tacky addition. We weren't the only ones staring in shock at the wall of floor-to-ceiling mirrors, which clashed badly with the Grecian columns on either end of the mantle. I snapped a picture.

"Shocking. Why didn't Susie consult a stager?" Cornelia closed her eyes and put her hand to her heart.

"Oh my God!" I heard a woman's voice shriek, from what sounded like the other end of the apartment. "Help! Someone!"

No one in the living room said a word.

"What's wrong?" I called out. Everyone, including Cornelia, just looked bored, as if they were in a scene from an Agatha Christie play. I had to do something.

Heart pounding, I ran through the dining room toward the voice. Near what must have been the maid's room, in the back outside the kitchen, I found Patty Baylor, another Huntley parent, sobbing and panting like she was in labor.

"Patty!" I grabbed her by both arms and shook her.

"Deep, slow breaths. Tell me what's going on." Patty pointed past me. At first, all I saw was a marble bathroom in a repulsive shade of mauve. After Cornelia's reaction to the mirrors, I thought maybe the color alone upset Patty. Then I looked down.

Sprawled between the toilet and the shower was Karen Sheldon, a former Huntley mom I recognized instantly, though her kids were older and had left for public schools a few years earlier. Her long-sleeved, expensive-looking silk paisley dress was short, exposing her model-skinny thighs. Wavy auburn hair, freshly blown out, was spread around her white face, which already had a horrible bluish cast. Thick mascara fringed now bulging eyes, and a slash of deep red lipstick outlined the tortured grimace of her mouth, making her look like a Japanese Kabuki actor.

Shaking, I stepped into the bathroom to look closer. Behind Karen's ear, I could see staples from a plastic surgery midlift, split open and oozing blood. Her surgery must have been done less than a month ago; it clearly hadn't healed enough to take the force of whatever had happened to her. I grabbed onto the sink while my stomach lurched. The sight of even tubes filling during a blood test repulsed me.

Why had I run toward the screams instead of freezing like everyone else? I needed caraway for my stomach and valerian to calm down. I didn't have anything. I took a deep breath and knelt to pick up Karen's limp wrist. No pulse, but her skin was warm and soft. She had died not long ago.

I thought about Ralph, the playground caretaker, who was cold and clammy and looked even worse when I'd found him a year ago. Detective Levano had made it really clear I should have known not to close a victim's eyes. I followed those orders now. But Karen's eyes would haunt me.

"Oh, I knew I shouldn't have come." Cornelia had arrived at the bathroom door, along with several other parents. "That poor woman." Cornelia looked closer; her mouth dropped open. "My God, to have her staples burst like that for everyone to see. Dr Rodenbeich will never get another patient."

Maniacal giggles threatened to erupt from my mouth. In this group, everyone knew who had done whose "work," and having your facelift bleed in public was a fate worse than death. I pressed my lips together. A loud guffaw right now would label *me* the callous and crazy one. I forced myself to look down at Karen. She must have been in her late forties, yet she could have passed for thirty-five with her muscled calves, slim waist, and swimmer's arms. Her cheeks and mouth had that too-tight look from her recent lift, and there were dark red marks on both sides of her neck. Her bright red nails were broken. She had struggled with her attacker. I wondered what the police would find under her nails.

"It looks like she's been strangled. We need to call the police," I said.

Several women on their phones nodded at me. But Amanda Schwartzkopf was taking a video. She worked with a TV network. I jumped up and tried to block her view of the body. "No pictures." I sounded like a *Law and Order* episode."Have respect."

Susie, the host of this gruesome party, appeared in the doorway looking almost as white as the victim. "What the f…"

A hand quickly reached out and pulled Susie's arm, whispered in her ear. It was her assistant. I'd bet she was reminding Susie cursing was a bad look for an agent.

"Can we please say the Lord's prayer?" Churchgoer Sandra Crane commanded the crowd. Obediently, everyone chanted, "Our father, who art in…" A tall man in a white shirt and tie pushed through the crowd. His name tag said Anthony Rjek. I guessed he was the super.

"What happened here? Everyone, go into the living room." Rjek directed the crowd, which turned and backed up as one, like a choreographed flash mob. Some of this group would leave. That wasn't good.

"You can't let people leave the apartment," I said to Rjek. "Anyone could be a suspect. The police need to talk to them." He looked at me like I was crazy.

"I don't have the authority to stop them, Ma'am."

With his height and British accent, I was pretty sure he could intimidate anyone. But I was in no position to argue; the waves of nausea in my stomach were just about to crest, and the nearest usable bathroom was far away. I darted out of the mauve marble crime scene.

I saw the back of a tall, thin man in a badly cut blue suit; he might as well have been wearing a neon sign flashing "Detective." The police had arrived, thank God.

"No one is to leave without giving their information to one of my officers," he said, addressing a large group in the dining room. There was a rumble of protest, as everyone recovered from their gawking and now wanted to get on with their day. These were not the kind of people who wanted to be identified with a crime scene, or detained from busy schedules.

"Where are you going?" One of the officers stopped me as I walked quickly through the room.

"Bathroom," I managed to mumble. He backed away but followed close behind.

I found the master bath, this one clad in a dark green marble with black specks that did nothing to help my nausea. It looked like a mausoleum. No wonder this place was so cheap, I thought, as I hurled up my breakfast. What kind of crime reporter got sick every time she saw blood?

Returning to the dining room, past the smirk of the cop who'd been standing outside the bathroom door, I saw Cornelia, who glared at me because she was trapped by Sandra Crane talking her ear off. Now Cornelia would blame me for the whole disastrous morning. I looked for Patty Baylor but surprisingly didn't see her. Then, I heard Mr. Slick confer with his stunning wife.

"I'll lowball it. She'll never sell the place now. Offer three million cash today." He took out his phone and tapped out an email.

What a bloodsucker, cashing in at a time like this. But what did I expect? This was Park Avenue, where even a murder was just another way to make a killing.

Chapter Two

I stepped back into the kitchen and noticed the floor was all orange Mexican tiles. Shockingly tacky for Park Ave.

Stop. Two hours with this crowd and I'd turned into one of them. Karen's body in the bathroom was the shocking disaster. A detective's brusque voice smacked me back to reality.

"Who found the victim?"

"Patty Baylor screamed. I guess she did," said Susie. "Melanie ran to help Patty. Melanie was here a minute ago."

I'd rather eat gluten than go back into that bathroom. *Just don't look down.*

"Here I am," I said. The detective was angular and tall, probably six feet. Even his face was long and thin, with pale skin that could have used sunlight, thinly stretched and scarred from adolescent acne, I'd guess. Clint Eastwood, but not as attractively weathered. Why is it that male movie stars have bad skin and don't get destroyed on Twitter, but women always have to be perfect? *Stay focused, Melanie.*

"Would you mind telling me what you saw?" He took out a pad.

"I heard Patty Baylor shout for help. We all heard her." I looked around for confirmation. Susie, the only other person left in the room, was suddenly preoccupied with her emails. "I ran here from the living room. Patty was hysterical. I don't know where she went."

The detective's calm exterior made me nervous. Levano, from the 24th precinct, would have exploded by now, since suspects likely had already fled the scene. This detective's badge said Robert Chilton. Sounded like a prep school. Only on the East Side would they make sure to have a white, male, calm, Protestant detective with a name and appearance that could pass at an old-school investment bank like Solomon Bros. If he had on a suit from Brooks Brothers.

I glanced at Karen's body. And surveyed the bathroom. Something was missing.

"Where's her bag?"

"What bag?" Chilton eyed me suspiciously.

"Look around. Every woman here has a pocketbook or briefcase. I don't see Karen's."

I could see the apartment's back door from the bathroom. It would have been simple for Karen's attacker to leave through the rear door with her bag.

"What's your name? Are you a housewife, homemaker, I'd suppose is the right word?" he asked.

"Melanie Deming, writer for a newspaper." I didn't have to tell him, but his crack about housewives annoyed me.

Chilton's left eyebrow lifted just enough to show me he was surprised. "Are you the one who got involved in that playground murder last year? Levano and Brown's case?"

"The very one."

"I've read your column. What are you doing here?" I couldn't tell if he thought my column was laughable or worthy of a Pulitzer. The Wild Westsider wasn't the NYTimes or the Daily News, but it was read by more upper Westsiders than any other small paper.

"I came for the open house. Susie invited me." Chilton looked puzzled by a crime reporter hanging out with Park Avenue moms.

"Were you looking to buy?" He was annoyingly amused.

"Nope. Social outing and being nosy. You know, see how the other half lives." Susie let out a muffled snort.

Chilton ignored her. "There's no pocketbook or briefcase here. We'll look around the apartment."

"If it's gone, that could be a motive, right?"

He shook his head. "Jumping to conclusions is not how crimes get solved." A flush of embarrassment made me turn red. He examined the floor.

"Here's her phone." He put on a pair of plastic gloves and took out a Ziploc bag. Bending down, he carefully removed an iPhone from under Karen's foot. I would have liked to scroll through that.

Susie edged closer to the door. The reality that Karen would not get up off the floor was hitting us.

"Please go into the dining room so my team can get in here. " Chilton said. Susie was out the door before he stopped talking. A sale might await her."Don't leave without getting your ID photographed by the officers," he called after her. "I suppose we already have your ID, Ms. Deming,"

"Probably." *Shut up and leave*, I told myself. But someone had to get this guy to check out the whole building. "That's the back door. Whoever did this could easily have used it," I nearly shouted.

"Maybe," Chilton sighed, bored. "But did you try the door to see if it was open?" He walked over and turned the handle, still wearing his plastic gloves. It was locked. "Unlikely a murderer would leave and have a back door key to relock it. Never assume anything." His condescending smile was like a bullfighter's red flag waving in my face. I jumped in too loud and too fast.

"Maybe the attacker had an accomplice who locked it after the murderer left. Or the door is one of those where you push the button on the inside of the frame, and that locks it." This guy negated everything I said. The fact that I'd fought a killer and gotten the mother and son convicted meant nothing to him.

"Some of her nails are broken. A woman like Karen would never let her nails break unless she was fighting for her life." The muscles around Chilton's mouth moved slightly as he held back a retort. He was just like every other cop, but with a coat of Park Avenue polish. He motioned for me to leave the bathroom. I ran out the door but heard him order an officer to search the building.

Back in the huge kitchen, where I bet only caterers had ever actually cooked, there was a Viking double stove. A SubZero refrigerator was hidden behind a front panel that matched the creamy beige cabinets, complete with narrow columns down the sides. It was a rich person's fantasy of Provence.

There were at least twenty people, mostly women, standing in clusters

13

around the dining room devoid of any furniture. There should have been a huge dining table to show off the room and give everyone a place to sit and talk.Chilton, if he was smart, could get information he'd now take weeks to find.

I recognized a fellow West Side Huntley mom, Gabby Marshall, dabbing at her eyes with a tissue. Her daughter was in Chloe's grade. I wondered how she'd known Karen.

Everyone talked in the hushed tones you hear at a wake, except for Susie's voice, trying hard to whisper but failing. Real estate agents lack the whispering gene in their DNA. Rachel, her assistant, listened intently.

"Karen just got the Harrington mansion listing. A huge coup. She was asking $45 million. I wonder whether the Harrington family will stay with Marc Olmsted's agency, now that Karen's gone."

Poor Karen's body was not yet cold, and Susie's mind was on money. I'd read about this mansion, a Beaux-Arts beauty and one of the few remaining untouched. I was surprised Susie wasn't dialing the Harringtons at that minute. But the big news to me was Karen was a real estate agent.

Their heads were now close together. I stepped as near as I dared.

"Karen wanted sixty percent of the commission. So, the agency would only have forty percent to split with the client's agent. Even if Marc Olmsted found his own buyers, he'd still never get his usual cut. Nobody gets sixty percent except owners, right?" Her assistant's head bobbed furiously. Susie continued.

"I heard she and Marc had lawyered up. They were barely speaking. Karen got the Harringtons to sign an exclusive with her alone. She must have offered them something. Marc couldn't get them away from her for an exclusive with him. He was furious. You know what he's like."

This was fabulous insider information for my column. Karen's colleagues at the Olmsted Agency would certainly be brought in for questioning. I was dying to text Devon, but Cornelia was still here. She already suspected Devon was more than a writing partner, and I didn't want to be grilled again.

I approached Cornelia, who impatiently scrolled on her phone, irritated to still be here.

"Did you know Karen was a real estate agent?" I asked.

Cornelia looked up. "Yes, she called me a few weeks ago to see if I was interested in selling. Very pushy, even for an agent. I'd never use Olmsted, even if I wanted to sell, which I don't."

"Why not?" I asked.

"Really? All right." She looked at me with the same slightly astonished look she'd used when I had to ask what SI and E meant when she described a diamond. Now I know it's the rating system for clarity and color, not that I'd ever be in the diamond market.

"Tom's grandfather was a founder of Christie's auction house, which now has a real estate division. So, of course, we would only use Christie's. Karen should have done her homework." Cornelia sniffed. Tom was Cornelia's husband, a banker with Morgan and Stern. Cornelia looked at her watch. "I really have to leave. My Pilates instructor is waiting."

What Cornelia said didn't make sense. Karen wasn't a pushy type.

"You sound like you don't like this Olmsted agency that Karen was with. Am I right?"

Cornelia gave me a raised eyebrow look. "Do I sense you're detecting again? I know you have this column thing. Bless Daniel for putting up with it all."

I was not getting baited into a fight. I waited.

"All right. If you insist. The Olmsted agency gives kickbacks from their fees to their clients, which makes it harder for all the other agencies not to do the same. They've been known to fight over the co-broker fee with agents who bring them buyers, even when it's all in writing. Marc Olmsted will swoop in and grab a client who's about to list their apartment with a competing agency. Let's say Corcoran and offer the client a reduced fee. But in the end, Olmsted will get his full fee. He'll take it from someone else. It's all the usual real estate double dealing but worse. And don't quote me, Melanie."

"Of course not, Cornelia. Never."

I did the math. Six percent commission on $45 million was $2.7 million. Karen had demanded sixty percent of that $2.7 million, which would have meant $1.5 million for her. If a real estate agent killed her, 1.5 million could be theirs. Money was a likely motive.

The crowd thinned out as each person gave their information to the police. They even had fingerprint kits for those who were willing. Never saw any organization like this on the West Side.

"Cornelia, before you leave, one more thing." She looked at me and at her watch. "I don't remember Karen Sheldon being a pushy type at Huntley, do you?"

She shrugged. "Going through a divorce, having to wait for alimony and child support, tends to make people aggressive. Karen threw herself into real estate because she needed money. She and Greg were divorced this year. Or maybe they're still negotiating. I heard he has a girlfriend, of course."

"So that's it. I didn't know."

"You're not a gossip Melanie, I will say that about you. It's admirable, but it leaves you clueless." She laughed.

"That's why I have friends like you." I sighed. "But Karen's dead. Who could have done it? She was pushy and maybe desperate about money. Do you think her ex would kill her because she wanted more alimony? Or is it something to do with real estate and that huge listing I heard she just got?

"Not the time or place to discuss such things," Cornelia said in her haughty tone, reminding me I had committed another faux pas. She placed her emerald green Gucci bag on her shoulder.

"Call me. Let's have lunch if you insist on pursuing this thing. But I'll remind you, the last time you got involved, you were close to being as dead as Karen!" She put her hand on her chest and sighed deeply.

"Cornelia, are you sure you're not related to my mother? Right now, I swear you're channeling her." Cornelia looked mildly offended.

"Someone's got to do it. You're lucky it's me." Her chin went up, making four carats' worth of diamond earrings glitter.

"I say prayers of gratitude every night," I chuckled.

As she turned to leave, I foolishly went to give her a hug.

"Melanie, what has gotten into you?" she said, jumping backward.

"Murder, I'd imagine. Sorry about that." She was impossible, but I knew growing up as a rich man's daughter with an absent mother and being raised by nannies had not been fun. Cornelia never hugged since hugging wasn't part of her picture. Murder wouldn't change that.

I stayed to see what other information I might get. Hanging out in this nearly four thousand -square-foot apartment was not bad as long as I stayed out of the bathrooms. I texted Devon.

Murder in Park Ave. apt. I was second on the scene. Do I have bad karma?

We have wonderful karma together. Wish we were horizontal. Sounds like a scoop for you, or us.

Devon's text started a heat wave racing through me. I couldn't think about him now. I replied.

I'm at a murder scene! And jammed my phone into my bag. This could be a scoop.

Who would Chilton notify if Karen was divorced? The thought of her children was so gut-wrenching I craved ignatia amara, an herb used for grief, which was back home, of course. As for her husband, or maybe ex-husband, I remembered Greg Sheldon. He'd looked like an aging ski bum when I'd seen him around school a few years ago. Patterned sweaters, leather jackets, jeans with boots year-round. He was either a plastic surgeon or a dermatologist, catering to the Botox and laser crowd. His girlfriend was probably a twenty-four- year-old model.

By now there were five people left, besides the police and Susie. Gabby, the West Side parent from my daughter's class, had stopped crying but still looked grim. I approached with a smile.

"So are you jumping ship and moving East?" Better to start with small talk. Gabby's husband was a partner at a big law firm. They could afford to buy this place.

"It would save so much time, not having to walk across the park to Huntley. But after this disaster?" She shivered. "I'd never live in this apartment."

"Did you know Karen? I only knew her to nod and say hello. It's been years since I've seen her," Gabby said.

Tears welled up again. "I was friends with her. We swam at the same pool. We'd have lunch occasionally. But she stopped returning my calls last year, when the trouble started with Greg. I should have kept trying to reach her."

"Whatever happened had nothing to do with you. Your calling her wouldn't have stopped her death." I put my hand on her shoulder gently. She looked up.

"Karen had problems with her oldest daughter. The girl had an eating disorder. The therapist thought there was some kind of trauma. Karen was very worried. She really needed friends, but she stopped calling me."

An empty feeling raced through me. What a mess. A husband who left for another woman, a daughter who had serious problems. Now, Karen murdered. I had to do something to help.

Gabby clenched her fists.

"Could you believe his girlfriend had the nerve to come today?

Damn, do I dare take out my notebook?

"That's a hell of a nerve. But real estate doesn't follow Emily Post.By the way, which one was the girlfriend? Was she here when we found Karen?"

"She left right before you got here, I think. Gray tight suit. Pink blouse. Made a big entrance just as the open house started."

"The woman I passed at the front door," I said out loud. Early thirties, maybe. Ten years younger than Karen,successful looking. That must have hurt.Both gorgeous, but the new one didn't have stress lines around her mouth and eyes. Not that Greg couldn't have fixed those.

"Was there a scene?" I asked.

"Karen stayed away from her. Marlena Shenko is her name. She's a man-hunter. Greg gives her injections weekly. He was here, too. I think he's looking to buy a place for the two of them and his kids. Did you see him? You'd remember him if you were here."

I shook my head. "I never saw Greg. He must have left early. "Did something happen between Greg and Karen?" My heart pounded.

"Oh, they got into it. I heard Karen say, 'I can't believe you brought her. You knew I'd be here.' He yelled, 'I can bring her anywhere I want.' Karen got louder. 'Bastard, terrible father.' It was quiet until she burst out with something about the kids' trust funds and money missing. A few minutes later, Greg Sheldon walked out. Marlena was in the living room, so she

18

heard them.

"What time did you get here today?"

"I was one of the first, before eleven. I guess I hoped this apartment might be the place." She looked sheepish.

"And when did the argument happen?"

"I heard them somewhere in the kitchen as soon as I got here. I think it was near where Karen was found."

This was more than a story. This was a motive. Chilton really needed to hear Gabby's account.

"Gabby, tell the cops what you just told me."

Gabby looked down and minutely studied her clear pink nails. "Marvin is not going to like this." She looked up resolutely. "But he knows the law. I really won't have a choice, will I?" She started tapping a text. Marvin, her lawyer husband, would take charge.

I flashed back to high school and the gossip and fear that ruled the social scene. Same fear, bigger stakes now.

Why did I care about the cops getting this information? My job was to write a story for the paper, maybe write a screenplay. But Karen's killer had to be found. I looked around. Others heard Karen's last fight with Greg. Susie and her assistant would never rat on a potential client, so they were out. Breathe. I needed to stay focused, not emotional.

"Do you remember who else was here and heard the fight?" I asked Gabby.

She chewed on her thumbnail. "People were coming and going. I don't remember. Buffy and Fawn were here, but I don't know whether they heard the fight. They left quickly."

Buffy and Fawn were in the lobby when I arrived at 11:45.

Chilton was headed for a rough time with this crowd, with their layers of financial obligations. Social status at school and connections at work were intertwined. Karen and Greg had kids at Huntley for only a few years, but they still had friends there. Some women would have sympathy for Greg because he was a good-looking man. Or they went to him for Botox.

But there were women who would suspect or blame Greg. If he hadn't left the marriage, Karen wouldn't have been a real estate agent at all. She wouldn't have created enemies, and she wouldn't be dead.

"Aftermath," my column about how crime affects the people closely involved, gave me an entrée to meet the key players. But this group was as hard to break into as a Vegas casino. Marlena Shenko and Greg Sheldon were at the top of my list. Somehow, I'd have to cross paths with them. And Marc Olmsted, Karen's boss.

The buzzer from the intercom blared. I moved closer to the kitchen and heard Chilton's voice. "All right. Send him up. One of you come with him."

Within minutes, loud voices came from the gallery.

"Who would do this?" a distraught male voice shouted. "I want to see her. How could she be dead?"

Greg Sheldon burst Into the dining room. He had less hair than when I'd last seen him, but his boyish face looked no older. The perks of being in the filler business. He wore the same boots and leather jacket. Wild-eyed, he pushed aside the cops until he reached Chilton at the edge of the kitchen.

Chilton took his arm and walked him through the kitchen, speaking quietly. In a few moments, I heard Greg sobbing, "No, no." He sounded genuinely shocked. We looked at one another—Susie and I, and three others—with the same discomfort. We shouldn't have heard this kind of grief. It felt too intimate. Don't poets say the surrender in sex is like dying? I was getting morbid standing around here.

If Greg had anything to do with Karen's death, he should get an Oscar for playing the bereaved husband. But he was no longer her husband; he was her ex, and he'd just been in a screaming match with her. Plus, he made a living creating false appearances.

I texted Rebecca, my closest friend. *At an open house on Park Avenue. There's been a murder. A former Huntley parent, Karen Sheldon, strangled in the maid's bathroom.*

OMG, why does this keep happening to you? I'll meet you at the usual. Just say when. Have till pickup.

It's only twice! It could happen to anyone, right? Karen's ex is here, Greg. He sleeps around. Tell you later.

I arranged to meet Rebecca in an hour at our regular diner.

20

A lean, fit-looking woman with short, dirty-blonde hair and a deep tan talked to Susie in a hushed tone. I heard "very interested." and "willing to wait till this is over." She had stayed on just to ask about the apartment. Now, there'd be a bidding war while Karen's body was being carted away. I felt sick again.

Greg came out of the kitchen with Chilton, his face wet with tears or perspiration. I heard fragments.

"Bastard Marc...he'd do this....vicious temper...jealous of the listing."

Dr. Greg Shedon stopped short when he saw the six of us. Susie and her assistant, the runner, Gabby, myself, and Anita, who was scrounging for info for the network. Greg broke into a smile, like we were guests at a party and he was the gracious host. He switched his grief off shockingly fast. Susie went to him and offered her condolences. He nodded, holding her hand between both of his, as he probably did with ten patients a day. He then walked to Anita, took her hand. Then started toward Gabby. Big mistake.

"You don't fool me for one second, you SOB. You're to blame. You're happy she's gone. I heard you. Now you have more money," Gabby shouted. She turned and ran out of the room. I cheered silently. Greg Sheldon got a look of rage but quickly transformed back into a grieving husband. "She's clearly unbalanced by this," he murmured. Chilton gestured to a sergeant to follow Gabby out.

The coroner's team walked in, men and women in white coats with a body bag and a stretcher. It was awful, but I felt happy to see them. They had a job to do, and they did it with dignity. They weren't bidding on real estate or disgusted because their day had been disrupted. I felt a surge of love for them.

Column or not, I refused to stay to see her wheeled away. The air in the condo felt frigid and stale, like a morgue. No one cared much about poor Karen. They only cared about how much money could be made. I gave the sergeant my ID, told him they had my fingerprints already from last year's murder and got the hell out.

Chapter Three

"What did you expect? Sobbing, hugs, casseroles? You've been stuck among those Prada devils for years now. They're never going to change. You couldn't fill a soup spoon with the tears they shed in a lifetime. They only cry when the market drops. Maybe."

Rebecca took a large bite of a toasted bagel spread thickly with cream cheese. She could eat anything without ever getting sick or gaining an ounce. If I didn't know her I might hate her, but she was my best friend; we agreed on almost everything, especially bad-mouthing the idle rich. We were in our hangout, the Argo diner.

"But to bid on the apartment when Karen's body was still there? You couldn't pay me a million to live there. The bathroom colors are putrid, anyway."

I took a sip of hot water with soy milk to soothe my lurching stomach. Oat works better, but in this place, I was lucky to get soy. I could break my rule about eating wheat flour. Poor Karen looked like she'd never eaten bread, but it didn't make her any less dead.

"If someone paid you, of course, you'd live there. I'd take the million, retile the bathrooms, and take the bedroom furthest from Peter. It would be heaven," Rebecca continued. Peter was Rebecca's husband, an underemployed research doctor. Their marriage was perpetually in a state of either full-on war or mild sparring while they each planned their next affair. A chess game of a marriage, with sex as the pawn. Crazy but more honest than most. She took another bite.

"I need a small piece of your bagel," I pleaded. Rebecca looked shocked.

"Sure have the whole thing." She pushed it across the table. "You must really be shook up if you're eating gluten." I cut off a tiny piece and handed it back to her.

"I'm ordering you a muffin. You need it." Rebecca called the cute waiter over. I didn't protest.

"My stomach's doing cartwheels. I think I'm jinxed." I had been known to lecture about the evils of gluten and dairy in gourmet stores, causing arguments, especially with my food writer husband, Daniel. But murder changes everything.

My cell phone rang, showing an unfamiliar string of numbers."I'm gonna take this. I think it's Devon. I'll just be a minute."

"You're not letting me listen to Wonder Woman and her hot assistant? Don't be cruel." Rebecca knitted her eyebrows and clutched her heart.

I rolled my eyes at her as I stood and walked to a quiet corner, too nervous to have her listen in.

"Hi."

"Are you there? Can you hear me?" Devon asked.

"I'm here."

"I've been in Africa for three weeks and haven't seen one dead body. Unless you count vultures eating roadkill."

"Nope. That's recycling. You want a murder, you have to come to Park Avenue. Unbelievable, huh? I was in the right place at the wrong time. Or maybe the right time. Is this my karma?"

"Who cares? You've got the inside track again." He paused. "If you want to take it." He was right to wonder. I wasn't sure myself.

"The opening scene writes itself. And there are so many players. Victim's ex-husband was at the open house and had a screaming match with her just before she was murdered. His new Russian girlfriend was there, too, but left after he did. There are greedy real estate agents. The victim just got a $45 million listing. She was fighting with her boss over the commission." I heard a crackling sound. "Are you still there?"

Devon's low, husky voice broke through the static. "I'm here, but I wish I was back there. And not just to work with you on this story. Maybe we could find an empty apartment."

Warmth surged everywhere like a grenade going off. I wanted to jump through the phone and be next to him. It was torture.

"You've got to cut this out," I murmured. *Pull yourself together.* "After today, an empty apartment is forever off my list of places for a lazy afternoon. Anyway, I thought we both agreed no more."

"You agreed. I didn't sign anything."

"I have a more complicated life, remember?" I could sound tough with Devon eight thousand miles away. I sighed dramatically. "Can you get information from the cops about Karen Sheldon while you're over there— wherever *there* is?"

"Zimbabwe, and yes, I can call my guy at the 23rd precinct. No problem."

"Great. I'll try Detective Levano, too." A wave of sadness came over me. "It was awful. Such a young, beautiful woman."

"I'm sorry. I really am," he said. "You can let this one go, Mel. Take a break. Our screenplay just sold."

This was the caring, sensitive side of Devon that, combined with our chemistry, made being around him risky. I felt the pull to jump on a plane and leave my life with Daniel and Chloe. That would be a disaster.

"You're right. I could take a break. We got a decent amount for *Playground Hero.* But I have a column to write. And I know you, Devon. If you were here, you'd go full tilt on this. A Park Avenue murder is too good to let pass, as sad as her death is."

I said goodbye quickly, to avoid lingering murmurs. The curly-haired waiter was flirting with Rebecca. She waved him off with a smile and looked at me sternly.

"I will remind you, you've told me a hundred times you won't leave Daniel and you're never sleeping with Devon again. So don't go there. I can see it in your face."

"Why would you think that? It's just about work."

Rebecca gave me an eye roll that would have made an eighth-grader jealous. I loved her, but it wasn't easy having a psychologist friend who could read my mind. She pushed the corn muffin at me.

I took a bite and sat back in my seat, one of those fake leather banquettes found only in diners. Pure comfort to go with all that fried and cheese-laden food. I loved diners, even though I rarely succumbed to the food. Why would you ever want to leave a diner where prices were cheap, all problems seemed fixable, and you could come dressed as you were?

"I'm never leaving Daniel," I confirmed. "Nothing has changed. Now tell me about Greg Sheldon."

Rebecca shook her head vigorously, flinging her blonde hair in the process. "Only if you tell me what Devon said. I'm between guys right now and need some excitement. Did he say he can't wait to hold you, feel you, smell you... Anything like that?"

"He's in Zimbabwe. And you know what men say better than I do. Just replay your own life. Come on, give me the goods."

Rebecca sat up straight and took another long sip of coffee. "All right. But you owe me."

She put down her cup. "Greg Sheldon has always had affairs. He's just too cute and charming, with too many beautiful women around. Everyone in the private school, plastic surgery crowd knows this. Except you, of course."

Cornelia said the same thing. But Rebecca smiled with affection.

"The question is why Greg decided to leave Karen for Marlena Shenko. Some people say Marlena threatened to tell everyone details of their affair. Which would be no big deal, really. Just embarrassing for him. She's single, so no liability on her side. Others say it's because she has money, and Greg needed cash. The sad part is, Karen didn't want a divorce—even with Miss Russia and her amazing cheekbones around. She went to Finster and Finster, the best divorce lawyers in the city. They told her to wait him out, the same thing they tell every woman. A woman who's been deserted gets more sympathy from a judge. And more money." Rebecca looked smug and finished off her bagel.

"So what about their legal separation, or were they really divorced? I heard he wasn't making support payments. You know Gabby, the other west side mom, was there. She reported a loud fight between them, about the kids' trust funds. Karen accused him of dipping into their money."

Rebecca sipped some coffee, her eyes wide. "Wow, the trust fund thing is news to me. That sounds like a motive." She paused. "I think they were wrangling an agreement about support payments, so no finalized divorce yet. He must make at least a million a year, just from the laser work and Botox."

"Jesus, a million a year from Botox? With that kind of income, you'd think they could come to an agreement about child support. Daniel and I would just split it and never have to worry again. These people do go to pricier haunts than this place I guess." I watched piles of fries and gobs of whipped cream carried by a waiter.

I started adding figures in my head. "Greg was looking at $4 million dollar apartments, so he'd need a lot more than a million a year. The down payment alone is eight hundred grand."

Images from the morning started flashing in my head. "I forgot to share some gruesome humor. Karen had a mid-lift, and everyone saw the staples bleed."

"A fate worse than death for that group, right?" Rebecca chuckled.

"Exactly. I had to grit my teeth not to laugh at Cornelia's shock. As if Karen could care anymore."

"So if Greg was in bed or on the examining table with everyone, jilted women could be suspects. Marlena Shenko, his fiance, was there. She was brought by a real estate agent, though, so I can't see how she'd kill Karen." I said.

"A jilted woman wouldn't have a motive for killing Karen. She'd kill Greg, wouldn't she?" Rebecca sipped her tea.

I thought about this for a minute.

"His divorce from Karen wasn't final. One of his women could be crazy enough to think if she helped free Greg of his wife, she'd become the special someone. Anyway, jilted women love to talk. Let's make a list of anyone you know he's slept with." I took out a pad.

"You've got your bloodhound nose on the trail again. You'll be surprised by the names. Let's start with Sandra Crane."

I stopped with pen in mid-air. "You're kidding. Church lady? She was definitely at the open house. She led everyone in the Lord's Prayer." I played with the packets of sugar.

"It makes sense. Sandra has sex with Greg to get back at her own husband for *his* affair. The new emerald ring he gave her wasn't enough. I don't think Sandra would be capable of killing Karen, but I can speak to her and see what she knows. Who else?"

Rebecca giggled. "You'll love this one. Your old enemy, Buffy Clifford."

I laughed so much my eyes watered. "Stuffy Buffy with Greg? Must have been during a Botox appointment. She doesn't like to waste time. This could give me a way to get her to talk to me. I can't see a motive for her either, but she would rat out anyone if she felt cornered." I smiled happily at Rebecca.

"You've saved this day from being a depressing sinkhole. Too bad I can't say who Greg slept with in my column. But I will mention that there was an undercurrent of tension toward him. How do you know so much?" Rebecca smiled slyly.

"Jackie—you know, West Side mom with a fabulous place at the Beresford? She talks to me a lot. She's a member of the Greg Sheldon Sex group. I doubt she was at the open house, though."

"No, I didn't see her. Ask Jackie about Greg's marriage to Karen, if you can find a way to drop it in the conversation."

Rebecca looked at her watch. "I'll try. She's over-the-top jealous and acts like Greg dumped her for Marlena. I remind her that she's married."

"Why would she be jealous of anyone when she has that handsome actor husband?" It immediately struck me how naive I sounded. "Never mind, I get it. Of course, he's having affairs on the set."

"Now you're catching on." We both eyed our phones. "I've got a session coming up. I have to go," Rebecca said, but her usual sparkle had vanished.

"What's going on? Speaking of marriages," I asked quietly. Rebecca had a lot of compassion for others but didn't like talking about herself.

"Peter and I are both in between affairs for the moment. We're not even seriously flirting with other people. It's boring and uncomfortable for both of us. Too much time together without any third parties." She laughed. "That sounds ridiculous, but it's the way we work. Maybe I should take on some extra research with Dr. Greg."

My jaw dropped. Rebecca chuckled.

"Melanie, you're so gratifyingly gullible. Don't worry. Greg's not interesting to me. He's been around the block too much. I have my eye on a new young psychiatrist at the clinic. They're never great in bed. But the pillow talk is deep. And they send me terrific referrals of wealthy patients afterwards. It's like a two-for-one special."

I laughed. "You go, girl." We hugged goodbye.

I wished I could talk this case out with Devon. Damn him for turning me on with talk of being horizontal. I had to stay focused, get my hands on the sign-in sheet that Susie had of who was at the open house. Was Marc Olmsted, Karen's angry boss, even there? That back exit door bothered me. Anyone could have come and gone that way. Maybe it was unlocked from the start of the open house. No one heard anything, apparently. Karen was killed without a noisy struggle.

Agents at an open house always have a sign-in sheet. Getting a look at the sheet would be a start.

There was a huge nagging problem: Daniel. My husband only liked risks of the culinary, the souffle may fall, kind. He reluctantly accepted my writing a column about the aftermath of crimes. He'd be up in arms if I investigated a murder again.

Yet it seemed preordained. All *I'd* done was go to an open house on Park Avenue in a respectable building with white-gloved doormen. It wasn't *my* fault if the lives of those immaculate East Siders were just as messy on the inside as the rest of us looked on the outside.

Chapter Four

Scarred wood floors, paint so thick the kitchen cabinets can't close, a desk shoved against old rattling windows. Our classic six (realtor lingo for old) two BR on the Upper West side screamed cramped and shabby compared to Park Avenue. Its only good feature was the absence of dead bodies. So far.

I fell on the couch. *Pull yourself together.* I clicked on my meditation app with the gorgeous guru and listened to his soothing voice remind me of gratitude. *Grateful I'm not dead.* I took valerian, California Poppy, passionflower.

The self-pity attack went away. I made a list of everyone I knew at the Open House—fifteen names. There had been more than forty people. I swiped through pictures on my phone. I wasn't any Richard Avedon, but the right person could identify people from these. I clicked on Cornelia's number.

"Hi, Melanie. Let me guess why you're calling." I heard papers rustling. She read three newspapers every day and then called her broker.

"I was going to ask how you were, but never mind," I mumbled.

"Oh, *really*. When you actually want to talk about that disaster on Park Avenue so I can help you with your *investigation.* Your *column.*" Suddenly, my column seemed trite. I heard her call out to someone. "Not that bathroom, the one down the hall." She returned to me. "I want Karen's killer brought to justice, too. But the men in blue can handle this without your help."

I paced around the apartment. "Like they did last time, right? That crazy woman was right here in my apartment. Come on. I just want you to help me identify who was there. Look at a photo on my phone. You know everyone." She was silent. Flattery wasn't working.

"What if I gave you something in return?" My desperation was pathetic.

"I'm waiting breathlessly." Cornelia laughed, but sounded intrigued.

I regretted the words as soon as I said them. "I'll give you the names of restaurants that will get rave reviews from Daniel, before anyone else reads them."

I didn't have a clue how I'd do this. It would probably involve digging through his office. Or maybe if I just pretended to be interested for a change, he'd tell me. He was the chief restaurant critic for *Food Lovers' Inc.* magazine. What I'd just proposed to Cornelia was like leaking stock tips for insider trading. But the top-secret intel was all about ridiculously embellished, overpriced food, like a rack of something-or-other, with truffled orecchiette and a confit emulsion, which sounded to me like fuel for jet engines.

"All right," said Cornelia. "Bring Chloe over tomorrow after school. And your photos. I'll consider this the equivalent of a charitable donation, and I'll take those restaurant names."

"Absolutely," I said. "It may take a while, but you'll have them. But you have to swear you'll never admit where the names came from. And I'll never give you up as a source. Agreed?"

"Yes, yes. My God, it's like doing business with Saudi Arabia." *When had Cornelia done business with Saudi Arabia?* "I think Anna's free tomorrow. My secretary is out at the moment."

"My secretary quit because of lack of funds," I said drily. "But as I remember, Chloe's free. See you tomorrow. By the way, it's men and women in blue these days." I clicked off. Rich people rarely gave a dime without getting something in return.

My foot tapped with a sense of urgency. I had to do something now.

I called Harold, my editor at the *Wild Westsider*. "Just the truth" was the paper's motto. I told him what happened at the open house. He was practically orgasmic.

"You're a f—in' magnet for murder, Deming. Some people are great at finding a Picasso in the trash. You hang out, and murders come to you."

30

"Nice, Harold. Such a flattering comparison."

"Come on. In our business, it's like having the Midas touch. So, when can I have a column?"

"Calm down." I took one of many deep breaths. "I'm just checking in. You'll have the first one by tomorrow. But since you mentioned the Midas touch, we need to talk about money."

"You sold a screenplay. You have like 40,000 followers. Isn't that enough?" He launched into the speech used by every bedraggled editor when a writer asked for more money. "You're asking too much. I can barely keep this place going. You're lucky to have a byline."

But I'd just had a lesson in demanding more from Cornelia. I needed money a lot more than she did. I strapped on a pair and battled on.

"You'll have the exclusive, Harold," I said. "You know I could get a lot for a Park Avenue murder from New York Magazine."

Harold coughed so loud it hurt my ear on the phone. "Nobody reads that junk. What do you want?"

"More than a column. The whole top of the front page. I heard enough at that open house to fill it and get some people agitated. Let's see what happens." A bolt of fear shot through my mind and vanished. "My usual salary plus five hundred dollars for this week."

"No way, I can't afford that. Four hundred."

That was more than I'd expected him to cough up. "Fine," I said. He slammed the phone down.

This investigation could get unpleasant for me with the parents at Huntley. Money would help cushion the blow when the inevitable argument with Daniel blew up.

The landline rang. I waited till I heard the voice on the machine before picking up.

"You're screening your calls. Who are you avoiding?" asked Cornelia.

"Not you. What's up? Are we off for tomorrow?"

"No, but there's been a change of location. Don't you ever check your emails? They've announced a meeting tomorrow morning for ignorant parents on how to handle Karen's death with their kids. I had a strong feeling you'd want to be there." She laughed her tinkly laugh. "Afterwards, I could identify some of the same parents who were there today."

"Doesn't this meeting sound like a made-up excuse to gossip? Karen's kids left Huntley three years ago. Chloe has no idea who they are," I said. "Who called this get-together?"

"Come on, Melanie, take a guess. The Parents' Association. That means Buffy."

"The vampire slayer. I wouldn't miss this for anything. I'll record it on my phone."

"Don't involve me, that's all." I heard her clicking a keyboard. You'll love this even more. Another email just came in. The meeting is at Buffy's house. She has that enormous living room with the twenty-foot ceilings."

I'd been there once for a parent get-together. An entire townhouse on a street adjacent to the Metropolitan Museum. There were no pricier locations in New York. "Her elevator is too small for this crowd."

"Don't you run up stairs every day?" She laughed.

"What time did you say?"

"I'm not your secretary. Eleven AM again."

"The same time as the open house today. I won't forget that." A thought was developing. Maybe the meeting wasn't Buffy's idea. "So, who's attending from the administration?"

"One of those children, the school counselor. Perky Hawkins." Cornelia sighed with admirable contempt.

"I think her name's Phoebe. Always wears pearls," I remembered. "Her whispery voice makes me want a Valium. Can you imagine her trying to calm down a room of hysterical Huntley parents? It could be a bloodbath." I felt a shiver as Karen's face flashed before me.

"Watch your language. After what happened today, everyone's a suspect." Cornelia hung up.

"How was the open house and Cornelia?" Daniel walked into the kitchen and opened the fridge. I had no idea he was home. My heart beat faster. Damn, I'd hoped this would seep out slowly. I relaxed when he took out a large bowl of double chocolate mousse made with a new Jacques Torres chocolate that had been delivered two days ago. Three pounds of chocolate for making mousse. It was all in the bowl. It might just save the day.

"There was a problem at the open house," I mumbled.

"People fighting over it," he chuckled.

"Something like that but worse." I ran out of the kitchen and into the bedroom and pulled on leggings and a T-shirt.

"What do you mean worse," Daniel asked, standing at the bedroom door with his mouth full of chocolate mousse.

"I'm going for a run. I'll be right back." I tried to slip past him and not get covered with mousse

"You're avoiding the question. Did you and Cornelia have a fight?" He followed me into the foyer. Cornelia's husband's firm held shares in the company that owned Food Lovers Inc. Daniel fawned over Cornelia. At that moment, I felt sorry for him. He took another scoop of mousse and offered it to me. I shook my head, though what I was about to say might go down smoother with mousse.

"No. Nothing about Cornelia. Now, don't get upset. But a former parent at Huntley, Karen Sheldon, was murdered at the open house. No one knows what happened, but one of the mothers found her in a bathroom."

Daniel's mouth with the mousse hung open. He had a graying beard and, of course, some mousse stuck to it. Not a pretty sight. He swallowed hard. "You're kidding me right? No you don't kid about murder. It's your bread and butter."

"Very funny. It was awful, actually." I let my shoulders slump and tried to seem near tears. It worked.

"So tell me about what happened." He actually put the bowl of mousse down on the rolltop desk that had rings on it from years of coffee cups. And put an arm around my shoulders. He nuzzled my neck. I felt something sticky. Oh yuck it was the mousse in his beard. I slipped out from his arm and strapped on my phone holder. I grabbed my keys.

"The police came. They took everyone's info. The detective had read my column. The coroner came. Everyone left." My hand was on the door.

"Come on. You're holding back." He walked toward me, finger-pointing.

"You're already doing the detective thing, I can tell."

I opened the door and stepped out. "No. The police are on it."

"I don't believe you. You look guilty as hell," he yelled.

"Really? Of what?" I yelled back. Doing a job I liked, and was good at, shouldn't be a crime just because Daniel saw it that way.

I might have stopped here had I known then what path the murder investigation and my marriage were going to take. Many people told me to stop here. But of course I didn't.

Chapter Five

"Are you all right? If you need to talk, we have a wonderful priest at the church." Sandra Crane, in a pleated tartan skirt and white blouse, which looked eerily like the Huntley girls' uniform, gave me a look she probably gave the homeless guys at the church shelter.

"I'm fine, but how are *you*?" I winked. Sandra had been screwing Dr. Greg Sheldon. My mind exploded at the thought. She pursed her lips and marched into Buffy's townhouse.

I watched swarms of mothers arrive at the meeting the next day dressed in coat-length Rag and Bone freakishly expensive cashmere cardigans and knee-high boots from Stuart Weitzman. This dressed-down look had to cost two thousand dollars. Patty Baylor, who found Karen, arrived looking like a ghost.

It was only three flights up to the living room. Buffy and her hedge fund husband and their two perfect-looking children, who were not too bright, according to Cornelia, occupied all five floors of the townhouse. This home off Fifth Avenue was almost double the width of its poor brownstone cousins on the West Side.

Buffy held court in her enormous living room with its double-height ceiling. Her gang, Fawn, Bia, and Mandy, surrounded her. Huge swaths of beige silk shantung hung from the massive windows. Three large, overstuffed brocade-covered couches and forty folding chairs were arranged in neat rows. I stood by the windows and took in the billionaire's view of the Metropolitan Museum down the block.

The assistant principal of the Huntley School, Joan Charles, wore a dark charcoal suit, a cream-colored sweater, and pearls. She sat in a corner of one of the couches with the school psychologist, Phoebe Hawkins, who looked to be on the verge of a nervous breakdown. Parents kept streaming in. I wondered what the fire code was for maximum occupancy.

There was a massive sideboard set with large coffee urns, pastries, and fruit. At least sixty parents had arrived by 11:15.

"Quiet, please," someone called.

I stayed on the edge of the group. This gathering felt more unsafe than the murder scene.

"You can calm down. I'm here," Cornelia said, coming up behind me.

"How did you know I feel like a mouse out of its hole?"

"Your shoulders are up to your ears." We found seats.

Buffy spoke first, using a wireless microphone I imagined she used to broadcast orders to her children.

"We are here today because of a tragic situation. A mother of two former Huntley girls who left the school a few years ago, was injured yesterday and died. The police say her fatal injuries appear to have been caused by another individual." I tried to stifle a snicker at this convoluted attempt to avoid the M-word. Two nearby parents gave me annoyed looks.

Assistant Principal Joan Charles jumped up, causing the couch to screech against the polished bamboo floors. Buffy shuddered. Joan grabbed the microphone.

"Let me be completely clear," she said, in an obvious bid for damage control. "What happened to Karen Sheldon has nothing to do with the Huntley School. Ms. Hawkins and I are here only to address your concerns about rumors your children may hear and told you. She is an expert. Please direct your questions to her."

Phoebe Hawkins clutched her chest as if she was going into cardiac arrest. Right on cue, the elevator doors opened, and Detective Robert Chilton, baggy suit and all, stepped off with a petite, slender woman in a well-cut, dark-blue suit, regulation light-blue blouse, and four-inch Aldo heels. She was not more than thirty, with Asian relatives somewhere in her background, far more attractive and elegant than any cop I'd ever seen. Good on Chilton for bringing a chic female detective to protect him from these East Side vultures.

"What's wrong with Perky Hawkins?" murmured Cornelia.

"She's dying rather than being eaten alive by this group of ravenous hyenas. Smart move," I whispered. Cornelia and I stifled giggles.

"Look at the detective with Chilton. Even in her regulation suit, she makes me feel like a poor relative."

"Everyone makes you feel underdressed, Melanie," Cornelia sighed. "A few thousand dollars toward a new wardrobe would solve that." Buffy took back the mike.

"None of us thinks the school bears any responsibility, of course. We're here to get advice about the children." Buffy gave Phoebe a withering look. She clutched her chest harder. Would Phoebe go all in and fake a coronary?

"Have they found who did this yet? My kids are terrified to even go to the playground," a suntanned father in an impeccable three-piece suit shouted.

"Is the school increasing security?" called Anita Massini, the doctor with three kids at Huntley who had checked Karen for a pulse.

I rolled my eyes. Huntley was already more heavily guarded than Fort Knox.

Parents talked loudly to each other. The noise level grew.

"It was Susie's open house. She should have had some kind of guard there," another mother said in a sharp tone. It was then I noticed Susie Carlbach standing in a corner near the elevator. If possible, she had lost ten pounds since yesterday.

"Why would they need a guard? The apartment wasn't a showplace or anything," A heavily made-up and slightly plump mom near me complained. "Shabby, really."

"But did you hear who the decorator was?" Her friend asked.

"There's another place for sale on Park for three and a half million. Twenty-foot gallery, three bedrooms, and a much newer kitchen." The heavily made-up mom took out her phone to show the listing. I stifled a laugh. A murder couldn't compete with real estate in New York.

A private school on the West Side had lost a child once in an outing at a zoo for several hours. Their admissions went down for three years. At sixty-five thousand dollars a student, that's a big loss. At the Fleisher School, a senior was charged with a rape of a classmate in Central Park on a Friday night. That school folded within two years. Joan Charles knew how schools got smeared. She had to keep this away from Huntley's reputation and reassure crazed parents.

Ms. Charles' neck got straighter, her arms rigidly at her side. "We have always had the highest standards of any school for security measures. A guard is at the door all day. There are two sets of locked double doors. Every person, no matter how well known to the school, has to sign in and present ID every time they're admitted." She paused and looked into the eyes of every parent, daring them to question the school's excellence.

"At pick-up hour, at least four men are working. One handling traffic, one at the door. Two on the street watching the children being picked up." She stopped short of saying they were armed. I'd heard they were but never saw anything. Anyway, the children of the richest of the rich, like the Forbes 400, were picked up by bodyguards. Everyone knew that.

"We have cameras in every area of the school, and our head of security watches those all day."

"Even the girls' locker room?" I whispered to Cornelia. She gave me a wide-eyed warning look.

"No one questions Huntley's excellence," said Buffy emphatically. She and her husband gave the school five million dollars last year for the endowment. "Ms. Hawkins will now give us some of her wisdom about how to talk to our children about this unfortunate death." She shoved the mike into Phoebe's hand. Her hand shook violently. She bolted upright, as if her job was at stake. Which it likely was.

She cleared her throat. I thought I heard her say, "Sorry, can't," or something in a whispery, undecipherable tone. Just then, the booming voice of God saved her day.

"If you don't mind, I'm going to jump in here. For those who don't know me, I'm Detective Robert Chilton, heading the investigation from the NYPD." The detective's strong and arrogant voice took over. Phoebe's lips parted. I swore she mouthed, "I love you." All eyes went to Chilton.

"I'd like to support Ms. Charles' reassurance about the school's security. We've worked with them for years. You don't have to worry about this murder somehow having anything to do with Huntley." Joan Charles allowed her thin red lips a hint of a smile. Huntley would make a larger donation than usual to the Police Benevolent Association this year.

"But I do need your cooperation in tracking down the assailant who killed Karen Sheldon. Some of you were at the open house and haven't returned my calls." He looked accusingly at a few people. "Help us out so we can solve this, and you won't have to be so frantic about a murderer on the loose."

He continued.

"And if you don't take my call, I will show up where you work or at your home. I guarantee that." He smiled broadly at the crowd. "Understood?" He watched. All nodded their heads, even the suits.

Cornelia whispered my thoughts in my ear. "Chilton told the school to have this meeting."

"Exactly. These parents are going to be pissed off. They've been duped."

The same three-piece suit father spoke up, but in a more respectful tone this time.

"We hear you, detective. I'll tell you whatever I can, but I wasn't at the open house and never met the woman. We have kids who are scared by all the talk. Aren't we entitled to get some help here? That's why we came."

Chilton's tone turned compassionate.

"I can't get kids to stop talking, but I've brought May-Ling Thomas with me. She is a forensic psychologist who specializes in childhood trauma. She'll take your questions." May-Ling walked resolutely to the mike. She gently took it from Phoebe, who fell back on the couch with tears in her eyes.

"I'm always glad to see parents who want to communicate better with their children," she said with a charming smile. "Some basic pointers in crisis intervention with younger kids. This event is the same as hearing something scary on the news. So, the first step is to gently find out what your child is thinking. They will have misconceptions. Don't try to correct these right away. Listen to them. This is extremely healing, in and of itself."

And almost impossible for parents, especially the Type-A's here, for whom every burp is an educational opportunity and teaching moment.

"Ask open-ended questions. Don't freak out if your child describes a scene out of "Night of the Living Dead." The line between fantasy and reality is often thin for children. They're sponges—a good thing when learning Spanish, but a problem when they overhear older siblings or parents talking about a murder victim. Don't do that around them. Save that for us. Don't toss around theories, even if the kids are in another room. They'll hear."

From the looks on the tanned and Botoxed faces, it was too late. All of these 'do not do' scenarios had already been done.

"Reassure them that nothing is happening to them or to anyone they know. Bad people will go to jail. The police are handling this. If they need you to sit with them at bedtime, go with that. It's temporary."

I wondered how many of these parents actually saw their kids at bedtime. Their babysitters were the ones who should be here.

"You said your child didn't feel safe going to a playground," Chilton chimed in. " Your kids may be getting yesterday's crime confused with the murder of the caretaker last year in the playground on the West Side. The people responsible for that are in jail now. It had nothing to do with any kids. The playground reopened two weeks after the murder. Children play happily there every day. Just ask your own Melanie Deming. She knows all about it. Helped to capture the perpetrators."

Oh, God. Why would he bring me into this? Eyes turned to me. I smiled meekly and waved a Queen Elizabeth wave. Then again, Chilton had just given me credit for solving the whole goddamn thing. Some of these princesses might actually talk to me now.

"You can stop beaming and waving, Melanie. May-Ling is giving us more Child Psychology 101." Cornelia sniped.

I took out my notepad and glanced at my list of open-house attendees. Deirdre Depke was here. Deirdre was at the open house. Everything she wore, including today's sweater, was tight and emphasized her large boobs and small waist. Those boobs had been added or lifted. I wondered if she had visited Dr. Sheldon.

My phone vibrated. Devon. I texted I was in a meeting. His reply startled and excited me.

"Returning next week for a short stay. Block off an afternoon for work and…."

We definitely had work now. Next week was so soon. A rush of heat came over me.

The meeting broke up. Cornelia and I headed toward the stairs.

"Melanie, can I talk to you for a minute?" Susie Carlbach appeared at my side.

"Sure." We walked to a quieter corner. Cornelia chatted with Joan Charles.

"This has been very bad for my agency, as you must realize." I nodded. I could see the bags under Susie's eyes. "And especially bad for me. Chilton just mentioned how you helped solve that murder last year. Would you come to my office at Rozen Real Estate tomorrow? Maybe we can help each other."

"Of course." I wouldn't turn down an invitation. "But the police are good at their job, Susie. Give them whatever information they want."

Susie looked offended. "Of course, we're cooperating with the police. But you need to know the truth about Karen Sheldon. We can help each other. How about tomorrow morning?" I agreed.

The truth about Karen? Susie was a NYC real estate agent. Truth wasn't really part of the job description.

Chapter Six

I walked hurriedly away from Susie to join Cornelia. Madison Ave was a two-minute walk.

"How about Nectar's?" I opened the door and herded her into one of the few surviving diners in Madison. "No Huntley people will be here."

"And yet here *I* am. What *I* do for friends." Cornelia closed her eyes and gave a martyr's sigh as she sat down in a booth, looking completely out of place. "That was a circus. We learned one thing. Perky only has her job because her grandfather gave Huntley a million, back when a million meant something. And that annoying detective planned the whole event."

We ordered tea.

"The chic May-Ling saved her." I sipped herbal tea with oat milk. Oat milk in a diner. Only on Madison. "Those parents will keep avoiding Chilton. He's dirty laundry to them." I took out my phone and scrolled through the pictures.

"I don't need any pointers from a forensic psychologist," Cornelia said, sipping her black Earl Grey. She made a face and hurriedly put it down. "My Elizabeth knows better than to cry about someone she's never met. She seemed especially upbeat yesterday." I didn't tell Cornelia that Elizabeth shared her problems with my daughter Chloe. Cornelia went on. "Everyone in that room will consult with a lawyer. He'll get nowhere with their vague answers."

I felt a familiar pressure in my chest that was saying *solve this now.* I showed Cornelia a photo. "Here's a shot in the foyer. Can you give me any names? How about this couple?" I pointed to the guy who'd tapped out a low-ball offer while Karen still lay on the bathroom floor.

Cornelia put on her Dolce and Gabbana fifteen hundred dollar reading glasses. "Just don't tell me what you'll do with this." She pointed a pearly violet nail at the photo. "That's Chuck and Jennifer Nelson. They've been renting for years. He must have gotten a large bonus at Yorkville Investment Group, so it's time to buy. She's trying to get onto benefit committees, Junior League. Wants her picture in the society columns wearing Versace gowns. This apartment would work for them. I don't think they'd kill for it, though." She gave me a pointed look over the rim of her glasses, then glanced back at the photo. "She's had a lift in the last year. Maybe they both did. Could be Reichenbach. Same as Karem. Think there's a connection?" She chuckled, enjoying her joke.

"You're an encyclopedia, Cornelia. What about this woman?"

I pointed to the petite, flat-chested woman with boyish hips and the gaunt face of a marathon runner—the one who told Susie she was ready to buy the apartment on the day of the murder.

"That's Peggy Fitzpatrick. Her son goes to Wheatley. Old family name and money. Big house in the Adirondacks, skiing in Switzerland, polo ponies in Southampton. Husband owns an architecture firm, but her family money supports them. She would never have met the Sheldons. She's as straight and by the book as they come. But she'd be able to tell you whatever she observed in laser detail. Not sure where you could casually run into her, though." Cornelia paused as she looked through her brain's extensive database. "Doyle's auction house. She loves auctions—they're like tag sales for old money. Go to the next jewelry and small painting sale. She'll be there."

"Brilliant. Sounds like fun, as long as I don't raise my paddle. I heard her tell Susie she wanted the apartment while Karem's body was still there."

Cornelia shrugged. "Maybe they got tired of living in the suite of rooms her family has had for ages at the Carlyle. I'd think they'd go bigger, but they spend a lot of time in the Hamptons." Cornelia looked up suddenly and stared out the window. "That's Karen's daughter."

"Who? Which one? What's her name?" I followed her line of vision and saw an auburn-haired beauty with thin, long legs like Karen's, talking to a guy. "Those leggings show her rear end. Her jacket is too short," Cornelia scowled. " I think her name is Jennifer. One of those "J" names. Really, to show her backside like that. Her mother just died."

I stood up. "I'll be right back."

"Melanie, you have no business…" I didn't hear the rest. With my phone and bag, I was out the door. She was only a few feet from the restaurant entrance, Probably deciding if the diner would give them the privacy they needed. I walked up to them. Jennifer and the guy stopped talking. The dark circles under her eyes struck me first. And she was too thin. I had a mother's urge to feed her.

"Hello, I'm Melanie Deming. I'm so sorry about your mother. I was at the Open House, and I'm a parent at Huntley. If you need anything or would like to talk, here's my number." I held out a card.

Fear and desperation crossed her face. "I don't need…" she stammered. "Let's go," the guy ordered. She grabbed my card, he grabbed her hand. They took off running down the block toward the museum. I pictured a feral kitten running under the bed if you touch it. Maybe she was sixteen. The guy was much older. Mid twenties, at least. Dark longish hair, expensively casual dress. I noticed the Moncler label on the shirt. Four hundred dollars, at least.

I had never seen this young girl before. She was so thin the bones on her arms stuck out. She didn't get that thin in two days. Her problems started way before her mother was murdered. Gabby said Karen worried about her daughter. Was the murder somehow connected to her daughter's problems? At least she'd taken my card.

* * *

"Are you perhaps convinced now that this meddling achieves no good end?" Cornelia sniped as I sat down.

"You were the one who pointed her out to me," I said dryly. "The girl needs help."

44

"She'll get over it." Cornelia sounded cold, but no one ever helped Cornelia when her mother died.

We identified a few more people from my phone's camera. I had a growing list of women who'd been to Greg to lift their sagging faces and ended up lifting their skirts. Of those I knew for sure, Sandra Crane and Buffy Clifford were at the open house.

* * *

The next morning, dressed in gray tweed slacks, a silky green blouse, and makeup, I went out to meet the sharks at Rozen and Olmsted real estate.

Rozen Real Estate was a medium-sized firm. Quick research showed they'd closed $200 million in sales the previous year. Although that sounded like a lot, the agents in total had closed one hundred and fifty deals to reach that number. So 962 Park Avenue, at $4.6 million, was a big sale to them. But Susie supposedly closed a twenty-five million dollar deal this year, putting her in a different league. She might be looking to leave Rozen and join a major player like Christie's or Brown Harris. The Harrington Mansion would catapult her. Of the hundreds of real estate agencies in the city, only seven agencies made a billion dollars in sales each year. Rozen and Olmsted were both way below that bunch.

Rozen's waiting area was a light-filled, glass-enclosed room with the usual fake suede couches and armchairs. Issues of *Architectural Digest* and binders filled with their listings were arranged on a glass coffee table. Stock market quotes and photos of apartments flitted across the flat screen of a TV monitor mounted on the wall. Not a huge operation not a sleazy walk-up agency on West 72nd Street, either.

"Ms. Carlbach will see you now. I'll take you to the conference room."

A young guy in a white shirt and tie but no jacket led me into the back rooms, which were filled with standard cubicles and private offices partitioned off a long hall. He seated me in a conference room with a glass wall.

Susie looked even more exhausted than yesterday. She wore beige slacks, a peach sweater, and the same gold ball earrings. She collapsed into the leather armchair next to me and rubbed her eyes. Susie wasn't sleeping.

"Thanks for coming, Melanie." She looked around to make sure no one was going to barge in. "I'll get right to the point. We need this murder solved quickly to get it off the news. They're dragging the agency's name into every article. To think this happened at one of my open houses…horrifying." I wondered if she meant a murder was fine at an open house, just not at hers.

"I am impeccably honest," she continued. "I do everything by the book. My referrals come from other customers. *Nothing* was wrong at that open house."

Nothing was wrong except Karen had been killed on her watch. On the verge of tears, Susie looked up at the ceiling, seeking Divine Realtor Guidance, I supposed.

"My reputation is at stake, Melanie. That's where you come in. Have you already solved the crime?" She looked at me hopefully.

"I'm not Miss Marple, Susie," I said, already annoyed. "Put pressure on the police, not me. I have some questions. Was the front door open the whole time?"

"Yes. That's standard practice." Susie was wary.

"Was someone always at the front door? The police assume the killer was someone who came for the open house."

"Rachel and I have a good idea of who arrived when, but it was one of the largest crowds ever for an apartment at this price range." She looked smug. "We gave the police a copy of the sign-in sheet, but it never includes everyone. We added names of people like you, who arrived later. We were just too busy to stand at the front door every minute. And there's a doorman, remember."

"What about the back door? Did you open it to show?"

Susie tapped her nails on the boardroom table. "I did open the back door once. I was annoyed about it, actually. Who cares about the garbage area?"

"Do you remember who asked to see it?" Susie twisted a ring on her finger. She was nervous and stalling.

"There were so many people." I waited.

"Maybe Greg's fiance looked outside," she finally said. "But I think there were others. I can't remember." No harm casting suspicion on Greg's girlfriend, I thought. He'd never buy the apartment anyway now that Karen had been killed there.

"Did you relock the door after you showed it?"

"Maybe? I'm not sure. Too much going on. Anyone could open it though from the inside."

"It was locked when we found Karen's body. What about a key?"

"From inside, you don't need a key," she scoffed.

Exactly what I said to Chilton. "But from the outside, you would. Did you leave it unlocked? That's important."

Susie knew what she had to say. "I did not. But anyone could have gone out on their own. Anyone could lock it or unlock it."

"It was locked when the detective tried it. So either the person came and went through the front door. Or there were two people involved. One left through the back door, while the other relocked the back door after the murder took place." Susie looked even more pale when I finished. Two murderers at her open house. What I really needed now was that list of names she said she gave the police. I bet she held some names back.

"Susie, what is it you want from me?" She played with the gold chain around her neck, deciding about me. We both felt an urgency to find the killer, but for totally different reasons. "Who do *you* think did this?" I asked.

"If I had to bet, I'd say it was someone at her agency," she said. "Marc was furious at her. They were fighting over how the agency's commission on the Harrington mansion sale would be divided. Karen wanted sixty percent. That's unheard of." Nothing new. I waited.

"Marc has this loyal assistant who'd like to be a lot more than that. Shane Warbuck. Marc's not openly gay, although everyone in the business knows he is. Shane is totally in love with him. He'd do *anything* for Marc." She looked at me pointedly.

"Was either of them at the open house?" I asked.

"I arrived just after it started, but my assistant Rachel was there at 10:45," said Susie. "Rachel told the police that Karen Sheldon came early. Shane arrived a few minutes later with a client. Karen was alone."

"I doubt Shane killed Karen in front of his client. Can't be good for business." Susie shook her head.

"You're not letting me finish," she said. "Shane came back after leaving with the client. Ten minutes later. I saw him when he came back, alone. He told Rachel he came to get more listing sheets. But we never saw him leave. It's a starting point, wouldn't you say?"

She clearly wanted to shift the rumors away from Rozen carelessness or worse, and over to Olmsted. I would see Marc and Shane for myself next.

"The police will be able to tell if he left on the elevator through the lobby or not. Is there anything else?" I asked.

"Karen was very pushy and not well liked in the industry. She was obsessed with getting listings."

"But aren't you all? Isn't that the point of the business?

Susie looked surprisingly uncomfortable. Was she struggling with her conscience—not something I'd ever known a real estate agent to possess?

"Of course, this is off the record," she said finally. "But I think Karen slept with prospective clients to get listings. Married men. I don't know which ones, but there have been rumors."

Sure, I thought. *Slander the woman after she's dead.*

"I need specific information and leads," I said.

"That's what the police wanted. I don't have anything yet, but I'd rather give names to you than to the police. They'll charge in and embarrass a lot of people."

"The same people who could become your clients." My comment sailed right past her. Susie swiveled in her chair and continued.

"You know some of the people in this crowd. Perhaps you'll hear something. We could make it worthwhile for you." Susie saw a call coming in on her phone but ignored it.

"You want me to be a paid informer, like a spy." I almost giggled. Look how far I'd come since my last gig teaching toddlers to scribble in a playground.

Susie shook her head. "One hand helps the other."

"Same thing," I said. I really wanted to know how much I was worth to them. I couldn't give Susie secret information if I ever got any. Rozen Real Estate might have been involved in Karen's death.

"I'll need a list of the people who signed into the open house." Susie sighed and pursed her lips.

"I'll have to ask about our liability before I can give you those names."

I fumed. "I came to this appointment for names, not to hear a load of gossip.

"You said you wanted to give me information so that I could help this murder get solved quickly. But the information I need is on that list." I glared at her. "You really asked me here to get me to interview men Karen slept with, or to trap Marc's assistant into a confession."

"I said we'd make it worth your time," she said with a shrug. "It could be a lot of money."

I stood up. "You're insulting me." I looked back down at her.

"By the way, are the police allowing you to show the apartment?" Susie gave me a haughty stare.

"We already have an accepted offer."

"No grass grows under your feet," I said. "Or on Karen's grave." She looked at the window blankly, impervious to shame or compassion. A dead body in the bathroom was a fly to be flicked away.

"One more question, since we're being so honest and open," I continued. "Is there a possibility that your agency will go after the Harrington mansion listing, now that Karen's dead?" The very slightest movement of her head meant I'd struck a chord.

"I'm not at liberty to discuss that," she said and turned away from me. The Harrington mansion listing was too delicate to discuss, but Karen prostituting herself for listings was a respectable topic.

. She said she'd try to get me that list. I wouldn't hold my breath. Susie's purpose was to get the heat off. Blame Karen for getting herself killed. That sounded like blaming the victim. For a working girl, she wasn't too liberated.

Chapter Seven

I walked fast and hard down Park Avenue to Olmsted Realty. *I hate these people.* My phone buzzed.

"You didn't return my calls," Devon said in a low voice.

"I've been busy." So I lied. Writing with him was great and turned out to be profitable. But his eyes, his body were also great. Chemistry A+ And that was the problem. I was married to Daniel. Not happily, but still married. Daniel knew Devon. They wrote for the same magazine. I met Devon at a publishing party with my husband.

I could escape to dreams of Devon and have hot fantasies, none of which involved beards crusted with mousse. But all involved guilt.

"Mea culpa. It's been a crazy two days," I babbled. "I just left Susie, the agent who threw the open house. She's desperate to get this solved so she doesn't look bad. And desperate to take a mega listing away from Karen's agency. Get this—she offered to *pay* me to give her information to find the killer. To talk to men Karen slept with to get listings, to find dirt on the Olmsted Agency. I'm on my way there now."

The silence went on too long. "Are you seriously thinking of taking the money?" Devon asked. He was doubting me?

"Of course not!" I yelled. "I didn't even ask her how much." I took a breath. "Though I wanted to know. I bet you'd like to know, too." He laughed. I went on, still irritated. "Why do you doubt my ethics?"

"I don't. Though it would be hard to resist a cozy studio to sweeten the deal," Devon said in a low voice. "I'm coming back next week like I texted. Why does it feel like you're less than thrilled?"

"I'm excited about seeing you. I've missed you." I paused to cross a busy street. Delivery guys shot across the intersection in the wrong direction. It was death-defying to talk and walk in NYC at the same time. "But you told me your ex wants to get back together. You know what it's like to have a history. I have a daughter." I sighed. " I dream about being with you all the time."

"I'm never getting back together with Alice. I'm not that person anymore. Let's make us happen when I'm there next week. Just tell me you'll think about it."

He still talked to his ex. She would keep pushing.

"I'm thinking about it already, but I'm also drowning in suspects. Can we talk about this murder? There's the husband and his jilted lovers—four women I know who already slept with Dr. Greg. And his separation from Karen was bitter. He apparently took their kids' trust fund money. Karen herself had many other enemies, if she slept with married men to get listings. And the Harrington Mansion, which was her exclusive listing, has a feeding frenzy of sharks waiting for the kill. You see how many suspects there could be? I need help narrowing this down."

"I'm right there with you, Melanie. We're partners. I'll be there next week."

"Detective Chilton gave me a shout-out at the Huntley meeting. 'Talk to Melanie,' he said. She knows her way around a murder. I have to tread carefully. I worry about Chloe at that school.

"I can do interviews. Women like to talk to me. Did you notice?"

"Nope. Never noticed." Of course I noticed. I wondered if he saw other women.

"The Fitzpatrick old money buyer who likes auction houses would chat with you. But these real estate people are a different story. I have to convince Marc Olmsted I'm a prospective buyer. And see if his assistant, Shane, is really so in love with him he'd kill for him. I need acting classes for this job."

Devon's voice boomed over the line.

"Remember you're there as a reporter. We always play a role to get a story. Was this Shane guy at the open house?"

"Twice, according to Susie. But she only saw him leave once. I don't believe her. The good news is, I'll be looking at gorgeous apartments."

"Check out what's available for a long, lazy afternoon."

"Don't make me drool. I've got to look well-groomed and haughty for this interview. Which days will you be here?"

We arranged two days to meet. My body said it wasn't all about work. Sugar cravings I could get rid of. Devon cravings were way harder to shake.

* * *

Marc Olmsted wore bow ties every day, judging from the poster-size photos of him in the agency's posh waiting area. Marc with the Mayor, with a former Vice-President. Marc with Oprah was the centerpiece. But it was the bow ties that got your attention. They drew you right to him. An embroidered burgundy tie; a light green swirling hand-painted looking abstract pattern.

Since I was kept waiting twenty minutes in an enormous burnt-orange suede armchair, I did a quick check of Saks Fifth Avenue's website. Those patterned silk bow ties, mostly by Valentino and Lanvin, were at least four hundred dollars apiece. Which wasn't much, I supposed, considering the Armani suits went for three grand.

If you were going to get the mega-million listings, you had to look like a million. Marc did. The books fanned out on the leather coffee table were a testament to his success, the showpiece being an entire leather-bound volume devoted to the Harrington mansion. "Price upon request." Ha! Everyone knew it was forty-five million dollars.

By the time a young, slim blonde in a creamy pencil skirt called my name, the décor had accomplished its purpose: I was thoroughly intimidated. The thick carpet in the hallway created a hush, as if we were in a church. And then there he was, Marc Olmsted, welcoming me into his spacious office, larger than my living room.

"Mrs. Deming, so lovely to meet you." Marc's wide smile was pleasant enough, but his gleaming white teeth reminded me a little too much of the Wolf in *Little Red Riding Hood*. His handshake was firm. What I didn't expect was his height, six feet at least. His nearly black hair was slicked back from a face that would have been handsome, but for an overly long jaw and eyes that were slightly too small. Today's bow tie was a subdued purple, the suit a dark navy, the shirt white with a hint of pink. Was this a mourning look for Karen?

"Thanks so much for seeing me. My husband and I are brand new to the idea of owning in Manhattan, but I did some research. I heard you were the best."

Marc's face was warily pleased. "I can't imagine where you would have heard that." I didn't offer any names, as there weren't any. "Why don't you have a seat, and we can chat? Page, can you get us some coffee? Or would you prefer tea?"

"Herbal tea would be perfect," I said. *Perfect,* I'd noticed, was every twenty-five-year-old's favorite adjective. Everything from a coffee order at Starbucks to a job offer is "perfect." And I wanted to come across as young and naive. The blonde assistant nodded and walked out. I had the feeling I was in a James Bond movie, having tea laced with a Roofie.

"So, where do you live now?" Marc asked as we sat down on the Swedish modern couch. The rug had red and black interplanetary swirls.

"The Upper West Side. You couldn't guess?" My act was carefree housewife hoping he wouldn't know about my column and Chilton appointing me amateur sleuth for the wealthy.

"Don't you love Central Park West? We have some fabulous apartments up there. Stunning park views."

"A partial view might be more in our range. But I'd love to see what you have."

As soon as I mentioned a budget, he looked askance at my slacks, which showed signs of wear. He was deciding whether to pass me off to a lesser associate; it was a mistake to mention money at this point. Marc walked to the door and called to an outer office.

"Shane, would you bring the mid-priced listings?"

Time to reel him back in, Melanie.

"Do you consider four million mid-priced?"

Marc's head snapped around, and he gave me a sly smile. No associate for me just yet. He spoke again into the hallway.

"Bring the Central Park West listing at 82$^{nd.}$ And the Riverside Drive four-bedroom."

Shane appeared in the doorway, and his appearance, based on Susie's description, did not disappoint. He wore an Armani suit like Marc's, but in a lighter shade of gray. His shoulders bulged against the sheen of the fabric. No tie, shirt unbuttoned to show a hint of perfectly tanned, smooth chest. His curly brown hair had been streaked with a few blond highlights, and his face conjured a thirty-year-old Brad Pitt. Shane was Marc's secret weapon to help seduce clients, male or female.

"Here are four of our listings," said Shane. "An offer may be coming in on the Central Park West, but it's still available for now." Gorgeous Shane smiled at me, but his eyes were hungry for Marc.

"Is the car here?" Marc asked. A look of panic crossed Shane's face.

"I didn't know you needed it. Naomi took a client. I'll call her." He took out a cell phone and punched in a number.

"Just call an Uber." Marc gave Shane an irritated look before turning his toothy smile back on me. We don't want to keep Ms. Deming waiting." Shane hit more numbers on his cell.

The phone on Marc's desk buzzed. Shane, holding his cellphone in one hand, leaped to answer it. He listened for a moment and put the call on hold. He darted back to Marc and whispered in his ear. I could have sworn I saw his perfect lips form the word 'Harrington.' Marc's eyes widened.

"Would you excuse me for a moment while I take this call in the conference room? You can make yourself comfortable and look at those listings. Shane will answer any questions."

"Of course."

I was enjoying this show so much; looking at overpriced apartments would be boring. Shane watched his lord and master leave the room. When he turned to me, he was transformed into a relaxed, charming companion.

"You know," I said. "I think I saw you the other day at an open house on Park Avenue," I watched his face. Shane looked down and licked his lips. When he looked up, his expression was innocent.

54

"I thought you looked familiar. What a tragedy." I wasn't sure if he meant the apartment or Karen. I'd stick with Karen.

"Yes. I met her briefly, years ago. But you must have known her well, since she worked here. How long was she here at Olmsted?"

"Well, I've worked here eighteen months, and she came after I arrived. I guess one year?"

"You must all be in shock," I said, though no one appeared to care at all.

"Oh, yes. Such a terrible thing. Such violence." He closed his eyes for a second and placed his hand on his chest. Opening them, he smiled and said, "But you're looking for an apartment, and that is a hopeful, blessed event. Like the birth of a child." Shane was very good. Between the looks and the lingo, he was like a sexy saint. I was determined not to get distracted by the hot salesman.

"Was Karen well-liked here?" I tried to keep my face neutral.

"She hadn't made a lot of friends," he said carefully. "She was so busy with family problems. Divorces are nasty, aren't they? How that woman suffered."

"What do you mean, suffered?"

"I try to understand a person's behavior instead of judging them." Shane leaned in for a confidential chat, having established himself on the right side of God. "Karen had serious financial problems after her divorce. You know, with her husband not making support payments. That's why I understood the way she acted."

Now, we were on the right track.

"How exactly did she act?"

"Oh, so cold and nasty to everyone. Clutching at money that wasn't hers, demanding more than her share. It was awful to see what Marc had to go through."

"Did they argue?" I asked.

Shane sighed deeply. "I prayed for it to end. Marc was so patient, but who can take that much tension and fighting? I worry about him. He is the most generous boss."

To Shane, Marc was a demi-god. It was easy to imagine Shane would do a lot more than pray for Karen's demise to please his idol.

"So their fighting really upset you?" I leaned in like a therapist.

"Whose fighting? No one at this firm." Marc strode in furiously. If he could have grabbed Shane and slapped him, he would have. "You're supposed to be showing Ms. Deming our listings. You are, after all, here to buy an apartment—isn't that right?" Marc turned his intense gaze on me, which made me shiver. I heeded Devon's advice and remembered I was there as a reporter. I tried to act comfortable being badgered by an enraged man, which I wasn't. I flashed back to my father and brother hitting each other before my brother moved out. I took a breath.

"Of course, I'm here to buy an apartment." I smiled. "But I was at the open house the other day, and someone told me that Karen Sheldon worked for your firm. I knew Karen years ago. I was just saying to Shane, what a shock and a loss for you all."

"Yes, of course," Marc said. "But life goes on. And if you still want to look at a few apartments, my admin has arranged for you to see two of them. The car has been returned. You can go back to your desk now, Shane."

The chastened Shane left, tail between his legs.

"That sounds great. I have about an hour." We left Olmsted's office and got into the elevator. Marc turned to me.

"We all have to forgive Shane for his assumptions and misperceptions. He's shared with me about his abusive family in the Midwest. There was violence and worse. Sometimes, he gets mixed up and becomes dramatic about relationships when, in reality, everyone at Olmsted is one big happy family. But we love and accept him here. I don't know where Shane would be if I hadn't taken him in when I did. But then I've been accused of being far too generous with employees." Marc put his hand on his heart. Nice touch.

I nodded sympathetically and even patted him on the arm. And the award for humanitarian of the year goes to…

Marc's impressive but small operation, by New York City standards, did one hundred and sixty million dollars in sales last year. It sounded like a lot, but at six percent commission, their take was only nine million dollars. From this amount, he had to pay his brokers, who actually brought in a property, their forty percent commissions. At best, he'd be left with sixty percent, which would be five million four hundred thousand. Running the agency could be two million or more. And the figures most likely had been inflated to impress.

Marc needed that Harrington commission and that phone call just now had alarmed him. He didn't give a damn about her death; that was obvious. Maybe he had even orchestrated it, using his puppet, Shane.

Chapter Eight

The driver opened the door to the black Mercedes sedan with tinted windows. I laughed to myself. Marc considered me a big enough client to get cream-colored plush leather seats and a bar stocked with Evian and Pellegrino.

"First, we're going to a rather unique four-bedroom, where the open living room, dining area, and kitchen all face the Hudson," said Marc. "It's an estate sale. The owner just passed away. Famous artistic family. Of course, I thought of you and your husband. The ask is $3.75 million. Not unreasonable, considering the sprawling size and view." Marc handed me a listing sheet.

"Am I supposed to offer the price? Is real estate still a good investment?" I asked, putting on the persona of a clueless buyer.

Marc gazed out the window, then turned to me.

"New York City real estate is the best investment anyone can make. There have been dips, but over a period of even two years, the owner will always make money when they sell. If you're interested, I'll guide you through any offer. Ah, here we are." The car pulled up to Riverside Drive and 84th Street.

Sure, I thought, New York real estate was a solid investment—unless the stock market crashed, then the bankers stopped paying top prices, and the real estate market would crash too as it had before.

The small but elegant lobby was attended by a doorman plus an elevator man. The contrast with my rental building blew me away.

Marc nodded at the doorman, who waved us to the elevator man, who glided us silently to the fifth floor. Marc opened the door painted a rich red. I stepped into the apartment. A large mirror framed in oak hung over a Mission-style sideboard. The antique sheen of the wood gave an immediate sense of warmth and history. A worn kilim rug with reds and greens covered the wood floor of the entryway. To the left from the foyer spread an open kitchen and large living-dining room.

My jaw dropped. It was like being in the Hudson River. A wall of windows lined the entire length of the open space, providing a picture postcard view. The water sparkled. Boats sailed by. A baby grand piano occupied a corner without overwhelming the room. I felt like crying. I already loved this apartment, and I'd never be able to live here. And who would I live here with anyway? Chloe and me. *Shape up; you're not here to buy.*

"You'd probably want to redo the kitchen," said Marc, striding into the space. "Some people have talked about changing the layout, putting the kitchen on the other side away from the front door, but frankly, once you start moving gas and water lines, you might as well buy a $5 million dollar apartment."

What? I wouldn't change a thing. This felt like home. The walls were covered with family photos. There was an original Hirschfeld caricature of an actor who looked familiar. *Martin Stone,* I realized. Oh, my god, this was his apartment. The Broadway and film icon had just died a few months earlier, at ninety years old. Looking more closely at the photos, I saw that they were from film sets and backstage at Broadway theaters. What a life of fame and fortune he'd led.

"Are you going to look at the rest of the apartment?" Marc was suddenly next to me, breathing impatiently down my neck.

"Oh, yes. Sorry. I was just surprised this was Martin Stone's place." I quickly stepped away from Marc and sprinted into the kitchen.

"Is that a problem?" he asked, once again inches away from me. Marc Olmsted was creepy, even in Armani.

"Absolutely not. I was just suddenly transported into Stone's amazing life." *Change the subject.*

"The kitchen seems very well equipped, actually. The chef's stove, the Sub-Zero fridge. My husband would love this." I ran my hand over the huge slab of wood that formed the ten-foot island, separating the kitchen from the rest of the room.

"And this view. I might actually cook a little, just to watch the boats." Marc smiled politely. He had no sense of humor. Marc took a phone call.

I walked back through the foyer. Marc waved me over to the other side of the apartment as he talked. I peered down the hall at what seemed like an endless line of rooms. First was a huge bedroom with a king-sized bed and two big easy chairs. A cluster of awards stood on a dresser, including one I was pretty sure was a Tony.

Returning to the hallway, I saw Marc was still on the phone. I strode deeper into the apartment, getting lost in a maze of rooms and hallways. I emerged from another bathroom—classic black and white tiles, but with a modern pedestal sink and gleaming copper fixtures—and ran smack into Marc. Startled, I laughed. He didn't. In fact, he seemed to be blocking my way down the narrow hall. Suddenly, I was gripped with fear. If he was responsible for Karen's murder, I shouldn't have come here alone.

"So you were at the open house where Karen was murdered." He must have overheard my talk with Shane. Damn. His stare was unnerving.

I smiled stupidly and nodded. "A friend dragged me over. I'd never buy on the East side, though. This is more my kind of place."

I tried to squeeze past him, but he didn't budge.

"I had no idea you knew Karen Sheldon," Marc said in the same menacing tone. I had to get myself out of this apartment.

"Not well. Her kids are much older than my daughter. " Did Marc seem to calm down? "I'd like to go back and look at the Master bedroom if that's okay."

I smiled at him brightly. He still didn't move. My heart was beating so hard I thought he might feel it, wedged as we were together in the hall. Where was a weapon? I could do damage with a shower curtain rod in the bathroom, but wrenching it off the wall would take too much time.

"I heard there was a big turnout of Huntley School parents at the open house, because of Susie Carlbach," he said. "And that the school called a meeting to discuss Karen's death. What was said there about her murder?"

He must have a snoop on the inside. How else would he know about the meeting? Did he know that I spoke with Susie? He might know Chilton announced to the group that I'd solved Ralph's murder last year at the playground. My cover as a prospective buyer was blown. I kept my voice chatty and light, which was not easy considering my growing terror. I couldn't get past Marc.

"The detective told the group to cooperate by giving any information. A psychologist detective talked about how to reassure children. A little about security at Huntley. That was all, really." My voice went from peppy to squeaky. I could feel Marc's hot breath on my neck. He was very tall and thin, but he carried himself as if he worked out. I didn't stand a chance if he wanted to hurt me. And he was oozing rage despite his terrifyingly level tone.

"How well do you know Susie?" he asked.

Seriously? We were going to play Huntley geography? How about going back to that lovely car now?

"Oh, everybody knows Susie. That's why the open house was so crowded. Not because of the apartment. I mean, that wallpaper, those mirrors. Appalling."

I almost sobbed as if awful decorators caused me unbearable pain. I deserved one of Martin Stone's Tony awards for this performance. For a precious moment, Marc was distracted by the tragedy of the decor at 962 Park. His body relaxed. I spotted two inches of additional space between his arm and the wall. I quickly pushed past him, nearly running to the front door.

"How many bedrooms are there altogether?" I stuck with my story of being a buyer even if Marc had learned differently during his phone call. I gathered up my things. Marc walked slowly out to the foyer.

"Four. One of the studies could fit a bed." His eyes narrowed. "Are you interested?" He shifted gears as he considered whether I was a serious buyer. Intimidating a client, it appeared, was not a recommended sales technique.

"I'd like to bring my husband back. You said you also have another apartment to show me?"

"I can't get there today. I have some pressing issues at the office."

I was not disappointed. Next time, I'd bring Rebecca. We went downstairs to the waiting car.

"I can walk home from here. Thanks for taking the time today. I know how busy you must be."

He looked at me coldly."I'm surprised you haven't asked me about Karen. You were so quick to discuss her with Shane."

Now that I was out on the street, I felt freer.

"Well, now that you mention it, people say Karen would never have been killed if her husband hadn't left her. She wouldn't have been in real estate at all. And business had something to do with her murder. Do you agree?"

Marc pursed his lips.

"I give everyone a chance. It is my downfall. But do I think she had the soul of a broker? No." *News to me that brokers had souls.* He gazed down the block. "She had a lot of rich friends, but that can only take you so far. If this horrible thing hadn't happened, I think she would have been out of the game as soon as she found a new, wealthy husband. She came on to every man she met, married or not." Marc's face was a picture of contempt. Susie said the same. I pushed on.

"Who do you think killed her?" I asked and watched his face.

Not a muscle changed. " Karen was her own worst enemy. She may have behaved badly with the husbands of her clients. That's all I'll say. She had plenty of people who disliked her."

Which husbands? I couldn't ask, but the cops would get her client list.

"What about the Harrington Mansion? There was a lot of speculation about whether your agency would still be involved, without Karen. Not that I'm in the market for quite that much space." I said this lightly, as if I just loved juicy real estate gossip.

Marc Olmsted looked down at me from his imposing height. "You probably heard that from your friend Susie Carlbach. She's been salivating about the Harringtons. They strung her along even after they'd given the listing to Karen. From what I heard, Susie had a full-on fit the day that listing became ours."

Marc continued.

"Did Susie tell you she and Karen went to high school together? They'd been rivals for years, and not just about real estate." He seemed even taller and flexed his arms under his suit. "Susie would have done anything to get that listing from Karen. She'd stolen clients from her before. She even tried to get Greg Sheldon way back when." His eyes darkened, and his mouth twitched slightly. "I wouldn't put anything past Susie. She knows people who know people for anything. You should be investigating Susie."

Of course. He continued.

"The Harrington mansion will be with Olmsted until it sells. Our reputation does not depend on any one agent. You might do some homework before you come barging in, asking questions of my staff and making outrageous assumptions." He opened the door to the car.

"I can find anyone a dream apartment. That is what I do better than anyone else. Though I doubt you're really in the market." Marc's face turned dark. Fear swept over me again. "For any other issues, keep away from my office."

"I expect a glowing report about Olmsted in your column." He lowered his 6'2" frame into the back seat. "And don't underestimate me. My legal team can destroy you." He slammed the door shut. Thank God the car pulled away.

As I walked up West End Avenue, I felt anger building. Marc Olmsted was a bully. Maybe a murderer. I would not underestimate him, but I could go around him.

Chapter Nine

"So, you're involved in another murder."

Daniel threw out this opening grenade while grilling turkey, duck, lamb, and God-knows-what sausages, delivered a few days before from a Vermont farm called *We Love Our Animals*. Their slogan is, 'We give them the best from birth to your belly.' Gross.

This farm wanted to gain traction with the natural restaurant market in New York and they wanted Daniel's seal of approval. Five pounds of sausages cooking in the morning were a pungent reminder to me that we were the odd couple. Fifteen years ago, we couldn't keep our hands off each other. Now, when I looked at Daniel, all I saw was his curly, graying hair and growing paunch spattered with sizzling meat.

"I thought we declared the kitchen a demilitarized zone," I quipped, trying to keep it light. He must have seen my half-page story in the *Westsider* this week. I was more shaky dealing with Daniel than with a potential murderer.

"Demilitarized, meaning I'm not allowed to question why you're jumping into another murder, but you're free to lecture me about fat and calories?" Daniel looked up from the sausages long enough to give me an accusing stare. He had a point, annoying as it was; he was a writer.

"Cutting down on calories and fat saves lives," I argued.

"Staying away from murderers saves lives, too," he countered. "You almost bought the farm a year ago. Not to mention what could have happened if Chloe had been home during your fight to the death with that crazy woman, right here in our foyer." Daniel's outrage made his ruddy cheeks even redder.

This was partially true. Nobody had died, though. It wasn't my fault the killer walked into our apartment.

"That won't happen again. I swear," I said weakly. Marc Olmsted in that hallway flashed in my mind. I went to Daniel and put my arms around his shoulder. "I have a feeling it was scarier to hear about afterward than it was in the moment. And now we lock our doors." I kissed his cheek.

"I've never been terrified in my life," Daniel insisted, pulling away. This, from the man who made me trap a mouse at a summer rental. I took goat yogurt and nuts out of the fridge and prepared to leave for fencing. Good for aggression and your butt.

"Anyway, Daniel, whoever killed Karen Sheldon wouldn't be caught dead in our apartment. We're not even shabby chic to those folks, just shabby." I grinned. Daniel looked crushed.

"There's nothing wrong with this apartment. It's a classic six. It could use some new furniture, that's all. Why don't you spend some of your screenplay money?" He glared at me as he tenderly turned his sausages.

"So I could hang a sign saying 'Newly redecorated classic six—open to Park Avenue killer'?" I burst into laughter. Daniel smiled thinly.

One thing we used to share was a total lack of interest in what our surroundings looked like. But Daniel worked now in a world of splashy book launches and posh restaurant openings. He'd been raised with money. Maybe he was serious about new furniture. The only furniture I'd spend my money on was a desk and chair I bought for my writing nook. Still, I was grateful. Decorating had replaced the feud about Karen's murder.

The smell of sausages made me sick. I left for the gym. Daniel said nothing more. Maybe the kitchen was the perfect place to argue.

* * *

"How can I find out where Karen Sheldon went to high school?" I asked Rebecca later in the day on the phone.

"Why? You think a high school sweetheart carried a grudge for twenty years? No guys I slept with in high school cared that much about me, or anything else, ten seconds after we'd done it." Rebecca laughed.

" Really. I wouldn't know," I mumbled. I hadn't had sex till college. "Not sure her sex life at seventeen is the issue. Marc Olmsted said Karen and Susie have been enemies since high school. Allegedly, they feuded about guys, including Dr. Greg. Olmsted insisted they fought about listings, too."

Rebecca was silent for a full minute, a record for her.

"So Marc Olmsted thinks there was a cauldron simmering under the surface of what appeared to now just be acquaintances. Most people are killed by someone they know. Fascinating that Susie was a Greg Sheldon groupie, too, from high school. This club just keeps getting bigger," Rebecca snickered. She went on.

"Wait a minute. When I told Paul what happened to Karen Sheldon, he said he remembered that name, that she had gone to a high school near him. He went to Croton High in Westchester. I'll text him now. What do you know, my husband might actually be useful. Hold on, I'll be back."

"Eastchester High," Rebecca said when she returned. "That's where Karen went."

"Great intel, Rebecca. Does Paul know Susie, too?" Rebecca texted him again.

Then she was back. "Here's the story. He thinks Susie was at Eastchester also, or nearby. Paul's buddy is married to a woman who went to Eastchester. Paul thinks he can come up with some dirt. It could take a day or two."

"This is more than enough to start with," I said, excited. "I'm going to another Susie Carlbach open house. I'll find a way to bring up the subject of high school. See if I get any vibe from her. Speaking of vibes, Marc Olmsted was beyond creepy yesterday. He's one angry guy. Gorgeous apartment, though. The late, great Martin Stone's, with panoramic river views."

"Melanie," Rebecca said sternly. "It's too dangerous, being alone with suspects and provoking them. Cut it out." She paused and chuckled. "Or take me along. Martin Stone's apartment. Wow."

"Exactly. I need you to help me decide which $4 million place to buy." I didn't want to admit how terrified I was in that narrow hallway.

"It might be the last time I see Olmsted, though. He's caught on that I want information more than an apartment.

* * *

The open house the next day was at a single-family brownstone on East 93rd Street near 3rd Avenue—an expensive neighborhood, but not as elite as Park Avenue. Susie was one of two listing agents. The open house was in the afternoon, and the townhouse was near enough to Huntley for me to make it in time for pick-up. Susie herself had emailed, urging me to show up since Shane would be there with a client. But it was Susie and her high school days that were in my sights, not Shane.

Maybe I'd taken too much DHEA, a hormone that promotes energy. I was panting with excitement at the thought of confronting Susie. This should have been a big red flag for me to slow down. It wasn't.

I walked down East 93rd, more annoyed than usual by how clean the street was compared to the West side. I took a gum wrapper and let it deliberately fall onto the sidewalk. Let them see what garbage looks like. Definitely crazy. Stop, you're acting crazy. Go for a run.

Instead, I marched up the steps of the brownstone to the double front doors like a process server in search of prey. Brownstone doors were made of a rich, varnished wood, with arched panels elegantly harking back to a more gracious era. Not here. Two slabs of thick glass behind ornate metal gates embellished with signs of the Zodiac. Asking to be smashed, I thought. Inside, there was a fountain spilling into a small pool of koi fish destined to be dead within a few hours. The foyer ceiling was at least fifteen feet high. The floor, for some reason, was poured concrete. The effect was Wealthy Buddhist Retreat. Maybe I'd crossed a portal and was in Marin in northern California.

The place was blinding white. Every shred of 19th-century dignity had been erased— ornate cherry moldings, wood paneling, sconces, stained-glass windows. Nothing of the era remained except the brown sandstone facade, which had likely only been left intact because of landmarking laws.

Stark white walls surrounded an open floor plan, with a frightening huge black gas fireplace. A gigantic kitchen island of stainless steel and granite rose from floors of white wood. Floor-to-ceiling cheap sliding glass doors led to a backyard, which had probably once been lushly overgrown but was now covered in multiple layers of decking and concrete. I saw an eight-burner gas grill. A single tree was left—a Linden, very common all over the city. But this one was surrounded by huge clay pots filled with waving straw plants, as arid as the desert. I returned to the foyer and up a floating staircase with metal railings and clear glass steps. A stairway to heaven or a good way to break your neck.

Shane was in the hall outside one of the bedrooms with an emaciated older woman hanging on his arm. She'd had too many facelifts; her lips barely moved as she asked Shane what he thought of the house.

"It's perfect for you," he said. "Elegant, clean lines—it's like a canvas waiting for your unique design." I recognized the woman. It was Caroline Bach, the iconic designer of outrageously expensive clothing. She was a fixture at the annual Met Ball. She could certainly afford the $8 million dollar price tag here.

Shane's eyes widened when he saw me. I nodded and continued on. Susie was my target today. Another couple, from India, the woman in a gorgeous gold threaded sari, walked through without saying a word. The husband was decked out in an expensive black suit and white shirt, no tie. I saw them confer with Rachel, Susie's assistant as she took down their information and I think wrote down a number. Was everyone but me a multi-millionaire?

Susie was in the master bedroom, which—no surprise—was bright white with one beige accent pillow. There were a few women milling around, two of whom I recognized from Huntley. I'd bet neither was looking to buy, just snooping and waiting to see if another murder happened. By now, I was so irate at so much money being spent to make this empty shell that I forgot why I was here.

"Is there somewhere we can talk?" I asked too loud. Susie had her back to me, deep in a conversation with someone. She turned and motioned with her eyes that we should leave the bedroom. I followed her out to the staircase. Susie wore white pants with a filmy white sleeveless blouse and her usual large gold bracelets.

I was fixated on the glass staircase. "This brownstone is a tragedy. These were irreplaceable sources of 19th-century architecture."

Susie gave me a withering look. "This particular irreplaceable source was a rundown SRO for years. The plumbing and wiring were gone. There was no kitchen. The chimney had caught fire. If it hadn't been landmarked, it would have been torn down long ago." She sighed. "Is this why you interrupted me—to lecture me on New York architecture, about which you clearly know nothing?"

I didn't know it had been an SRO, but she didn't have to be so nasty. I jumped in with both feet.

"Why didn't you tell me you had a feud with Karen going all the way back to Eastchester High?"

Real estate agents and police officers have a lot in common. They all go to similar type schools that taught rigid facial control. Susie stared at me. Her face showed no shock or any emotion. But her neck tensed for a nanosecond. In that moment, I knew she'd been at school with Karen. In another nanosecond, she regained her bitchy composure.

"Who are you to come here and confront me like this?" she hissed. "I'm working. I don't have time for your silly games."

"You haven't been straight with me. You've known Karen since high school, and you've always hated her, is what I heard." I was bluffing; I didn't have any real information yet, except for what Olmsted had told me. Paul's source hadn't come through. Yet I barreled on. "You and Karen fought about everything, from guys to property. Did you want her dead?"

Maybe it was the DHEA I'd taken, or that I just didn't like Susie. This was a ridiculous accusation to make so soon in the investigation. Accusing her in public was dangerous. Susie almost looked pleased at the invitation to fight. She was an expert.

"I don't know what you're talking about, Melanie," she said loudly. "Karen and I were cordial friends and colleagues. High school was a long time ago. Marc Olmsted feeds you lies, and you gobble them up like an amateur. We don't need someone like you working for us."

"I don't work for you," I retorted. "You tried to bribe me into giving you information, remember? Well, I'm giving you information now."

Susie stuck her chin in my face.

"Look, sweetheart, be careful making crazy accusations. There are rumors already about you. Lots of people walk in Central Park besides you and your sexy guy. Look around sometime." The smile she gave me was pure evil.

My heart stopped. I backed away from Susie and almost tumbled down the abominable floating stairs. The two Huntley mothers emerged from the bedroom to watch. I grabbed hold of the steel railing and ran down the stairs like a mortified teenager at a sorority hazing. I'd taken more than a few walks in Central Park with Devon. Now I knew someone had seen us.

Stop running. You haven't killed anybody, I yelled at myself. I slowed down and pretended to be calm as I walked out the door and down to the sidewalk. My heart was pounding so hard it hurt. My phone buzzed. "Hi! I'm here! When can we get together?" Devon chirped.

Chapter Ten

"Never again unless you have a bunker sunk in the Atlantic," I yelled so loud a babysitter pushing a sleeping child shushed me.

Ouch. My foot smacked a stone planter outside the entrance to a brick apartment building, catapulting me onto the evergreen in the planter. I grabbed for dear life like it was a redwood. It wasn't. Shaking pine needles from my hair, I looked up. Two doormen and an elderly woman couldn't stop laughing. Great. I put my head down and scurried away.

Devon chuckled, which felt like a warm, soothing blanket.

"I can make a bunker happen," he said. "How about Queens? A friend lives on the water." I was silent. He got serious. "What happened?"

"I'm wrong for this work. I just went after Susie Ohrbach, and she went after my neck. She warned me that if I accused her of any wrongdoing with Karen she'd tell Daniel someone had seen me with you in Central Park. Several women were listening. I'm turning in my detective badge." Out of breath, I started hiccuping. Devon was silent for a brief moment.

"You're panicking for no reason," he scoffed. "We didn't have sex in Central Park, and it was a year ago, anyway. You were upset because Nadine was badly beaten. I gave you a hug. Nothing else happened. Anyone who saw us knows that."

My pulse and my feet slowed. "I attacked her first. That's the problem. I practically accused her of murdering Karen."

"Melanie, slow down. You tell everyone to breathe and meditate. So you charged in. So what. You didn't lose anything." He paused and added. "You don't seem to have trouble with slow and easy in other areas," Devon

71

murmured, and my cheeks—along with other body parts—grew warm.

"We can't even risk being seen at a diner now, even with manuscripts all over the table, so don't get all X-rated with me." I stopped at 93rd and Lexington, a noisy corner, at 2:30 in the afternoon. Buses, cars, and an ambulance blared.

"We wrote a screenplay together. Now we're working on a second. We're business partners. Don't let the bad guys get to you. Then they win." Devon struggled with kids at school, and with his father. This was personal for him.

"I was just threatened in public. Susie wants to stir up trouble with Daniel. These brokers are coiled snakes." I took a breath and went on.

"Devon, you interview some of these creeps. I'll stay with the Huntley moms. I already got a call from Sandra Crane. She read my first piece about the murder. She asked me to come over with Chloe this afternoon. I can't mess up too much at her apartment with the girls running around for a playdate, right?" I sounded pitiful.

"Who cares? Meet me tomorrow for lunch. How about Midtown? I know a tiny Japanese restaurant. No East Side crowd."

"Not Midtown—someone could be going to a matinee. Uptown near Columbia. Friedman's, at 118$^{th.}$ It'll be all students." We made a date and hung up.

I had too much adrenaline pulsing through me. With thirty minutes before pickup at Huntley, it was time to add some steps to a measly 6,892. My cropped cotton pants, and white sneakers would work for a quick run. I headed to the Central Park reservoir track. Susie's threat faded away as I stripped off my sweater and joined the other runners. I sailed past the ducks and the familiar skyline surrounding the man-made lake in the middle of New York City.

A full lap, 1.6 miles, brought me to 10,255 steps. I arrived at Huntley only mildly sweaty, just as the fourth graders came out. Great timing. I didn't have to make chit-chat with Size Zero Laura, who today wore a silk jumpsuit and cashmere wrap that would have looked more at home lounging on a settee at the pool. I gave her a wave. Gabby, my fellow West Sider, was decked out in Lululemon running gear that looked brand new. We nodded hello, fellow conspirators, after our conversation the day of the murder. I wondered what she told Chilton about Karen's last fight with Greg.

Patty Baylor, who found Karen, was there also, picking up her son. She looked grim. She saw me and ran over. "I need to talk to you."

"What about?" I asked.

"The back door at Park Avenue," she whispered.

"What about the back door? I can't talk now. Can you call me?" She nodded yes. I doubted Patty had anything much to add. I found Chloe, and we joined Sandra Crane and her daughter Tiffany for the short walk to their Madison Avenue apartment.

* * *

Sandra's apartment was nowhere near the sprawling opulence of Buffy's townhouse or Cornelia's duplex. Roy Crane was an investment banker, but not in the same stratosphere. Sandra came from a working-class family in Pennsylvania. She said they had issues, and she didn't see them often. She and her husband were politically conservative and had been above gossip until the previous year when a rumor circulated that he'd been seen leaving a Midtown hotel with a voluptuous younger woman. Suddenly, the Cranes were in the front pew at church on Madison Avenue every week. And Sandra sported that large emerald ring.

They'd combined two apartments, putting the kids on one end and the master suite on the other, with a great room in the middle. The place had been expensively decorated, but it struck me as utilitarian, not a showplace. School bags hung neatly in a cubby near the front door. The girls grabbed granola bars and ran into Tiffany's bedroom. Sandra and I sat at her large granite-topped kitchen island. To my surprise, she immediately started to cry.

I waited through her quiet sniffles, wondering whether the tears were for Karen or for her own marriage, or because her daughter had not gotten an A on a math test. You really could never tell with these people.

"I try so hard to be a good Christian in this awful, sin-filled city." *Amen,* I

73

mumbled.

"Roy is so depressed about the ethical wasteland here. He comes from Des Moines, where his family ran the bank, and no one ever broke the law. You wouldn't believe the pressure he's under to do illegal trades. Which he would never do." I nodded. His family had money. He could afford to be ethical.

"Is that what's upsetting you?" I asked.

She let out a deep, martyred sigh. "No. It's about Karen's death. I need to tell someone what I think." She looked at me with tear-filled hazel eyes. She was attractive, well-groomed more than pretty, with a head of expensive cherry-blonde highlights and a retro pouffy haircut that belonged on her grandmother.

"I'm all ears. But you know you have to talk to the police, right?"

She looked at the floor, then back up, shaking her head. "This isn't *evidence*. It's embarrassing, and you have to swear you'll never tell anyone." I was sorely tempted to say that everyone already knew.

"No problem," I said.

Sandra suddenly got the urge to straighten her already neat counter, which was lined with cute ceramic jars stenciled with farm animals.

"Greg Sheldon is not the man he appears to be," she finally said. She looked at me for a response. I bit the inside of my cheek to stop a loud laugh.

"Well, most people aren't. And...?"

"He cheated on Karen for years."

Tolerance, Melanie. Patience. I could hear Devon. "Actually," I said, "I've heard that from a few sources, so you aren't betraying any confidence."

"Well then, don't you see? He must be the killer," Sandra said urgently.

"That's not necessarily true," I said. "Greg and Karen were already separated, nearly divorced. Why would he kill her?"

She cleared her throat. "I know things about Greg that other people don't. We were very close." She sounded like a script from *One Life to Live*.

"Sandra, did you have an affair with Greg?" She looked as if I'd ripped off her dress. Her pale blue eyes widened.

"Yes. But it's not what you think. It only happened once or maybe twice?"

Oh really. "It was after his usual hours. He'd give me a special appointment time, after his nurse left." I wondered if she had to pay extra.

"Other than the fact you had a fling, what is it that makes you so sure he's the killer?"

Sandra squared her shoulders and crossed her hands in her lap, twisting the emerald ring on her finger. "He was very stressed about money. He actually asked me if my husband could get him a loan, or if I had money stashed away for a rainy day. That was the last time we met after hours." Such a delicate way to say hooking up. I squelched a laugh.

"There are other people who knew he had money problems, so you're not betraying him, Sandra," I said. "And I have to say, asking you for money is pretty sleazy, considering you were having sex."

"Shh! I don't want the children to hear."

"They're making a lot of noise," I said. " I doubt they can hear anything. Should we move into your living room?" Sandra stared intently at a pot on the stove that had a smudge. She really wanted to get up and clean it. She turned to me.

"I was shocked when he asked about a loan. He said my husband must be doing well. That hurt. He'd told me I was unlike any woman he'd ever met. This was last year, when I was at a low point. So, I fell for it. Now I think he didn't care about me at all. He was just looking for money." She waited for me to contradict her. I didn't.

"What else do you know about him, Sandra? Since you were close. Ever hear him threatening Karen?"

A sad expression crossed her face. She had really liked this gigolo. Her words came out in a whisper. "He said once that death was easier than divorce. And the surviving spouse ends up with all the money." Useful information, but everyone has probably had that thought in a rancorous marriage.

"And Greg said he'd have to declare bankruptcy if he couldn't pay off his loans from medical school. Can you imagine still having two hundred and fifty thousand in school debt at his age?"

To me, it sounded like a good way to get sympathy from a woman who thought a Yale education was the key to holiness. I suspected Greg's loans were long paid off. But he might need money for other reasons—to keep Miss Russia happy, because of bad investments or gambling debts, or to live like a high roller in New York City.

"Did he mention any other debts, or anything else in your afternoon... appointments?" I was positive they'd done it more than twice before he'd asked for money. Probably a few times afterwards, too, to see if he could convince her.

"He seemed nervous and in a hurry the last time we met. And he yelled at someone on the phone to stop calling him."

"Sandra, when was the last time you saw him? "

She looked a tad sheepish. "It was three weeks ago. I mean, I needed filler anyway." I laughed. An unadvertised two-for-one special. Later, as Chloe and I got on the bus, I realized that Greg Sheldon's fiancée, Marlena Shenko, might be eager to spill information about him. He'd been cheating on her with everyone.

* * *

The next day, Friedman's, far uptown, was filled with students and professors, since Columbia owned most of the buildings from 110th up to 135th. Still, I nervously checked out all the tables. Devon had secured a table in the back. My eyes took him in before he saw me. He was just as appealing now as when I'd met him a year ago. Same light brown hair with hints of gray. Same blue eyes, same sweetness to his face despite the rugged jaw. I could feel the solid muscles of his shoulders when he stood and enveloped me in a bear hug. It all looked friendly and innocent enough. But after ten seconds, neither of us wanted to let go. I pulled away first.

"It's been two months," he said. He was tan, and the stubble of a beard on his face was way too attractive.

"Time is actually the same here as in Zimbabwe, you know," I said. "Just behind by seven hours. So, technically, it's been seven hours less than two months." Damn, it was hard to look at him. "I wish I didn't feel so happy to see you."

"Nice seeing you, too, Mel." He reached for my hand, but I took it back.

"You know what I mean. And running off to exotic locations only ups the ante when we see each other. I can't even get tired of you."

"Some women might consider that a good feature."

The waiter came, and we both ordered. Scrambled tofu and gluten-free toast for me, A Beyond burger for Devon. We talked about the murder and outlined scenes for a screenplay. We were a good writing team. Devon was calm. I was unpredictable. He had more police contacts, but this time, I had my Huntley connections. We tried out different scenarios working backwards, changing who did it. It was easy to build a case against the real estate agents.

"I was a real estate agent once," Devon announced.

"In another lifetime?"

"When I tried acting for a few years, I used real estate to make money."

"You were an actor? Full of surprises," I pretended nonchalance.

"Very short-lived career. Two commercials. I liked writing more. End of story. But what I learned about real estate is all bad. Grabbing listings from each other even in the same agency. Constant pressure. Having to be available all day and night to show apartments to people who eventually bought from someone else. I think the pressure weeds out decent people. What's left are sharks."

"That sounds like the agents I've met," I nodded. "How desperate are they? Would Susie or Olmsted or Shane actually commit murder to get a big listing? "

" Maybe. We need to find out their personal financial situations. See if Marc was close to going under."

"Money or jealousy. The motive has to be one or the other. I want to meet Greg's fiancée, Marlena. I heard she gets her hair done at the Jean Le Claire salon. Hairdresser to the stars, at one thousand dollars a pop. Cornelia has a contact who can tell me when she'll be there."

"You're going to spend a thousand dollars on your hair?" Devon looked shocked.

"No way. Maybe after I've talked to her, I'll get an urgent call and have to leave."

Devon took my hand between both of his and stroked my fingers. The jolt went straight through my body.

"This is not a good idea," I said.

"No one knows you here." He didn't let go of my hand.

"Let's leave."

I took my hand away. We got the check. We walked across the street and onto the Columbia University campus, more parklike than you'd expect in Manhattan.

"Have you ever been to St. Paul's Chapel?" Devon asked, holding my elbow discreetly. We walked up the steps of the domed library and beyond into a quiet square of ornate buildings, in the center of which stood a jewel-like little church. Here, above street level, there was a hushed atmosphere as a few scattered students walked through to class. The chapel had three tall columns in front. Above the entryway were engraved the words Pro Ecclesia Dei. Atop the brick and limestone building sat a large dome encircled by stained-glass windows.

"Let's go in," I said, trotting up the steps. Churches in New York were often surprising gifts of beauty. The front doors were open. We walked softly into the magnificent empty space. I felt as though we'd stumbled into some heavenly old church in the hills of Umbria. My eyes unexpectedly filled with tears. Devon led me by the hand to an alcove off the main space, where it was dark and secluded. He grabbed me in a long, deep kiss. We kissed each other gently and then more urgently. Finally, I pulled away.

"I'm not taking anything off in a church," I said, my hand on his chest. "This is blasphemous enough."

"No blasphemy here," he murmured, kissing me again more intensely. I stayed with him, kiss for kiss. Touching him again, the world disappeared. I tried not to think about what that meant.

There were muffled footsteps. I pulled away.

"We can't," I said. "We stood together, breathing heavily, like after a fast run. "This is a really complicated murder. I can't think straight. You're only here for a week—I'll still be here in the middle of this mess."

We looked longingly at each other. I gave Devon a last lingering kiss and quickly walked out of the church, leaving him standing there. Outside, the campus shimmered with light and energy. I snapped a photo to capture the scene—the students and professors, the impeccable brick walkways surrounded by manicured lawns and trees. It was a long time before I looked at the picture and realized what I had seen.

When I got home, I looked up St. Paul's Chapel on Wikipedia. No wonder I'd felt transported. The church was only one hundred and twenty years old, but its interior was designed in the Byzantine style. The exterior was Italian Renaissance. The Latin over the door, when translated, proclaimed "For the Assembly of God." I could only hope God looked kindly on adulterous lovers.

Chapter Eleven

You owe me. I hate standing for three hours. I hate the misogynist storylines in these endless, crashingly boring screechfests."

Rebecca stopped ranting long enough to take a sip of her Merlot. It was intermission at the Metropolitan Opera House—one of two New York City cultural institutions nicknamed The Met.

"A woman actually enjoys sex, like in *Carmen*, and the guy who screwed her kills her." She took another big gulp of wine. "In Tosca, she kills herself because her lover is shot. In La Boheme, she dies coughing herself to death while the men screw around at the cafe."

Even in her contempt of opera, Rebecca still knew her stuff. Her outfit was as defiant as her attitude; she wore a short leather skirt and a fringed blue suede blouse that looked straight out of Woodstock. She was stunning no matter what she wore, with straight blonde hair and model-high cheekbones belying her razor-sharp mind. We stood in the lobby with our drinks. Rebecca ignored the open leers of the three-piece-suited bankers, who were accompanied by overdressed wives. I doubted they were looking at me, in fake suede pants and my only pair of chunky high-heeled shoes. These guys were probably all here on season tickets, paid for by their companies in case an important client wanted a night of high culture out on the town. And the wives came just for the excuse to dress up.

"You know why we're here," I said, sipping a wine spritzer that was mostly spritzer. "Buffy the Vampire Slayer comes to the opera. I have to catch her off guard."

"Melanie, you don't know for sure she's here. She could easily have skipped this bore. She doesn't pay for her three hundred and fifty dollar ticket, anyway. And we paid forty dollars to stand. Life is unfair."

Rebecca stared across the lobby and looked appalled.

"Do you see that hideous shirtwaist with the big black-and-white plaid? That dress might as well say, 'I have not had sex in years.' It's as stiff as a canvas. She should just hang herself on the wall."

I laughed. Rebecca was right. The woman wearing the monstrosity in question was also featured in fundraiser photos displayed downstairs. The Met was one of the most famous music houses in the world, but it was also a fashion runway. There was a fifty-foot-wide red-carpeted staircase leading down to the orchestra section. This was flanked on either side by curved red-carpeted staircases leading to an open promenade. A prime spot to check out the crowd and be seen. An enormous chandelier hung over it all. A glass wall of windows and doors provided a view of Lincoln Center's grand plaza and the dancing water fountain, a miniature of the one at the Bellagio in Las Vegas. Once you entered the Met, you were part of the show.

We sipped our wine and judged the fashion parade. Was anyone here for the music? I knew I wasn't. I scanned the crowd for Buffy, or anyone from the list of Greg's lovers, or anyone who had been at the open house where Karen had been killed.

"If you don't see her soon, I'm leaving," Rebecca announced. "I don't want to watch this young woman die a slow, painful death in the final act."

Just then, Buffy appeared in a gold-flecked sheath and headed toward the ladies' room. I followed her. The line from the bathroom snaked upstairs. I jumped in behind Buffy.

"Hi," I said. "I didn't know you liked Verdi."

Buffy turned her head, nodded, and turned her back to me. Suddenly, she whirled around and pinned me with her hawk eyes.

"Why are you and your hideously dressed friend here?" She looked at Rebecca, who was trying unsuccessfully to be discreet, twenty steps away. "And by the way, *La Boheme* is Puccini, not Verdi." The woman in front of Buffy gave me a look that could wither plants.

I was going to try a friendly approach, but when Buffy insulted my best friend, I saw red.

"We can't all afford your Valenciaga or Prado or whatever it is you've got on," I said, dropping my eyes over her dress with disdain. "Not that I'd wear something my mother-in-law would wear, anyway." Buffy gleefully accepted my invitation to fight.

"It's obvious that you know nothing about fashion, since you show up at Huntley day after day in the same jeans. And you can't even pronounce the most famous names in the fashion world. Doesn't your husband make enough to spring for another pair of jeans?" The woman behind me grabbed my arm.

"I know a great fashion consultant. She won't cost much.?" she said. Buffy grinned. I seethed.

I pictured grabbing Buffy by her long, scrawny neck and watching the breath leave her body until I remembered that's what had happened to Karen and that Karen was the reason I came to this opera. Karen was a victim, like Mimi in *La Boheme*.

Get back on track, I said to myself. Don't attack Buffy like you did with Susie. Not that we'd ever been friends. But I needed them to talk to me if I was going to make any progress in finding Karen's killer. Devon was counting on me to work my Huntley connections.

"Can we call a truce here, Buffy? " I said, trying a different tack. "You know, like a half-hour cease-fire?"

"Why would I do that?" she said, her voice ice cold.

"For Karen, how about that?"

Buffy's eyes widened. She sensed I knew something. "Karen was…a lovely woman with impeccable taste," she said, clearly grasping for something nice to say about a woman whose husband she'd been screwing in his office. "Did you see the paisley dress she was wearing the day she died? From Ralph Lauren's new silk collection. It was right in the window of the shop on Madison." Buffy sniffed and proceeded huffily down three steps as the line moved.

The woman in front of her, in a short cocktail dress, actually turned around to say, "Lauren's new silk shirtwaists are really divine. And so reasonable."

What was wrong with these people? Their laser focus on looks made me snort.

I hurried down the steps after Buffy.

"Fascinating," I said. "But I was thinking more about Greg. Speaking of fashion statements, he does the high-end cowboy ski bum look pretty well. I know that's an appealing look to a lot of women. Maybe to you?" I whispered this and kept my expression innocent. Buffy faced me with a look of shock and contempt.

"You're just on a fishing expedition. My relationship with Greg was strictly about dermatology." She took another step toward the bathrooms. We were getting closer. I had to speed this up.

"Really? Not gynecological? Come on, you weren't the only one. I'm not here to judge. I just want to know what intimate confessions he might have made that could help us catch Karen's killer."

When Buffy glared at me, I went for a look of sympathy that seemed to throw her off guard. Suddenly, she leaned in, almost touching my face, so close I could smell her perfume. *Soleil Blanc*, by Tom Ford. Six hundred and fifty dollar an ounce. Cornelia would be proud of me for recognizing it, I thought. I'd spent too much time with her at the perfume counter at Bergdorf's one afternoon.

Buffy whispered into my ear, making my face tickle. "I may not have been Greg's only fling, but I know I was the best. And you're looking in the wrong direction going to his paramours." She had her mouth on my ear by now. " Money's at the root of Karen's murder. Follow the money, and you'll find the assailant." She stepped into the bathroom near the stalls.

I was so stunned to hear Buffy whisper, a voice I'd never heard in all her years of tyranny at Huntley Parent meetings, that I missed my turn for the bathroom. With all those kegel exercises, I could wait. I turned around and left. Rebecca was lurking in a dark corner in the lounge.

"I thought she'd eaten you and flushed your remains down the toilet by now," she said. "You don't look so good. Did she make you retch?"

"Not this time. She basically confirmed what I already knew. But she said to 'follow the money.'Does that mean she knows who did it? " I rubbed my ear and scrunched up my face like a kid who just smelled sardines. "Her lips touched my ear. Yuck. I hope I don't have nightmares."

Buffy strode quickly out of the bathrooms and toward the stairs as the gong chimed for the final act. "I like your Soleil Blanc, by the way," I called after her. She turned, raised her eyebrows, and gave me a look of amused contempt. Score one for me, for now. But I knew she'd get back at me somehow.

"You knew her perfume?" Rebecca asked. I'm impressed. Now, can we go get something to eat at that divine bakery?" She pointed out the window to Bread, a hot place across the street. We headed for the glass doors.

"I don't see how women sleeping with Greg and giving him money, or not giving him money, has anything to do with Karen's murder. Tonight was a waste of *my* money," Rebecca complained. We walked back out into the balmy night, across the plaza toward the bakery. "And by the way, 'follow the money' is a line from like a million movies."

"Maybe. But let's say Greg needs money badly. Gambling, maybe, the greedy fiancée, who knows. Presumably, he'll be the kids' guardian and have control over their trust funds now that Karen is gone. He'd already been digging into that money illegally, and now he could get the rest. The cops should be investigating the trust fund angle. But are they?"

"The trust fund money buys the apartment where his ex-wife was murdered?" Rebecca chuckled. "That's tacky, even by Park Avenue standards."

"Susie already has a buyer. Who knows? There are plenty of other places. I'm going to another open house tomorrow. Come with me?"

"You sure that's safe? I'm not going if Susie's involved, after what she said to you."

I shook my head. "This one isn't Susie's. Get this—it's the Harrington mansion."

Rebecca looked at me in surprise. I went on.

"Normally this kind of thing is open to serious customers only. You have to show bank statements! But I got Shane to put me on the list. I said I'd do a write-up for the *Westsider*, with pictures and all, and he jumped at it. I guess $45 million mansions are harder to sell these days."

"We'll go in all-black attire, Addams family style," Rebecca laughed as we walked into the bakery cafe.

We brought our food to a long communal table. My mind was still on 'follow the money.'

"If Karen just found out Greg took money from the trust funds, she might not have had time to change her will and power of attorney for her kids. Maybe she was on her way to do that the day she was murdered. Maybe that's why her briefcase disappeared. Maybe it wasn't about the Harrington listing at all."

Rebecca pointed toward the counter. "Isn't that your boyfriend?"

It had been only a day since Devon and I had met and nearly broken our vow—*my* vow—of chastity. I stood nervously and walked over to him.

"We do run into each other statistically more than most people I know."

He turned and laughed and nearly put his arms around me. Even with a crowd around us, his blue eyes and warm smile made me sweat like a radiator had been turned on.

"I'm here with Rebecca, and I have lots of juicy information," I said. "Come sit with us?"

"I'll be over as fast as I can through this crowd." He grabbed my arm and squeezed. It was impossible to work with a man who attracted me like this.

I pulled away, leaving Devon looking like a boy caught with his hand in the cookie jar. I didn't mind being a cookie, as long as I was sugar and gluten-free. But this constant arousal, like I was eighteen, had to stop. My mind turned to mush. Maybe an herb. Chasteberry. That was the one priests used for turning off sexual desire. Scientists said it didn't work, but I was willing to give it a try.

"Your face couldn't be any redder or more guilty. And I know you didn't just eat one of those gorgeous scones in the two minutes you were gone. I'm guessing that's the Devon effect." Rebecca managed to take a huge bite of babka and still sound like a know-it-all.

"There are herbs, you know, that suppress sexual desire," I said. Rebecca's mouth dropped open.

"You wouldn't. You might start to grow a beard. It sounds unhealthy." Then she laughed. "Poor Melanie. Feelings you never knew you had. Welcome to my world."

"So, I'm invited to a girls' night out." Devon appeared with a cup of coffee.

"Women's nights are practically as boring as guys' nights out," said Rebecca.

I saw a text. *Don't say you heard it from me, but Karen Sheldon's briefcase was found behind basement pipes at 962 Park. Empty. A maintenance man is missing. What do your Park Ave friends say?* It was from Detective Levano, who had strangely become my informant in the police department. One year ago, I helped him arrest Ralph Duvet's murderer.

"Something wrong?" Devon's radar for my emotional state was acutely sensitive, unlike Daniel's.

"A handyman at 962 Park is missing. Karen's briefcase was found stuffed behind some pipes in the basement. It was empty. Levano wants to know what I know. Maybe I should tell him half the Upper East Side women were sleeping with Greg. And two sources say Karen slept with some of the husbands. I don't have to give names. Hopefully, the cops will know all of this by now, right?" I looked at them for reassurance. Nothing. My heart beat faster.

Rebecca's face got that stern mother look. "Or, you could keep your mouth shut and stay out of trouble, like everyone else is doing. You agree, Devon?"

"It's not that easy, Rebecca." He smiled, hoping to calm her, which would never work. "We have to stay on decent terms with the police. Give them something to help their case. We can choose what and when to tell them. Hopefully, we tell them after they already know, and nothing too specific. But I'll tell John at the precinct this time, Melanie. "

I was too busy biting my lips and jiggling my foot to hear either of them.

"This is bringing up bad memories from last year. You know I hate violence, right? I've never even seen *Psycho* and never will." They both nodded, as did a man in black tie at the next table. Great. I dropped my voice to a whisper and leaned in. "So why am I getting involved? I got away with taking risks last time. It was just dumb luck that I only got scratched by a knife. Why put myself through that again?"

Devon put his warm hand on my icy one. "You're not going to. When we get anywhere close to finding the killer, we back off and leave it to the police. I'm here for another week. Don't go running off alone to meet with a suspect."

"I didn't run off last year. The killer broke into my apartment."

My heartbeat sped up. What about after Devon left? The warmth of his hand was spreading to places I didn't want it to go. I took my hand away and googled Chasteberry on my phone under the table. I ordered a large bottle. But my mind was already on to next steps.

"Before the Harrington mansion tomorrow, Rebecca, let's go to 962 Park and talk to the super." I thought for a minute. " I can get Shane talking. Or you can, Rebecca."

Rebecca rolled her eyes. "Oh my God, you don't like danger, yet you're going back for more. You can't have it both ways." She looked at me and then at Devon, shaking her head. "You're like two jigsaw puzzle fanatics. You'll never stop till you have the whole picture."

Chapter Twelve

"If you'd just *call* Detective Chilton at the 19th precinct, he'll tell you we're cleared to go to the basement. I have his number right here." I shoved my phone in Rjek's face and pulled out Chilton's card. God help me if he made a call. "You come with us, to be sure we don't touch anything."

It was the next morning. Rebecca was with me at 962 Park Avenue. We wanted to check out the basement.

My jaw hurt from fifteen minutes of smiling. I heard Rebecca clear her throat loudly. Her lips and eyes suddenly transformed into those of a sexy, pouting teenager.

"You remind me of a boyfriend I had in high school. He was around your height, but you're Mr. Universe compared to him." She pursed her lips and fluttered her eyes at Rjek, whose face got red. "You're the big man around here. Your word is law." The flush on his face I bet spread right down to his groin. In a flash, he was a panting puppy. The way to a man's heart is not through his stomach.

"We agree that you are interested in buying the apartment and want to see the basement?" he said, his eyes devouring Rebecca. She nodded languorously.

"Imagine if I lived just upstairs from where you are," she purred. His mouth dropped open slightly.

"For you, I will do this, but I only have five minutes," he whispered to her. "There's nothing to see. Do not touch anything." We both nodded. Rebecca could get any man to do anything, except her husband.

"Nice job," I mouthed as the super walked ahead of us.

Even the freight elevator was wood-paneled, nice enough to be in a dining room. It was my first time in a Park Avenue basement, and to say that I could have eaten off the floors was an understatement. I could've had a dinner party here. The walls were smoothly redone, and tasteful art lined the passageways. The lighting was high-end Home Depot. The laundry room was spotless, with comfortable Pottery Barn armchairs and magazines to read while you waited for machines. It was like being in a Madison Avenue hair salon.

We passed the glass-enclosed gym with a sign that said EquiSport, an elite company. For a small gym, the Pilates equipment and spin bikes were impressive. Three residents were working out, plus a guy whose chiseled arms said personal trainer. This was a busy basement.

Rebecca looked at her phone. "I have to talk to a patient who is having a meltdown. I'll meet you in the lobby, Melanie. You've been wonderful." She purred to the super. He mournfully watched her strut to the elevator.

"How did the killer get from the Open House on the 8th floor down to the basement to stash the briefcase and not be seen?" I asked Rjek.

Rjek shrugged. "Walked, maybe. There were no cameras in the back stars. The Board knows that."

"What about a camera in the basement?"

Rjek was about to answer, but one of his building workmen asked him a question. "Excuse me." The super and handyman walked over to a small closet ten feet from where I stood. Rjeck took out his keys and inserted one. The door swung open. It looked unlocked.

"Holy mother of God." The handyman backed away, crossing himself. "mierda." The super rushed into the tiny room.

"Call 911, call 911," Rjek yelled. I ran to the super. Lying on the floor face down was a man, blood crusted on his skull, blood on the walls. Nausea came over me in waves. I turned away and punched in the numbers.

"Help. 962 Park Avenue basement. A man has been badly hurt. Send police and ambulance now," I shouted.

"Ma'am, are you in danger?"

"No. I think it's a handyman from the building. He looks bad. Blood all over his head."

"He's dead," cried Rjek. "Hernando is dead."

"The super here says the man is dead. Hurry, please."

"They're on their way. Don't touch anything," said the police operator. Touch anything? Not this time.

The super was crying. He didn't want to leave Hernando. I backed away from the door, afraid one more look and I'd throw up where I stood. The closet was five feet wide and maybe ten feet long. Hernando was sprawled out in the back. From the blood, it looked like Hernando fought, but his attacker threw him against the walls. Maybe there was a knife wound with all the blood. I wanted to see if he had been strangled like Karen. But I'd contaminate the scene.

I had a sinking, desperate feeling and called Devon. It went to voicemail. I texted.

You should be here. Handyman is dead. I called police.

Devon replied. *Crap. Get out of there if you can. Not your problem.*

Not my problem. But it was my problem. Leaving now made me look guilty of something. I had to stay. Within minutes, the ambulance arrived. The medics rushed into the closet. Moments later the police with Chilton, of course, arrived.

"Another open house, Ms. Deming? Don't leave," Chilton yelled to me as he joined the group in the small closet. I called Devon. "Chilton told me not to leave. Do I need a lawyer? "

"Melanie, when you're trying to get information, you have no idea what will happen. You're a writer and reporter. You didn't do anything." Devon strangely sounded impatient.

"You sound annoyed, like this is my own fault.

"Sorry. I have a deadline. I'm not there with you. I should have gone instead of Rebecca."

"She's upstairs talking to a patient." I felt a flicker of fear. " What could have been so important in that briefcase that the killer risked coming back to get it and then killed this innocent bystander in order to shut him up. We

90

have to find out what was in there." A familiar fear gripped me.

"I don't know. But the murderer is an amateur and panicked. Not smart." At that moment, Chilton strolled over to me. I got off the call, texted *speak later.*

"The super tells us that you wanted to see the basement. Would you mind explaining why?"

"I write about crime. I wanted to describe the basement for my readers. They're following the story. "

"Why come down to the basement?" he asked coldly.

"Because I knew you found the briefcase in the basement. And that Hernando was missing. I wanted to see how someone could get in and out of here without being seen."

"So what's *your* assessment?" The question was sarcastic. Of course, I answered.

"It wasn't possible this time. The handyman confronted the killer with the briefcase. Otherwise, Hernando would be alive." The coroner's team arrived.

"I'm giving you one last warning, Ms. Deming. Stay away from anyone and anywhere connected with these murders. Next time, you'll be charged with obstructing justice or worse. You may have to come down for questions. Don't leave the city."

That did it. My stomach flipped over. "Am I free to find a bathroom?" I squeaked. Chilton waved to a female cop.

"Please escort Ms Deming to a bathroom if there's one here and then upstairs and out of the building." Thankfully, I found a really nice basement bathroom and lost another breakfast. Officer Cardoza accompanied me to the lobby.

* * *

Rebecca sat on a suede couch in the immaculate lobby while she chatted with the doorman. I fell into the seat next to her. She squeezed my hand but looked at me like a disappointed schoolteacher.

"That's the third body. You say murder follows you. But this time you went looking for it. These people are killers. Like sharks out for blood. Take up a hobby. Kick-boxing.Or ballroom dancing. Just stay away. All Hernando did was interrupt the killer looking for the briefcase, and he got killed? You could be next." The doorman must have told her.

"I'll be fine. Just too much blood. I don't know about kickboxing, though. Sounds so violent." I tried to laugh.

At that moment, Susie Carlbach walked in through the double doors. Not sure which of us looked more shocked.

"What are you doing here? We fired you" she said so everyone could hear.

"You can't fire someone who was never hired," I yelled. "Do you know what just happened? You probably lost another two hundred thousand."

Susie stormed past me, deliberately banging into my arm.

"Nice people you hang with," Rebecca shook her head.

"She's awful, but I don't think she's the killer. One down anyway."

"Are we still going to see the mansion?"

I blanched. I forgot after seeing Hernando.

"I get it. Too much after another murder."

"No, no. I have to go. I can't stop now." But It felt indecent after seeing Hernando.

* * *

There are a handful of limestone mansions in New York that are private residences. The Harrington mansion looked frozen in time, around 1904 when it was built in the Beaux-Arts architectural style. This Gilded Age mansion was steps from Central Park between Fifth and Madison Avenues on East 74th Street.

"Isn't forty-five million low for the whole place?" Rebecca asked as we took in the opulence from the outside.

"It's a steal. We should grab it." I laughed. "I think the ten bathrooms are only partially renovated. The kitchen needs work."

I saw Shane at the double black front doors, embellished with swirling brass handles and a matching brass door knocker. Shane made tsk-tsk sounds.

"You're late," he said. "I can only give you fifteen minutes. Take some pictures of me in the living room and the garden. We have serious potential buyers coming soon, and they want a private tour. Marc wants final approval of the finished column and any pictures you use."

"No problem." I was only here about Karen's murder. And now Hernando. Shane didn't seem to know about Hernando. I'd write one paragraph. "Let's get started, then," I said. Shane held a door open. Rebecca stared wide-eyed with lips parted at Shane. He was gorgeous. I shook my head. He belonged to his boss.

Chapter Thirteen

A grand marble staircase rose gracefully from the center of an inlaid marble floor in the foyer with a twenty-foot ceiling. Fred Astaire could come tapping down the stairs. I took a picture of Shane with his chest so puffed up his buttons almost popped. We continued on through the grand space.

Just beyond the huge entry was a ballroom-sized living room with a fifteen-foot ceiling. Multi-paned windows looked out on the patio and garden. Double doors led to a twenty-five-foot-long kitchen. Renovated at least ten years ago, it was an eyesore with black counters and dim lighting. The appliances were the usual high-end stuff: Miele dishwasher, six-burner Viking stove. There was a separate area for four wine refrigerators. The kitchen did not scream forty-five million.

From the living room, we walked out through the glass French doors, which needed work. But, money had clearly been spent on the huge stone terrace, which boasted a wall of built-in appliances, including a gas grill, sink, and fridge. A complete outdoor kitchen. A pergola covered half the patio. A made-to-rent $15,000 a day party venue.

"You have to see the terraces," gushed Shane. "The view is to die for." Not an especially PC choice, considering. We walked up two flights of outdoor stairs and arrived at a large terrace. There were massive urns, but the trees in them were almost dead. Any stager could find gorgeous mums.

From the terrace, we had the $45 million-dollar view over the treetops of Central Park, which was all the way to Central Park West. Shane left us for a moment. Rebecca and I gazed in silence. It wasn't a view I would die for.

"Rebecca, this place is creepy.

Rebecca stared dreamily out at the park. "Burnt orange, deep crimson, gold leaves crown the trees, why in heaven's name would I ever leave." She was in poetic mode.

"How about $45 million and monthlies of $50,000, not including food or electricity or Wi-Fi or doctor bills? That's why you'd leave. I'm not feeling the glow."

Rebecca came back down to earth, shaking her head. "All this detective work is taking away dreams." Definitely true.

"Have you seen enough, ladies?" Marc Olmstead, wearing a red bow tie with his gray suit, sauntered out onto the terrace. I hadn't seen him since my harrowing apartment tour. "Enough to do a fabulous report on this ravishing historic mansion?" His narrowed eyes appraised me and Rebecca. Our time must be up. I gave Marc a big smile.

"Such an incredible find here in Manhattan. I'm sure you'll have no trouble selling it," I gushed, as if real estate turned me on. It worked. He preened.

"And you haven't even seen the screening room. It's on the main floor as you leave. Your readers will love that. I'm told the first movie shown here was *Gone With the Wind*. Cecil B. Demille himself came to the party. Of course, it's been totally renovated since then. Digital equipment, reclining leather seats, retractable screen, a full bar…" He turned to Shane, who suddenly appeared. "Please show Ms. Deming and her friend the screening room on their way out."

I had not won him over.

"You know, Marc, I've never been kicked out of any place quite so elegantly. Did you hear about Karen's briefcase?" I asked casually.

Not a muscle moved on his face. "Of course. I have my own informants, as you do. Not that it mattered at all to me. There was nothing in her briefcase that impacted our business here. And we have copies of anything she might have been carrying from the office." His mouth twitched slightly. He was lying.

We followed Shane down the stairs to the main terrace and, through the glass doors, back into the kitchen. He stopped as we passed through the foyer.

"You know what else is fabulous? Look under the staircase. All you see is molding, but there's a door that opens to a little storage room. I heard the Harrington children used it as a hiding place, the way kids do. I hid from my parents." He looked pained. I peeked under the stairs, but it just looked like molding to me. Shane insisted we keep moving. We got to the screening room.

"I'll be back shortly. Look around." He slammed the door.

"Did he just lock us in?" Rebecca shouted. She tried the door. It was locked.

A flush of panic rose in my chest. I dug into my bag and found my vial of California poppy. I opened a cabinet and found a brandy snifter.

I filled the glass with water from the tap and thirty drops of poppy. I gulped it down.

"I'd take some of that, too if it was whiskey," Rebecca said. She searched through the cabinets. "There's nothing but old movies here. Steve McQueen in *The Thomas Crown Affair*. There's got to be some alcohol somewhere." She frantically opened and slammed cabinets. "Maybe this is a trap. We're going to be sold as sex slaves to some fat tribal leader somewhere." She held something up. "Whoa, look at this." She held a CD. "It says Eric's party night, June, Mansion. What the hell could that mean?"

I googled the Harrington family. Eric Harrington popped right up. Stocky guy with lots of greasy hair slicked back. He had young girls on each arm outside a club. "Eric Harrington looks like a grandson gone bad. Look at this." I showed her the picture.

"Yuk. He is the sex slave type. We should look at the video."

I looked around and found a CD player. I put the CD in and turned it on. A blurry but visible picture came up. A video of a guy standing with two very young girls all laughing. All had drinks. The most important clue was the black and white floor and the staircase. "He was drinking with underage girls right here. One of them looks familiar," I said. I heard noise outside the room, We frantically turned off the TV. I threw the CD in my bag. Rebecca raced to the window.

"I am not going to sit here and wait for someone to douse us with chloroform. This is big Melanie. He served alcohol to teenage girls right here. And probably had sex. You have the evidence."

"Maybe Karen knew about this." I said. Eric with these girls was revolting. I thought of Chloe. "So, what's your plan? To overpower whoever tries anything?".

"Right. You do your fencing thing. I know some karate."

I didn't even see a curtain rod. Overpowering some hired kidnapper wasn't going to happen. "Rebecca, there's got to be a way out of here."

The windows were covered with retractable shades. I pushed one aside. There were no bars on the windows. "Look. We're just on the first floor. We can climb out the window." Rebecca seemed to relax. I heard voices in the foyer. I put my ear to the crack between the door and the doorframe.

I heard a woman's voice, then a man's. Then Marc's pompous boom. "...zoning to subdivide is almost ready." Another voice. " I have connections..."

After that I couldn't hear anything else.

I moved away from the door, beckoning Rebecca to come sit near me in one of the huge leather chairs facing the screen.

"Those bastards," I whispered in her ear. "They're planning to turn the mansion into apartments. I wonder if the Harringtons know. Marc Olmsted will get a percentage of the profits from the condo sales, not just a commission for selling this white elephant. "

Rebecca sprang up from the buttery leather recliner as if she'd just heard me. "Let go of this, Melanie. Under-the-table zoning changes means a huge financial gain. People would definitely kill for that. And now we have a CD that could put one of the Harringtons in jail. And the handyman was killed because he saw too much. The police are trained, and they get paid for it." She looked at her watch. "We should get out of here. I'm going out the window."

She began wrestling with an old lock on a window. Just as she mastered it, the door to the screening room opened.

"What are you doing? You could set off the alarm!" Shane shouted.

"I could die from lack of oxygen, too. You locked us in here." Rebecca glared at Shane and shoved past him out to the front door. I smiled and put my hands up in surrender, as if to say, *what can I do?*

"She has to get to work," I said. "Did you know you locked us in?"

"Why would I do that?" Shane said, looking at the door handle. "The lock must have been pushed in by mistake."

I almost believed him.

"There we have it," I said. "No ill will intended." I peered out into the ballroom-sized entryway. It was empty. Rebecca ran out the door. "So, Shane, do you think you have a buyer?"

His Brad-Pitt-sexy-baby face assumed a guarded but excited expression. "Oh, yes. They're committed. They've been here a few times. There's so much to take in. You never saw the upper floors, with the palatial bedrooms."

"I'd love to see them, but it seems like Marc wants me out of here."

"Marc is busy with his customers. That's the only reason. He's nice to everyone.".

"Sure. I totally understand," I said, holding back a snort. "Marc needs to focus on his deal. God knows I don't have $45 million dollars. I'm curious, though, about the types of people that *do* have that kind of money."

Shane perked up, as I hoped he would. "Oh, you'd be surprised. For the Arabs, this is small change. Also the Russians. Oil money."

"But why would they want this huge place that needs so much work, when they could buy a triplex looking out on the park?"

Shane sat on the deep windowsill, his posture beautifully erect and his crossed legs revealing bare, hairless ankles and alligator loafers.

"You don't get it," he said, shaking his head at my ignorance. "This building is worth far more than the asking price. So much can be done with it. Landmarking doesn't prevent anyone from creating grand apartments. Why, we have—"

"Shane!" Marc burst into the screening room. "I need you upstairs now. Ms. Deming should have left thirty minutes ago." When his eyes met mine they were filled with rage. "Our business here is not anyone else's business. We are confidential real estate brokers. What has Shane told you?" Marc stormed over to me. He looked even taller and larger than in the narrow hallway of that apartment. When this man's fuse blew, he was an atomic bomb.

Fencing teaches you to parry and move fast. I sidestepped his hand reaching out to grab me. And was out the door.

"Melanie, where the hell have you been?" Rebecca was on the front steps, her face grim. I gulped in fresh air for a few minutes.

"Wait here," I whispered.

I reentered the huge foyer. and hid behind a pillar. I peeked into the ballroom-sized entryway.

Marc was talking to three people near the staircase. One was a barrel-chested, muscular man in a tightly stretched suit. His head was shaved. He looked like every picture I'd ever seen of a Russian oligarch. There was a tall man with horn-rimmed glasses, graying hair, and an air of academia. His clothes said old money. And there was a woman with her back to me. Long, shapely legs; a snugly-fitted black suit with a short skirt, and perfect blond streaks over light brown hair. The look was familiar. These were Marc's buyers, I assumed. I snapped a quick picture and retreated outside.

Rebecca was on the sidewalk.

"You've got a death wish, Melanie," she said furiously. "I was about to call 911. After they locked us in that room, I fully expected to be given an injection and wake up in a basement strapped to a chair, with a buzz saw coming toward me."

"Maybe you should write thrillers instead of poetry," I laughed. We walked down the block past impeccable townhouses with window boxes full of brilliant mums in every color. My mind processed what I'd just seen and heard.

"They are subdividing that place. Maybe they can even get a variance to add another floor or two. There are five floors. Ten apartments at fifteen million each with terraces and views. That's a hundred and fifty million." My mind raced.

"They stand to make a profit of at least sixty million, maybe even eighty million after construction costs. Marc wasn't fighting with Karen over the commission split. He wanted a piece of the eighty million profit with developers. If she stood in his way, that's more than enough reason to kill her."

I looked back at the mansion, and saw the leggy woman emerge, walk down the steps, and get into a waiting town car. I saw her face. It was Marlena Shenko.

"Rebecca, that's Greg Sheldon's fiancée. Let's get out of here.I don't want her to see me." We raced down the block.

Rebecca whistled. "She's the whole package. *I'd* even kill for her. like *The Postman Rings Twice*, that movie where she gets the guy to kill her husband."

A bell went off. "Greg could have killed Karen for Marlena. I'm going to see him in his office. For Botox, but not really." Rebecca stopped and grabbed me by the shoulders.

"Melanie, wake up. The CD in your bag. The zoning changes. Now Marlena. You have to tell the cops. Stop interviewing suspects." I gently ungripped her hand.

"Not yet. I need to talk to Karen's husband, Dr. Greg. He has multiple affairs, a fiancee involved with this mansion."

"Stop. Too dangerous," Rebecca yelled at me as she walked into the subway.

But I couldn't stop.

Chapter Fourteen

E state auction Doyle's four today. Come. Friends might be there, Devon
wrote.

Devon should chat up Peggy Fitzgerald, the old money runner
who was at the Open House, without me. But I wanted to go. God, I was
back in high school. I shook my head like a dog shedding water.

I texted Devon. *Be there at 4.*

Since I had on every New Yorker's loafers, really sneakers-in-disguise
shoes, I ran to the park and slow-jogged up the reservoir path, dislodging
Devon from my brain. My steps were at 10,243 by the time I got home. This
could be a fifteen thousand step day if I ran back across the Park to Doyle's
auction house.

I ran up the four flights to the apartment, grabbed my notebook and index
cards, and jotted down a description of the mansion. You couldn't pay me
to sleep even one night there. I wrote Shane's comment that the value of the
mansion was in subdividing. I jotted down Marc's words when he exploded.
This was the third time I'd seen his anger and the worst. He knew that I
knew about his deal.

I took the DVD out of my bag and hid it in my underwear drawer. Was
it time to tell Detective Chilton and his sidekick, May-Ling, about the real
estate end of this? Or the underage sex parties at the mansion? Chilton
would threaten me again with legal action.

My leg jiggled. I couldn't sit still. I mixed ten herbs, added extra California
poppy and rhodiola. Rhodiola has the odd distinction of being able to keep
people focused while calming them down. It didn't make sense, but the

KILLER CONDO

drops worked.

I put on my one other pair of pants I owned that weren't jeans and race-walked back across the park. 14,281 steps total.

* * *

Doyle's Auction House occupied the ground floor of an unattractive concrete and glass building between Third Avenue and Lexington. A Grecian bust on a pedestal table stood on a gorgeous oriental rug in front of a window. Hanging nearby was a large painting of an ancient ship crossing the ocean, spilling over with desperate, drowning souls.

There was nothing elegant about Doyle's compared to Sotheby's, the most revered auction house in New York. At Doyle's, a handwritten note on a chalkboard announced the four p.m. start of the next auction. I followed a sign into a large room. At the front were counters filled with jewelry. Rows of chairs set up for perhaps one hundred. There were around fifty potential bidders already seated. The counters were staffed by attractive, well-made-up women and some men. The mostly female customers were dressed in everything from jogging outfits to well-tailored suits.

I spotted Devon chatting with a too-skinny woman. I immediately recognized her as Peggy Fitzgerald from her severely short, dirty blonde hair and Fit2Run pants, the kind serious runners pull on after a marathon. Her gaunt athletic look made her easy for Devon to pick out using my description. She'd probably just finished fifteen miles. One glance at her and my fourteen thousand steps seemed silly.

I sidled over to the counter near them and examined the jewelry in a glass case. Most of the bracelets and pins on display were embellished with large, jewel-studded animals. Turtles with ruby eyes, ladybugs covered in diamond chips, cats with emerald spots. Loading thousands of dollars' worth of jewels onto these endangered creatures seemed so ridiculous I had to laugh. A man behind the counter eyed me suspiciously.

"Gorgeous, totally," I chirped. "Just looking."

I took a few steps closer to Devon and Peggy.

102

"The polo in Southampton is the best in the country," Devon said as if he knew all about the game. "Does your husband play?"

Peggy first looked disgusted then animated. "No, it's my son who's a brilliant horseman. We'd have him out there all year with his coach, but his school is here. We think Colgate is very fine." I listened more closely.

"Oh yes, Colgate. I heard a rumor that a former mother from there had been killed. Is that true? At an apartment showing?" Good segue, except he knew Karen's kids went to Huntley.

Peggy seemed confused, then drew closer to Devon, making it harder for me to hear. "You must mean Huntley. Everyone is saying...." That was all I heard. The auctioneer's loud, nasal voice—doing a poor imitation of a British accent—broke in.

"Our first item today is from the Angling, Decoy and Americana Collection of John Parmly. We have seven wooden decoys. Who will start the bidding at one thousand dollars—do I hear one thousand?" One paddle was raised. In a lifetime, I thought, no one would ever shoot enough ducks to pay for these decoys. $1,000 would buy a lot of duck dinners. More paddles went up, and an elderly man with a checked hat won the ducks for $4,000. A guffaw burst out of me, so loud that the last row of bidders turned around to shush me.

The auctioneer gave me a disapproving stare before moving on to the jewelry. "Here we have a unique snail clip-brooch by David Webb, a fine designer from the nineteen-fifties. It's from the estate of Mollie Aster Brewster, and made of 24 karat gold with more than a carat of diamond chips. Who will start the bidding at $5,000?"

A curvy, thirty-ish blonde woman in a clinging knit dress raised her paddle high enough that the diamond bracelets on her wrist caught everyone's eye. The auctioneer looked like he'd just won the lottery. He beamed at the woman as again and again her paddle went up. The bid was up to $6,000 when Peggy Fitzgerald jumped in with a $6,200 bid. After a brief battle, Peggy snagged the diamond snail away from the blonde with a $6,800 bid. It seemed funny to me that a runner would covet a snail.

The blonde looked at Peggy with loathing. Peggy ignored her. Their bidding war was repeated over a garish gold leopard with diamond spots and emerald eyes. After the leopard came a hideous toucan. Each time they fought it out, Peggy stayed in until she had all three. $18,800 for the whole menagerie. Was this a kind of money laundering, or did Peggy have an animal fetish?

I raised an eyebrow at Devon and motioned I was leaving. I waited just down the block. In five minutes, he joined me.

"You'd make a really bad millionaire," he said.

"What was done to those animals in there is almost as bad as climate change," I protested. "The diamond-encrusted leopard, the snail. Give the money to save the Amazon, for God's sake."

"Peggy Fitzgerald wasn't even there for the jewelry," Devon said. "She was there for a pair of 19th-century enameled tables for their Southampton house."

We walked rapidly away from Doyle's, in case Peggy came hunting for Devon and remembered me from the open house.

"So she only bid on those animals to make sure that blonde wouldn't get them." I would never cease to be amazed at the follies of the rich. "Did she know the blonde?"

Devon shook his head. "No, that's not part of her game. Peggy Fitzgerald is competitive in every ounce of her emaciated body. The way she talked about her son and polo, I had the feeling nothing would stop her from making him a polo star."

What I wanted was information about Karen's murder.

"But, anyway," his voice brightened. "Peggy spilled a lot in there about the open house. She's certain she heard Karen yell, 'You took the children's college money.' Greg yelled, 'You have no proof.' And Karen said, 'The statements are all here.'"

"You got Peggy to tell you all that? You really know how to charm women into confiding," I blurted and immediately regretted it.

He shot me an amused look. "You have me pegged as some Don Juan type. If I'm God's gift to women, why are we standing here on the street instead of lying down in a hotel room, where I could show you what a prize I am."

His mouth looked angry, sad, and luscious all at the same time.

You can't mix sex and work; that was the moral of this story. Where was the chasteberry I'd ordered?

"We're not in a hotel," I continued, "because this is New York City, where we could be easily seen, and we have a lot of work to do together, and I have to pick up Chloe in ten minutes." My voice was too loud. A dog walker with four dogs stopped to enjoy the drama. I put my hand on Devon's arm.

"With *two* murders, we have a lot to work on." I smiled. He smiled, and the bad moment disappeared.

Why was it so much easier to have an argument with Devon than with Daniel? Of course, I was married to Daniel for fifteen years. Arguing with Devon was a relief, really. Talking about whether to have sex and when and where was way better than arguing about chocolate mousse and whether crime reporting was a hazard to the family.

"If Peggy is telling the truth, then Karen had evidence with her that Greg had stolen from the trust funds," I said. "But it doesn't make sense that Greg, knowing everyone may have heard the argument, would return to the apartment, kill Karen, steal her briefcase, and then come back *again* to put on a grieving husband show. "

"Murder doesn't have to make sense," said Devon. "He could have done it. He needed to get the briefcase. Peggy told the police what she heard and they haven't arrested Greg."

We were two blocks from Huntley. This was as close as I'd get to the school with Devon. That place was a beehive of gossip. Devon suddenly took my arm and guided me into a large hardware store on the Upper East Side. It wasn't the sort of place I would expect to see Huntley mothers, but it still felt dangerous when he put his arms around me.

"At least it's private," he whispered, burying his face in my hair.

His body against mine was too much. Dammit. I'd better change the subject.

"We've got to find out what they saw on the security tapes from the morning Hernando was murdered. The cops took the footage. Your contacts are the only way."

"Will do." His lips had found my eyes and were moving down to my ear.

"I haven't told you about the Harrington Mansion," I gasped, "and the plan to chop it up and make a fortune with Russian oil money." It was getting harder to focus. "Rebecca and I were locked in a screening room. She was sure we were going to be sold into slavery."

"You'd make bad slaves," Devon murmured into my hair and close to my neck. We'd be at it in a minute. I had to get out of there.

I slipped out from under his arm, though every part of me wanted to stay.

"Not now. Not here," I managed to say. "Marc Olmsted was furious at me. And we found a DVD showing a Harrington grandson I think having sex with underage girls in the screening room." His worried look was gratifying.

"What the hell, Melanie?! I thought our deal was that next time, you'd take me along for protection. That guy is going crazy again, and now underage sex tapes. This is dangerous stuff." His blue eyes turned dark gray.

"Rebecca was there. Look, not even a scratch." I waved my arms. "I'll give you the details later." I dashed out of the store.

I knew I should put a stop to the flirting. Okay, it was a lot more than flirting. But I didn't want to.

* * *

I racewalked to Huntley and brightened at the prospect of seeing Chloe. At the same time, an old song popped into my head, and I couldn't get it out. *You'd be so nice to come home to.... You'd be so nice by the fire...* My father loved to sing this, and it brought back the memory of a car ride, the radio playing oldies.

I arrived at Huntley and waited outside. Patty Baylor, who was the first to find Karen at the Open House, trotted awkwardly over when she saw me. She was attractive, but less elegant and slightly heavier than the typical Huntley mom. Today, she was dressed in running gear, including Hoka One shoes like the pros wore, and the usual Lululemon leggings with sheer panels and a speckled running jacket. She looked like a wannabe runner and probably a wannabe Park Avenue mom, too.

"Can you talk?" She looked around as though every parent was listening. No one had even glanced in our direction.

"Actually, I have a call with the FBI coming in," I quipped.

"Really? Is it about Karen?" Good grief. The lack of humor among these people was disturbing.

"Just kidding." I tried hard to sound polite. " What do you want to talk about?"

Patty took a deep breath and put her hand over her heart.

"I told the police, but I don't think they took me seriously."

"What did you tell the police?" I asked. Something about Patty made me want to flee. I prayed for Chloe's class to be one of the first dismissed.

Patty leaned in toward my ear. "I saw the back door close while I waited for the bathroom at the Open House."

"You waited for the bathroom?" I asked loudly. This was the first time I'd heard this. It seemed important to me. How long had she waited? Did she knock and finally ask if the person inside would be much longer? I'd assumed that when Patty got to the bathroom, she'd seen Karen on the floor. But of course, the murderer would close the bathroom door.

Patty hissed in a bad imitation of the Pink Panther. "I'm talking about the back door to the apartment, not the *bathroom*. I remembered that I saw the back door closing when I got there. I was in such a state of shock I couldn't think of anything but Karen lying there. But a week later, I remembered the back door."

" Did you see who went out the door?" I wanted to shake her.

Patty ignored my question. She had a script in her head. "Like I said, I was in shock for a week. But then it came back to me. I saw the back door close. Then it opened, and there was Peggy. Peggy Fitzgerald."

"Did Peggy say anything?" I asked, trying to contain my excitement. "What was she doing?"

"She came in the back door," Patty repeated slowly. "She looked startled to see me. Then she said, 'I was checking the garbage area. It's very clean. That's important to know about a building.' She walked past me and into the dining room."

"So you told the police. What did they do?"

"They questioned Peggy. She insisted she just looked at the garbage area. She said she'd take a lie detector test."

"And they believed her, I assume." Patty nodded. She grabbed my arm and held on.

"That's the problem," Patty continued with more urgency. "They shouldn't have just let her go. I don't believe her. I think *you* should investigate. You know how to get to the bottom of these things, right?"

"Once. That happened once." I took my arm back forcefully while trying not to interrupt Patty's flow. There was another important point she had slipped in, and I didn't want to lose sight of it. "You said the bathroom door was closed when you got there?"

"Yes. That's why I was waiting. Susie didn't want people using the main bathrooms." This was news to me, since I'd thrown up in one of them.

"So the door to the bathroom was closed. When did you discover that Karen was lying there?"

"After waiting a while, maybe ten minutes, I decided it was empty. I knocked, and there was no answer. I waited a few minutes more and finally opened the door. That's when I started screaming." Patty got a blank look and clutched her hands. I really didn't want to be near her if she started screaming again.

"You're doing great, Patty." I gave her a warm smile and touched her arm, which seemed to bring her back to the present. "I'll see what I can find out, okay?" She nodded. Her breathing slowed down quickly.

I saw Chloe's class, said goodbye to Patty, and gratefully took my daughter's hand.

"How was school?"

"She's the one who found the lady, right, Mom?" Chloe asked, pointing. Forget school.

"How do you know that?"

"All the kids said it was Freddy's mom. She's a little weird."

"Your friends are right. It was Freddy's mom. She's very upset about it. Which makes sense."

108

"Yeah, but Samantha said Freddy's parents fight more now. That his mom acts *crazy* now. Samantha went there for a play date." Chloe's little face scrunched up like the play date smelled bad. Then she looked up at me warily.

"But you saw that lady too, and you're not upset 'cause you're like a detective, right?". Chloe wanted to know if I was weird, too. Would I be there for her? I squeezed her hand.

"You bet it was upsetting. But I'm okay now. I talked about my feelings. You know that helps. But if you think I'm acting crazy, you tell me, okay?" She nodded. I stopped and put my arm around her shoulder. " Chloe, you know I'm not a detective, right? I write about crime, but I'm not a detective." She rolled her eyes. And she's only ten.

"Of course,, Mom. You don't wear a uniform or pack heat, but you figure stuff out. Like on Castle. He's a writer, too."

My heartbeat got fast. "Packing heat, okay. Do you like Castle? Is it scary?"

"No. It's pretty dumb. I always guess who did it before he does anyway." I laughed. Chloe smiled broadly.

"If you have any ideas, I can always use some help," I said. Patty was crazy and fighting with her husband. This was new information.

"Sure, Mom. I'm hungry." I grinned.

"Right, let's get a snack." Murder was not that interesting, anyway.

Chapter Fifteen

T he brass plate read Dr. Greg Sheldon, Plastic Surgeon, New York and Los Angeles. I pushed open the door of the private entrance to his suite off Park Avenue. Another door, also glass, opened into a pure white space.

"You're Melanie Deming?" asked the receptionist—Deedee, according to her nameplate. Blonde and petite. Her restylane-filled huge lips barely moved when she spoke. Her arched eyebrows were permanently set at surprise as if I'd walked in without an appointment, though it was unlikely they got walk-ins for procedures that started at six hundred dollars a shot.

"Yes," I said. "I have an appointment." Deedee's shoulders relaxed. She told me to have a seat. There was a display of packaged creams with Sheldon's picture on each one. Framed, on the wall, was an article where he discussed the benefits of laser surgery, complete with a photo of his younger, cocky self. The article was fifteen years old, but the guy in the photo looked almost exactly the same as Greg Sheldon, who'd walked into 962 Park Avenue to identify his wife's body. Greg must inject himself every time he looked in the mirror.

A thin woman wearing sunglasses and a floppy hat paid her bill; her face scraped red and pulled taut to her ear. There were no elderly people with walkers in this office, no women with children in tow, or a husband or boyfriend. Women came to a plastic surgeon either alone or in pairs, like a Botox party.

I waited impatiently for Cornelia, who had agreed to be my wingwoman. Where was she? There were brochures describing Botox, different kinds of fillers (who knew), and a gruesome photo album with before and after close-ups of baggy wrinkled skin followed by somewhat tightened areas. My phone buzzed.

Not coming. Leave there now, Cornelia texted. I felt a chill. Did she know something? Just then, a nurse stepped into the waiting room.

"Ms. Deming, Dr Sheldon will see you." I got up and followed her, texting furiously, *Are you kidding? Going in now. What do I say?*

I'm never kidding. Assume he knows who you are. Say for a consultation. I shoved the phone in my bag and pressed Record.

"You must be the famous Melanie Deming." And there was Dr. Greg, hand outstretched, big charming smile. A few wisps of blonde highlights accented his thick brown hair, which flopped slightly to the side, evoking John Kennedy or Tom Cruise. Boyishly sexy, and with a doctor's white coat to top it off. I glanced down. Yep, there were the cowboy boots. That was what really hooked the women, I thought. The charming doctor in bad-boy boots.

I shook his hand, which felt clammy.

"I'm famous?" I chuckled. "For what, exactly?" *Assume he knows why you're there*, Cornelia had said. Not happening.

Greg laughed and gestured that I should sit on the cushioned patients' table, with its raised back covered in white paper. I hoisted myself up. There was no nurse in the room, I noticed nervously.

"Rumors do reach me," he said, no longer smiling. "I heard you're the resident expert at Huntley on solving crimes. Parents were told to talk to you if they have questions about Karen's death."

"No one said that," I protested mildly. " I'm rather ordinary, not Wonder Woman, no superpowers here."

"Ms. Deming, you're too modest," Greg said, looking at me warmly now. He came closer to the chair and peered at my face. "You're a successful writer, and you're certainly the most attractive crime reporter I've ever met."

I knew I should be turned off by the flattery, but there was a little part of me turned on by this porn movie dialogue and scene, as if I was standing outside watching. I was appalled by the fleeting image. He was good at this game.

"I wouldn't call myself successful. Not yet. Anyway, I'm just here for a consultation."

Dr. Greg switched back to professional mode and examined my face.

"Yes, I think we can bring this face closer to perfection. It will only take two syringes of Botox for the forehead and the lines between your brows. I can also do a little plumping around the eyes, if you'd like. That will help with your crow's feet. And we could consider some filler for your cheekbones, but that's not urgent."

Crow's feet, lines between my eyes, what the hell? I jumped out of the chair and ran to the mirror on the wall. With my nose almost pressed to the mirror, I could see a single tiny wrinkle near my left eye.

Greg chuckled. "Now, what are you really here for?" He walked over and put his hand on my shoulder. "Not that I can't make you look like an auburn-haired Margot Robbie, if that's what you want. What *do* you want, Ms. Deming?" He was using his seductive voice.

I sure as hell didn't want him standing this close and touching me. If I turned around, I'd be right where he wanted me, face to face and body to body. I quickly took two steps to the side and ran back to the table.

"It's surprising you don't have a nurse present when you see patients," I said. Greg's phony but confident smile faded for an instant. "I wanted to ask you about these pesky marionette lines." Rebecca coached me to say this, even though I knew I didn't yet have those lines that form from the nose down around the mouth.

"That's not a problem for you *yet*," he said. "I'd wait a year and come back in. See what's fallen."

"Thanks. That gives me something to look forward to," I said, stalling while I decided what to do next. My phone buzzed. It was Cornelia. *Are you still there?* I quickly tapped yes. I looked up at Greg, watching me. "Sorry, my kid. You know how it is."

Have Botox or get out, came Cornelia's reply. The next bubble said *You could use it.* Seriously?

I looked at Sheldon and made a decision. "My friend said I should get

Botox. But since you brought up Karen, may I ask what theory you might have about her murder?" He folded his arms across his chest, and anger flitted across his face. I pushed on.

"At the open house, I heard you tell Chilton something about Marc Olmsted. Do you think he murdered her?" This was the easy question, inviting him to put the blame on someone else.

Sheldon leaned against the all-white counter, crossing his arms. "Karen was an aggressive negotiator. Marc hated her, especially because of the huge listing she had just gotten. So yes, he had reason to want her out of the way. Maybe he hired a hitman, or that flaming assistant of his did it. Or maybe Marc went into one of his famous rages."

So, I wasn't the only one to light Marc's short fuse. Greg's jaw clenched for an instant. "Karen had enemies everywhere," he sighed, glancing at his Rolex. "Who do *you* think did it?"

My recent experience told me to slow down and follow his lead. Don't confront him right now. "I have no idea," I said. "I didn't know Karen, but she seemed perfectly nice to me. Can you tell me who these other enemies were besides Marc?"

"No, I will definitely not give you any names." He gave me an icy stare. "There are women whose good reputation means everything to them. They had every right to hate Karen. She was a homewrecker, like one of those iron balls swinging into buildings. Only Karen didn't want to rebuild; she just wanted their apartments to list, and she would go to any means." Without my asking, Greg revealed there were women who hated Karen. He was also slandering the mother of his own children. He seemed to hate her too.

"When you say any means, what exactly did Karen do? Did she offer kickbacks? Or was it something else? Calling her a homewrecker is pretty harsh. That usually means she went after a married man." I wanted Greg Sheldon to come out and say what he was implying, especially since my phone was hopefully still recording us. But he didn't give me the satisfaction.

"You said that, I didn't," he said. "But I guess that's one definition of a homewrecker."

There was a dangerous direction I could take now. Of course, I plunged in. "So Greg, if Karen made some women hate her, did you make them feel better? "

I saw a moment of fear in his eyes. They definitely looked bloodshot. "When women look better, they feel better," he said tersely. "Every woman I treat leaves here feeling better. That's why I'm one of New York's top plastic surgeons." He waved his hand at his office, one of four rooms. We were in a tricky tango here.

"Some of your patients had their homes wrecked by Karen. Would that be accurate? I assume that's where you got your information?"

"I do not talk about patients. Read the medical code of ethics before you ask a doctor questions. And I'm afraid our consultation time is up." Greg strode to the door.

Well, of course, he wouldn't answer that. He and Karen could have been screwing the same couples. The wives complained to him. Then Sheldon, disregarding his very strict "code of ethics," raises their spirits and raises cash for himself. I suddenly felt like I needed to be hosed down with Lysol to get rid of the sleaze in his pure white office. Propolis, at least, would be a good, natural disinfectant herb.

"I know my time is up, but where were you when Karen was killed? You came to the open house and left. Marlena was just leaving when I got there." Greg's jaw tightened at Marlena"s name. I looked into his bloodshot eyes, and there were bags forming underneath.

"I came back here from the open house. I'm only ten blocks away from 962. It's why I was interested in the apartment, not that I'd ever buy it now, though Susie keeps calling. You can ask Deedee, my receptionist. I told the detective all this. If you have no special abilities, what are you doing here?"

Susie told me she already had a buyer. Another lie.

"I write a column about crime. I heard your relationship with Karen was not stellar. Do you agree with that?" I asked. Greg had one foot out the door, but stopped. I went on.

"Several sources heard you and Karen have a yelling match in the kitchen at the open house, about money that disappeared from your kids' trust funds. Would you like to confirm or deny?" I watched carefully. As Greg slowly turned around, I saw his mouth twitch.

"That is a lie," he said, shaking his head slowly, as if reprimanding a child. "As I told Detective Chilton and the charming May-Ling, Karen and I had an amicable separation. I make support payments for the household regularly. You can ask my lawyer." He opened the door, stepped into the hall, and looked me up and down like I was a hooker he was appraising. Yuk. "There'll be no charge for today," he said.

"Really, even though I didn't give it away for free like the others," I said. He looked back at me with hatred. And slammed the door.

I heard another door open and then a hearty greeting to his next patient. Greg Sheldon was as phony as the masks he created for thousands of women, but I shouldn't have given him that last jab. I shivered.

I already knew of three women who'd admitted to having sex with him and being asked for money. It was time to give my readers more information about the cast in this mystery without using the word 'suspects.'

"Do you want to make another appointment?" Deedee asked, her eyebrows raised as high as they could go.

"I'll call when I'm ready," I said.

"I'm sure we'll see you again. Eventually, all the women realize how special Dr. Sheldon is." Was she kidding me? I laughed right in her frozen face and walked out the door.

* * *

Back on the street in the bright sun, I gulped a huge breath of relief, as if I'd just escaped some sadist's dungeon. Come to think of it, Greg Sheldon could be called that. Dungeons or his office, you were at the mercy of an egomaniac who could torture you. Whatever he did, you had to take without a whimper and tell him how great he was so he didn't make you look like Cruella Deville. Even bribe him so he'd treat you better. And when you finally got out, everyone knew where you'd been and what had happened to you.

I shivered again at the bleakness of his Park Avenue office. My phone rang.

"How do you look?" It was Cornelia.

"Exactly like you," I parried. "He even gave me diamond studs."

"So you didn't have Botox." I could hear her disappointment. "I should have known. A waste of a visit."

"Not exactly," I reassured her. "But why did you tell me to get out of there?"

"I had a strange attack of anxiety. Suddenly, I was the type of mother I detest and worried about you. I never worry about anyone, even my Elizabeth."

"Welcome to the human race," I said. "What were you worried about?"

"That your flippant honesty would provoke some sort of confrontation and...." She didn't finish her sentence.

"He'd inject me in the neck with heroin, redo my face so I looked twenty years older, and throw me out a window onto Park Avenue?" I laughed. "His office is on the ground floor, Cornelia."

"You see, it does not pay to worry about people," she sniffed. My humor was lost on her. I hadn't thought it was possible to hurt Cornelia's feelings.

"Sorry. I appreciate you, but you did abandon me to the wolf. Is there some other reason you were worried besides that my big mouth might get me killed? "

By now, I had walked to Madison Avenue and faced a window filled with chainmail dresses and pants. They started at ten thousand dollars each. Fortunately, metallic wasn't my look.

"It will get around that you went to see Greg," said Cornelia. "His receptionist is not the most discreet. And I'm sure you were not tactful. What if he is a murderer? You're putting yourself in danger again." Cornelia didn't sound like herself today.

"It's Daniel, isn't it? You've been talking to Daniel." There was a long pause as Cornelia weighed her options.

"And what if I had?" she finally said. "The poor man is a wreck. He's afraid that Chloe is not safe, and his concerns are real. You fought off a murderer in your own apartment last year."

I felt red hot with anger at both of them. I didn't buy Daniel's "concern" for a second.

"So Daniel's the reason you didn't come with me?" I sputtered. "You've known me for years. Have I neglected her at all? Journalists investigate all the time. They don't get murdered. I'm not reporting on the cartel in Colombia."

My hand trembled. Even if I knew I could be in danger, I couldn't afford to act scared. Or be scared.

"I never said you were a bad mother. I don't want to be a buffer between you two. But Daniel confides his worries to me." Cornelia cleared her throat. I'd never even heard her sneeze. "Not that you take my advice, but you may remember my telling you that in marriage, you can do what you want, like everyone else does. But we all know to take care of our husbands first."

What sounded smart to me a year ago now sounded straight out of some 1950s housewife handbook. But Cornelia was savvy. She knew Daniel's *concerns* had little to do with safety and were more about jealousy.

"I don't know why Daniel cried on your shoulder," I said. "But I get why you didn't show at Greg Sheldon's." Her reputation might have been tarnished.

"I never get in the middle," she said back in her usual imperious tone. "And you still owe me that restaurant list." She hung up.

I was breathing hard. I really needed herbs. I frantically looked through my bag. Nothing. Daniel crying on Cornelia's shoulder scared me. He was fed up with my sleuthing. That scared me. The prospect of going onto his computer to steal her goddamn restaurant recommendations scared me. Greg Sheldon, Marc Olmsted, Susie Orbach, they all scared me. I felt desperate to talk to Devon and have him hold my hand.

You free? I have info about footage at 962. Like magic, his text appeared.

Yes, I am.

Can you come here?

Where are you?

380 West 52nd. Buzzer 1811

Okay. In 20.

Sure, he could have told me on the phone, but this felt like some kind of divine intervention by the universe. I needed to be with Devon, who looked at me with warmth and not disgust. He saw me as a whole person, not as a bad mother or a disappointing wife. I didn't ask whether the address he'd given me was his friend's apartment. I knew it was.

Chapter Sixteen

The fastest route to Devon was through Central Park. I ran the wrong way on the reservoir path, dodging runners and nasty looks, and raced bikes on the main road. I exited at Columbus Circle. Flanking the statue of Christopher Columbus is the giant Time Warner complex, where Chinese, Middle Eastern, Russian, and American billionaires and investors buy giant apartments through shell corporations to squirrel away tens of millions of illegal dollars.

I ran across busy 57th street. "Sorry, sorry," I yelped, dodging little older ladies and mothers with strollers. I headed toward Ninth Avenue. At mid-block, I suddenly had a weird feeling that I was being watched. I looked around. A car was keeping pace with me. A nondescript black Nissan driving at my speed is the kind of car used by Uber. I couldn't see the driver. I picked up my speed, and so did the car. My legs tightened.

I heard a thud and felt a dull pain in my hip. I've been shot. OMG. Then I realized I'd be a lot worse if it was a gunshot. The car sped away. At my feet was a rock the size of an orange. It was wrapped in a piece of paper held on with rubber bands.

"What the hell?" A loud voice interrupted my thoughts. "Now people throw things out of cars?" I looked around and saw that the Bronx accent belonged to a tall, forty-ish woman with bright red hair. She was chic in a garish way, carrying a big Gucci bag and wearing serious makeup. A total New York type. I grinned unexpectedly at my new best friend.

"Looks like it. And I thought I just had to watch out for concrete falling off buildings." I tried not to shake. I bent down, took a Kleenex out of my bag, and picked up the rock.

"You okay, honey?" the woman asked in that caring, rough NYC tone. I wanted to throw my arms around her and hold on.

"Think so. This blazer helped." I patted the spot to reassure myself nothing was broken and I wasn't gushing blood. "Did you notice the car?" I asked the forty-something redhead.

"Black, didn't notice the license.? I don't do cars. City kid." She paused. "I saw the hand that threw that thing, though. There was a glove. Beige. Good leather. Fashion I do know." I gathered as much from her outfit.

"The hand with the glove could have been a man or a woman," she continued. "But whoever it was knew how to throw. You got an ex wanting to get your attention? I wouldn't touch that thing if I were you. It could be a subpoena or divorce papers." I laughed nervously. "I'm an expert on divorces, too. Glad you're okay." She walked on, the clicking of her leopard heels and the smell of her perfume gradually faded away,

I looked at the rock. On the paper were large black letters. MYOB. Even my daughter would know what that meant: Mind your own business. I covered the rock with more tissues in case there were prints and dropped it in a pocket of my bag.

* * *

The apartment complex at 52nd and Ninth was made up of identical high-rise buildings that disappeared into low-hanging clouds; it took some sleuthing to find number 380. I took the elevator up to the eighteenth floor. The halls were quiet and carpeted, as if I was in a hotel. I was disappearing from my real life, less than forty blocks from home.

Devon answered, wearing sweatpants, his hair in need of a comb, and his T-shirt crumpled. I'd only seen him like this once before, the morning after we'd been together in Miami. My body remembered that night all too well.

"I know I didn't wake you," I said with a ridiculous laugh. "You called *me*."

"Sorry. I've been on the phone all morning." He ushered me in, his hand on my back. "Wait till you hear about the tapes from Park Avenue. Tea?"

While he fixed us some herbal tea, I looked around the apartment, an oversized studio with a partially hidden sleeping alcove. The room centered on the view. There was a floor-to-ceiling window: a forest of skyscrapers and blue sky. I watched people working at desks on the lower floors or at home in their kitchens on the residential upper section. In between buildings, you could see a sliver of New Jersey across the river.

My shoulders relaxed. I was, above all my problems, safe from rocks thrown from cars, floating in a stranger's apartment with Devon. I sat down on the brown fake-suede couch, just like the couches in all the men's apartments I'd ever known. I'd come here without thinking, without my usual guard up. What was I doing? All I knew was I didn't want to be at home, where I'd have to pretend I didn't know that Daniel complained to Cornelia. Pretend I wasn't sleuthing and writing another screenplay with Devon. Pretend I hadn't gotten the warning that was now in my bag.

Devon handed me a mug. He sat on the couch next to me, not in the armchair. I couldn't tell him just yet about the rock, or about sleazy Greg. I just wanted to be here alone with him now.

"What was on the basement security tape?" I asked. Devon's smooth cheek and his arms, with their just-right muscles, were heart-stoppingly close.

"Well, the big news is what's *not* on it," he said excitedly. "At 6:45 a.m., someone covered the camera. The cover was removed at 7:10. There's no sign of Hernando on the tapes, even though we know he clocked in at 6:50. Whoever killed him had this planned. It wasn't a spontaneous thing."

I felt like throwing up. The person who had carefully taken aim at me could be the same one who had calmly covered a security camera before killing an innocent man.

"I didn't tell you about Patty Baylor," I said, words tumbling out in a nervous rush. "She remembered that Peggy Fitzgerald came in the back door while she waited for the bathroom. She told the police, but they decided Peggy was just checking out the garbage area. Maybe you can bring up something if you see her again."

"Sure, no problem." He studied my face. "I know the camera being covered is creepy, but what's wrong?" Devon was always tuned into my moods. He took my hand. My body relaxed, but my heartbeat sped up.

"I've had a rough day," I confessed. "Cornelia stood me up at Sheldon's. She's on Daniel's side and bugged me to stop investigating. Daniel cried on her shoulder, saying that I was endangering Chloe." Just saying this out loud made me furious and teary. "Then Greg Sheldon denied any ill will toward his deceased ex, which I believed like I believe good genes are the reason for his forever-young face. He also told me I needed Botox and got a little too close until I snapped into bitchy reporter mode." Devon smiled.

"I implied he might be doing the wives of the husbands that Karen apparently screwed," I looked out the window so I wouldn't stare at Devon's arms. "And this was just thrown at me from a car on 57th Street." I took the rock out of my bag. The tissue was still on it.

Devon looked at the writing on the rock, and his face lost color. He put his arm around me and held me as if I'd just told him I had a fatal illness.

"We can stop," he said. " A ritzy Park Avenue murder is a good story, but you're a target."

"I don't even have a bruise," I protested, looking up at his lips. Then he was covering my face with kisses, and our mouths were doing things together that were borderline indecent, even with our clothes on. Every doubt and fear of mine, everything melted away except his hands on my back, my face, finding their way under my sweater. I knew where this was headed, and I didn't want to stop it.

Suddenly, the Harry Potter theme clanged loudly. My phone. The number said precinct.

"I'd better take this," I said, unwrapping myself reluctantly from Devon.

"Is this Melanie Deming?"

"Yes."

"Detective Chilton here. I think it's time we had a chat, perhaps exchanged information. Is now a good time?" It was a blissful time, but not for chatting. I looked out of the corner of my eye at Devon, mouthing *he wants to talk.* Devon shrugged, but kept stroking the back of my neck.

"I have to be on the East Side by 3:30."

"How about now? I can be at your apartment in twenty minutes." I stopped breathing. A detective in my kitchen again. Would Daniel be home?

"I'm not at home right now."

"How soon can you get there? Or would you rather come to the precinct? We aren't far from Huntley." *Why the urgency?*

"I can be home in thirty minutes."

"Why don't I send a car from the precinct? Where are you?"

Panic swept over me. Why would they send a car? Was I being arrested?

"Not a problem, I can get home. You can trust me."

"Until proven otherwise. See you in thirty minutes," he said and hung up. I jumped up; the room spun around. I grabbed onto the back of the couch.

"He was going to send a squad car to get me. What the hell? I just wanted some time alone with you to calm down. Is he arresting me? For what? Daniel might be home. I have a daughter. It's too much." I jogged from one foot to the other, finally collapsing into the armchair. I dug into my bag and found some hyssop oil, naturally calming, I dabbed it around my neck and chest. Devon quietly came over and sat on the arm of the chair. He massaged my shoulders.

"You're a brilliant writer and sleuth who happens to be married. You have a terrific daughter. Chilton's just trying to scare you off. Nothing wrong with you that I can see." He bent down. I couldn't resist his lips. This time he almost ended up in my lap.

"What time did you say you had to be home for the detective?" Devon murmured.

What was I doing? I needed Chasteberry.

"I've got a cop coming to see me. We have to stop." Maybe Devon was like all the men I'd known, whose needs came first. But I desperately wanted to stay, to run away with him and disappear.

"Sorry, but that call was a mood destroyer," I sighed. "The last thing I want is to rush being together." I untangled myself. " What do I tell Chilton?" Devon stood up, shifted back into investigative writer.

"I'll come with you," he said. I shook my head.

"I understand.," Devon realized. "Daniel. Though all of this is legit, Mel. We *do* write together." He sighed. "Okay, first find out why Chilton's there.

Why did he call today?"

"My guess is Greg Sheldon. Dr. Cowboy Boots got upset after I left and called his lawyer, who then called Chilton."

"Then he'll ask why you went to see Sheldon."

"That's easy," I said. "Botox consultation, but I chickened out. Conversation veered to the investigation when Greg said I was the most attractive journalist he'd met."

"I agree with the bad doctor on that. The detective may buy it. He'll want to know more, though." He cupped my face in his hands. "I want to be there with you."

"Don't tempt me." I put my shoes back on. " Telling the truth won't be a problem. Greg Sheldon didn't confess anything. Except for one slip about women hating Karen, because she bulldozed marriages. But he insisted that these angry women were fine, upstanding citizens with impeccable reputations.

Devon broke in here. "Remember Sheldon was in the middle of a divorce battle with Karen over money. The cops know he'll lie."

"Then why the rush to see me? Do I tell Chilton about the rock?"

Devon looked at the view and then back to me. " Maybe they can pull fingerprints from it. He's gonna want to know who could have thrown it, who wants you to mind your own business." He unfolded my clenched fingers and rubbed my cold hands. "Being safe is the priority. Who do you think threw it?"

"I don't know. I've annoyed a lot of people, but I'm not exactly hot on anyone's trail. As soon as I think it's Susie or Marc Olmsted, I jump to Greg, but I always come back to money. The plot to get around the zoning laws is the big news. I can tell him that. "

"You'll know how to handle this guy. What's in your best interest?" His confidence in me made me fling my arms around his neck before I left. I had ten minutes to get home.

* * *

Fortunately, Daniel was out when I got home.

I could feel the obsession to find Karen's killer building in me. My old shrink said it had to do with my family. The obsession and surge of adrenaline fueling my search were familiar. I'd never felt safe at home. My brother and father fought all the time. When they got physical, I'd try to stop them. My mother disappeared during their fights. I was eight, my brother was fourteen, and his fights with our father got so lethal they made Darth Vader and Luke Skywalker look tame.

Karen's murder got my adrenaline flowing, as if *my* life depended on finding who'd done this awful crime. Keeping the peace between my father and brother took that same crazy Red Bull kind of energy surge. It felt like life or death. My brother stormed out at eighteen and never looked back, leaving me with the wreckage.

But did I have to keep jumping in, putting myself in danger? I called Rebecca, this time because she's a psychologist.

"Hi, it's Melanie. You have a minute?"

"I can see it's you from this wonderful modern invention you've probably heard of, caller ID." Rebecca quipped. "You sound strange. Anything wrong?"

"Is looking for the truth a good thing or a neurotic thing? I get that my angry brother and father were scary. Maybe I'm just trying to fix the past. I shouldn't be out looking for murderers like an avenger. I should have a calm life. The kind Daniel wants."

"Oh God," Rebecca moaned and smacked her forehead. "You mean you're ready to go back to the same old, same old. You found a money-making way to take your neurotic stuff and do some good with it. Scorcese doesn't analyze why all he's interested in are mafia types. He doesn't care what any of his wives think. Coppola made a fortune on Godfather movies. Don't worry about what Daniel wants. Do what you want for once."

"That's why I called you. I'm about to have a visit from the police. And I almost did it with Devon again. I'm a mess."

"Since when does having sex mean you're a mess? I think my promiscuity is one of my finest traits." She almost sounded hurt. "It's always been all right for men to lust after anything with breasts, so what's wrong with women's lust?"

"On you, it looks good," I said. "Not so much on me. Like a bridesmaid dress I wore once. Some girls made it look sexy. On me, it was a lumpy nightgown."

"You're not lumpy; you're in great shape with all that crazy exercise."

My bell rang.

"That's Chilton. I have to go."

"Offer him a drink. Have one yourself."

* * *

I opened the door.

"You open your door without asking for a name? You have a death wish?" Selma, my elderly next-door neighbor, shook her head. Her hair was blue and green; the color palette changed weekly. She was an old-timer in the building. She held a Tupperware container.

"I'm expecting someone. We can chat later."

"You're kicking me out when I bring chicken soup for your troubled soul?" The chicken soup was a bribe for intel.

"Love to chat when I can." The downstairs buzzer rang. My stomach clenched. I picked up the intercom. "Yes, send him up."

Thelma turned and walked slowly and grandly back to her apartment with the soup.

"We all worry about you because you found that dead woman," she said, waving her hand to include the whole building. "Keep your door locked. Call me if you need help." I chuckled at tiny five-foot, seventy-eight-year-old Thelma doing hand-to-hand combat.

The elevator opened. Detective Chilton, May-Ling, and the last person I wanted to see: Daniel.

"These detectives are here to see you," Daniel scoffed. "Why am I not surprised?" He stormed into his office, slamming the door.

"Bad time?" Chilton smiled broadly. Punching him and spending time in jail might be the escape I needed right now.

"Damage is already done. Might as well sit down." I gestured to the carved oak kitchen chairs. Valerian root, passionflower, and rhodiola now, I thought. I took out a glass, put in a small amount of water, and added the drops. They watched me carefully.

"What is that?" demanded Chilton.

"They're herbs," said May-Ling. "We've made her nervous."

"You are police and you're in my kitchen? Not really soothing. Would you like herbs?" I held out the glass.

I reached into my bag and gingerly placed the rock, still wrapped with tissues, on the table.

"What have we here?" May-Ling asked.

"This rock was thrown at me from a moving car on West 57th Street today at about one p.m. The tissues were to save fingerprints, if there are any."

Chilton took out a plastic glove and put it on. He picked the rock up, letting the tissue fall away.

"Do you know what this means?"

"Of course. Any school kid knows MYOB."

"So, who do you think wants you to mind your own business?"

"I don't know," I said. "Probably someone connected with Karen Sheldon's murder? I wrote a column about that day. "

"We read it," said May-Ling. "There wasn't much new in it that the *Times* didn't say." Whoa, a nice punch in the gut. I hoped my editor Harold didn't read the *Times*.

"But mine was a first-person account. The *Times* didn't have that." I countered.

Chilton jumped in.

"This is beside the point," he barked. "We know you're talking to parties in this case. We got a call from Sheldon's lawyer suggesting he could sue you for libel. Sheldon's practice is based on his reputation. He said we should put a leash on you. That's why we're here. Why did you talk to Dr. Sheldon?"

"Wouldn't you talk to him if you were me?" I protested. "I write a column called 'Aftermath.', and he's been impacted by a crime. Plus, my friend suggested I needed a consultation about Botox."

127

May-Ling nodded while Chilton chuckled.

"Really? You don't seem like the type to me," he said. "What exactly did you say to Sheldon that got him riled up?"

"Who, what, where, when, and why," I said. "The usual. Where was he when Karen was killed? Who did he think did it? What was his relationship like with Karen? How were he and his kids doing? All the same things I'm sure you asked him."

"And what else?" Chilton persisted.

"Not much." I hesitated. "Just about the trust funds. But you know about that and the argument he'd had that morning with Karen."

Chilton laced and unlaced his fingers. I hated when people did that.

"You're getting involved where you don't belong," he said. "This is a serious and dangerous police investigation. You're causing trouble for yourself and for us."

"Sheldon must be nervous if he got his lawyer to call," I said, changing the direction. "Do you think he threw the rock?"

"Not at all," Chilton said dismissively. "He has lawyers who take actions on his behalf. Why would he throw a rock? But the point is, you have to back off, or you'll get hurt. And we can arrest you for interfering with a police investigation."

That lit my fuse.

"Asking questions is *reporting*, and it's protected by the First Amendment. I do this for a living. Maybe I should get a lawyer, too." My voice had gotten loud enough that Daniel strode into the kitchen. He clamped his hands on my shoulder.

"Don't raise your voice to the detectives," he said, smiling at May-Ling especially. "They're trying to protect you—and us too, by the way."

"Protect, or stifle." I shrugged off his hands. "Ask Detective Levano about how my 'interfering' helped him. I'm the one taking a risk here, not anyone else." I glared at Daniel. He glared back.

"Well, I can see you two have a lot to talk about." Detective Chilton jumped up and gestured to May-Ling. She pushed back her chair and glanced at my tea stash on the counter.

"Chinese teas are more effective remedies than any of these," she said. "You should check them out."

"What do you recommend for stress?" I asked, just to be polite.

"Lots of dried flowers with green tea," she said. "Chamomile, lavender, jasmine—"

"Passionflower is also good," I jumped in eagerly. "I love the idea of you in the precinct, drinking Chinese flower teas." May-Ling actually rolled her eyes.

"I think we're done now," said Chilton, hustling his partner out the door and closing it behind him. I stood there, still in shock. What a waste of time. I hadn't told them anything. They didn't ask. They didn't believe I could help. This visit was just a reminder not to cause any trouble. I heard a sigh of exasperation. I'd forgotten about Daniel.

"I'm going back to the office. There's a reading at Place Gallery at six tonight that you obviously forgot. You were going to bring Chloe. Cornelia will be there with her daughter. Remember? Any synapses coming to life?" He snapped his fingers at me. Good thing for him I wasn't a violent person.

"I remember. But are you sure you want a lowly crime reporter sullying your event?" *I had not one shred of a memory about this.* Cornelia again, so soon? She'd want one of Daniel's unpublished restaurant finds as payment. I still didn't have any names.

"I can separate what you do with this murder thing from the fact that you are my wife and the mother of our daughter," he said pompously. "I am capable of doing that."

"I'll wear an apron," I said, only half joking. "Maybe dark glasses and a wig? I could be the babysitter."

"I don't see the humor here."

"That's just sad, Daniel." I sighed. "What's the address, and are we going to some new out-of-the-way bistro afterward?"

He looked relieved. "Place Gallery. 410 West 21st. The only new restaurants around there are in Chelsea Market. Levan has a new bistro." Daniel suddenly was transfixed, his eyes glazing over as they did when he talked about food. Or had sex.

129

"The chef is a woman, Florence Fiori," he said, closing his eyes. "What she does with truffles and cream…" I wondered if he was actually having an orgasm.

I interrupted his reverie. "Chloe and I will meet you at the gallery. Just be sure you introduce me as your wife, the columnist."

Daniel stared at me as if I was an alien in a bad dream. At least I'd gotten a restaurant name and a chef. He left for the magazine. I sent a text to Cornelia, giving her the name Florence Fiori and Levan.

It's about time. I'll see you later, she texted.

Thank God now you won't starve.

The police didn't take me seriously. They got nothing from me. What they got was only "elementary, my dear Watson," as Holmes said. Sherlock Holmes and Agatha Christie's Miss Marple were in an honor society of amateur sleuths who were smarter than the police. Maybe I was, too.

Chapter Seventeen

"I'm wearing a stupid party dress. It's a school night. I need to do my homework."

I squinted at Chloe's face. Angelic, with a dose of teenager showing. She hated homework.

"Dad wants us here. You'll have fun with Elizabeth." Chloe took my hand and returned to her almost ten-year-old self. We walked the last block toward the Place Gallery at Tenth Avenue in the 20s. Nicknamed Chelsea, a once down-and-out neighborhood, was now New York City's art gallery capital.

We'd been summoned here by Queen Cornelia. She had to show up because her husband Tom's investment firm was part-owner of the publishing company that produced Daniel's magazine and had an investment in this event. What Cornelia wanted, Daniel did. A downtown crowd spilled onto the sidewalk from the gallery, a sea of black, including a gauzy, billowing outfit with torn sleeves and ragged hem as if she had flown in from Hogwarts. Inside, the crowd was a mixture of publishing types in business suits—accessorized with expensive eyewear—and the artsy set in spandex, glitter, Janis Joplin patchwork, and beyond. One woman's breasts were fully visible through the sheer fabric of her top. I wasn't the only one trying not to stare.

Chloe stopped short at the door. "It's a lot of grown-ups," she said. I thought the same thing.

With a high-pitched screech, Cornelia's daughter, Elizabeth, came running up and grabbed Chloe by the hand. Suddenly, my kid was perfectly willing to disappear into the mob. I followed reluctantly, satisfied at least that I would be barely visible in my navy silk blouse and black pants.

Daniel was nowhere to be seen, but I spotted Devon talking to a thin, muscular woman in a clinging leather dress. When she murmured something in his ear, he laughed so loud I knew he was faking it. He gave a raised eyebrow salute before turning back to Leather Dress, whom I now recognized as Peggy Fitzgerald, four inches taller in Manolo heels.

My dislike for this woman was not rational. Just because she'd outbid the blonde stranger for sparkly animal jewelry, she didn't want, because she'd made an offer on that apartment while Karen still lay dead on the bathroom floor, because she flirted with Devon because she'd inherited money instead of working for it. Rebecca's voice in my head said *of course we hate her.* She may have assaulted me the other night. She might be the killer.

I pretended to look at the exhibit entitled "Invasion of the Climate Snatchers." Huge photographs of the Amazon, of Antarctica, of polar bears on ice floes, of toucans and gorillas, all color treated with blinding neon shades of pink, orange, and purple. Superimposed over the treated photos were screaming faces, skulls, and images of hellfire. The cumulative effect was a three-dimensional jolt of *climate change is death and it's all your fault.*

"Attention, everyone," a voice said into a microphone. The crowd quieted. "We are honored to have with us the chairman of the Magazines Forever Group, Arthur Bradley. Magazines Forever is responsible for this exciting and important exhibit. Art must march forward to increase public involvement in saving the planet." There was polite applause.

That was a stretch. A huge amount of plastic and who knew what else had to have gone into the production of these 3-D visions, putting more than their share of toxins back into the atmosphere.

Chairman Bradley droned on for a few minutes about the responsibility of journalism and art to save the planet. *And to make money.*

"I am proud to present the Poet Laureate of Ecuador, Miguel Domingo, who will read from his new work, "What Have We Done."

The man who stepped up to the mike a graying, angry Antonio Banderas type. He began to read in an ominous voice.

"Like a virus, we invade

Like an army we destroy,
Like a fire we incinerate,
Like a tsunami we engulf,
Like a virus we mutate."

This cheerful verse continued for almost fifteen minutes. A buxom blonde near me wept openly. She might have been a paid actress. Some teenagers did break dance moves to the poet's uneven rhythm. People drifted to the bar until there was a line snaking through the gallery. For fifteen minutes, we stood and listened to the coming destruction of the planet via a poem that screamed 1970s Kerouac. At least the drinks were free.

There was polite applause when he finished. Then the crowd, like a virus mutating, transformed back into a loud, raucous bacchanal.

The smell of pot was very strong. When and why had marijuana started to smell like skunk. I scanned the crowd.

Devon finished his chat with Peggy and started toward me. But my eyes had found Daniel, leaning against one of those huge pillars you find in old loft buildings. I watched him laugh and smile as he hadn't with me for years. The object of his warmth was a small woman wearing a floral dress and platform heels. I knew instantly, the same way you know when you have a scratchy throat that you are in for a full-blown cold, that he was sleeping with this woman. I felt like I'd taken a knee in the stomach and might crumble in a heap, right there in this crowded room lined with hideous art. My old world dropped away. I knew the petite woman too well. Nadine Duvet. She was a baker—Daniel's partner on his last cookbook—and the widow of Ralph Duvet, whose body I'd found in the playground last year. I'd saved her life. She met Daniel, and launched her career, through me. And this was how she repaid me.

But who was I to feel bitter, or jealous or to be surprised? Now that I thought about it, I had seen him happy and relaxed a year ago. That was the night we celebrated the arrest of the mother/son killer team, my new column, and his forthcoming cookbook featuring Nadine's recipes. He proclaimed Nadine the best pastry chef in New York. I hadn't seen her much since that party.

"Are you thinking what I'm thinking?" Devon's voice startled me into breathing again.

"I doubt it. But try me."

Devon had an amused smile.

"I'm thinking you don't have to feel so guilty."

"Maybe they're just work friends," I said, not believing it for a second.

"I think I'm right," said Devon. "And I wish we could leave right now." He got so close I could feel the heat from his hand near my back. *Change the subject.*

"Any news from Peggy Fitzgerald? Did she bring a husband this time?"

"She wasn't sure he'd make it," he said. "I think he's a professor here in the city or out on Long Island? Any work her husband actually does, I'd bet, is just for show." He stepped closer. " Can you leave?" I shook my head.

"I have a nine-year-old somewhere. And we still haven't been presented to Queen Cornelia. I'd better look for Chloe." I wanted to grab Devon but instead touched his shoulder in a quick caress. I made my way through the crowd, giving Daniel a wide berth. He only had eyes for Nadine, anyway.

I sidestepped a guy in tight glitter pants who showed off a tango step and his bootie to two women with matching black pageboys. "*Tango for Dummies* has an advance order of ten thousand already," one woman said to the other.

Nothing I wrote would ever have an advance order of ten thousand. It was either this fact, or knowing Daniel was likely sleeping with Nadine, but a cloud of depression settled on me.

In a minute, I'd burst into tears, and I hadn't found Chloe. It was so crowded. I pushed past three men in suits, talking adamantly.

"These plastic boxes mean the end of civilization," the shortest suit said.

The taller suit with wild hair emitted an exaggerated sigh.

"The show in the Hamptons was more offensive, worse than a school science show." His accent was obviously fake British. He shuddered. I burst out in a loud laugh. The three turned together as one suit and examined me as if I was a piece of bad art. I hightailed it back to the entrance without Chloe.

The wild-haired man looked vaguely familiar, like a college art history professor.

"No sign of Chloe," I said to Devon. He looked past me. I felt a tap on my shoulder. There was Daniel breathing down my neck holding our daughter's hand.

"Chloe has homework. She needs to go home," he said curtly, with the slightest nod at Devon.

"Hi, Daniel. Nice of you to say hello. So I'm being dismissed? Cornelia gave permission?"

"She said she talks to you all the time, and she has to get Elizabeth home."

"Just when I was about to buy that piece with the skull and the fuschia icebergs. Imagine how it would look over the couch." Daniel remained stone-faced.

"Melanie, we'll give you a ride home," said Cornelia, who appeared suddenly in a bright blue suit. "Our car is here." Chloe and Elizabeth ran to the waiting chauffeur.

"Are you coming, Daniel?" I asked, already knowing the answer.

"I have to talk to Miguel about a poem he's completed about his mother's cooking, and I have chefs to meet," he said tersely.

"I noticed," I said, matching his curt tone. "Say hi to Nadine for me." I gave Daniel a peck on the cheek, just to be irritating. He drew back, startled, then caught himself. He tried a smile.

"Yes, of course." *Definitely screwing Nadine,* flashed in neon. Daniel got a nervous look on his face and hurried back into the crowd.

"I'm staying at West 52nd. Can I hitch a ride?" Devon asked Cornelia, giving her his never-fail charming smile.

"I suppose. We have the big car tonight." Cornelia's tone was icy. The three of us turned and walked out of the gallery. I had won, but also lost somehow. I grabbed Devon's arm.

* * *

In the limousine, Devon and Cornelia chatted about Zimbabwe. She had been there on safari, of course. We dropped Devon at his corner. The girls drank Perrier and giggled. At our building, Chloe ran into the lobby. Cornelia put her hand on my sleeve.

"I heard your comment about Nadine, and I noticed Daniel being rather attentive to her. Even if something *is* going on there, be careful. Do you want your marriage to shatter? Where would you live? Devon is away all the time."

"Thanks for the ride," I mumbled and jumped out of the car. Seriously, Elizabeth was in the car. If she heard Cornelia, she'd tell Chloe in a minute.

"Don't forget the Parents' Association meeting. It's about the Book Fair," Cornelia called out. Not happening.

Chloe and I rode upstairs. We were quiet. I wondered when Daniel would be home. I wondered why I cared. Chloe did her homework in the kitchen while I made hot chocolate for her and tea for me.

"So, Mom, are you and Devon like Castle and Beckett?" she asked, looking up at me. "She's a police lady. Castle writes mysteries. He's good at clues, and they solve the case together. Like you and Devon."

My stomach tensed. The TV series *Castle* Castle and Beckett eventually became lovers and got married. The Castle character had a daughter named Zoe.

"Not exactly like that. I mean, I'm not a policewoman. I follow clues sometimes." I smoothed her hair. "I can see why you'd think so, though. Where do you watch that show?"

"Samantha's house. Other kids." Her sweet face looked concerned. "Everybody lets their kids watch anything. Except you and Dad." Well, at least there was one area left where Daniel and I agreed. "You better not yell at Sam's mother."

I put my arm around her. "I won't. I mean, like you said, you have a mom who's a sleuth and writes about crimes. That's bad enough, right?" I realized with a jolt that Chloe's opinion about me was more important than Daniel's.

Her face scrunched up. "Bad? That's crazy, Mom. I think you're cool. Samantha thinks so, too."

"All right!" I high-fived her. "How'd I get so lucky to have you for my daughter?" But inside, my twinge of fear grew stronger. Would I meet up to her expectations? Was she trying to make sense of Devon and me?

* * *

Daniel came home a few hours later. Chloe was asleep. I jotted notes about the auction, Peggy's comments about what she heard, sorted index cards according to what people said. Daniel undressed and got into bed. Neither of us said a word. He stretched out and turned his back to me. He no longer had fat around his waist.

"I know you think I'm a male chauvinist, trying to hold you back from being successful."

"Not exactly. Maybe you're competitive?"

Daniel abruptly turned and looked at me like I was an idiot.

"Seriously?" He laughed coldly. "I'm a top editor and cookbook author, and you think I'm threatened by the stuff you write?" He snorted and rolled over.

God, I hoped I got extra points in heaven for not punching him. I did think about hitting him over the head with his and Nadine's giant dessert book. No one ever made any of those instant heart attack recipes anyway. I was right about his being competitive. Maybe screwing around with Nadine was part of it, getting back at me, tit for tat.

Daniel had criticized my writing for a long time. Four years ago, he'd been adamant that if I spent two weeks in L.A. doing a screenwriting job, it would do irreversible harm to Chloe. He traveled whenever his boss asked him to. He'd most recently tried to get me to take a secretarial job and give up writing for the Wild Westsider. It was my column there that had paid off with thousands of followers and the sale of a screenplay.

I lay in bed piling up grievances, fuming, unable to sleep. When Daniel snored lightly, I carefully got up and put on long leggings, a neon yellow shirt, and sneakers. Why not run out this energy? Before midnight, I could reach 20,000 steps. I quietly left the apartment and went out to the sidewalk. It was 11:30.

I stayed on Broadway, heading downtown, where I knew the streets would be more populated. When you're running, especially when you're angry, distance goes by fast. I wasn't the only one out there, either. Suddenly I was below 72nd Street and passing Lincoln Center, the lights over the auditoriums still burning brightly. The audience was just getting out of a marathon three-hour opera.

I felt my phone buzz.

You okay? Devon asked.

I didn't really think after that. I kept running away from Daniel to Devon. Suddenly, my left arm was being pulled wildly. I teetered like a bowling pin, trying to stay up. What crazy was doing this? I couldn't turn around. Thank God we worked on footwork at fencing class, I caught myself when I pitched forward, only scraping my hands. I pushed myself back up.

"Hey!" I screamed at the clearly female runner who'd zoomed ahead of me. The hooded figure turned and screamed back at me.

"Watch out bitch! Stay the hell away from what's not yours!"

"What?! " I yelled."What the hell?" But she was gone.

Was it Peggy Fitzgerald? The woman had come at me deliberately. I rubbed my arm. There was pain, but I could bend it. Nothing broken. Another warning. But this one was different. What did she mean, stay away from what wasn't mine—that stupid apartment I had no interest in? Ugly animal jewelry? Devon? But he wasn't hers, either, much as she might wish he were. It didn't make any sense.

Five minutes later, I was at Devon's building. The short Stallone-type doorman looked me up and down with disapproving eyes but waved me to the elevator. Then I was running down the hall on the eighteenth floor and knocking on Devon's door. The song "Knocking on Heaven's Door" played in my head.

"It's me," I panted.

He opened the door. I stepped into his strong arms, and he pulled me against his chest.

"Are you really here? I've been dreaming about this."

"I don't have much time," I said, collapsing onto him. My anger and adrenaline suddenly shut off, replaced by a wave of exhaustion and desire.

"We'll take what we can get," he said. I leave in two days." He took me by the hand. We fell onto his bed, mouths and bodies finally finding each other again.

"Ouch," I yelped as my bruised arm pressed against him.

"What's wrong?" Devon murmured, his lips on my neck.

"I ran here. I got mowed down by a runner. It could have been Peggy Fitzgerald." Devon stopped nuzzling me.

"What happened?"

"She crashed into me," I said. "It had to have been on purpose. But get this—she said, 'Stay away from what's not yours.' What could that mean?" I sat up and rubbed my arm, more from nerves than from pain.

"Here, let me do that." Devon gently took off my shirt and massaged my arm. His hands were warm, and all my pain eased. I felt again the mix of lust and exhaustion, and I wanted lust to win.

" Daniel's getting back at me with Nadine. It's all my fault."

Devon slowly and softly stroked my arm and neck so that I couldn't think straight.

"You're not the bad one," Devon murmured between kisses. He stopped and looked at me seriously.

" Daniel's angry. He wants you back to the way things were. He never thinks he's wrong. He doesn't try to make things right with you, to win you back. And isn't there a childhood trauma with his mother? Maybe it's his version of the Tonya Harding syndrome. That makes for destructive crazy."

Then, I was destructive and crazy, too. I went running way too late, was attacked, and ended up in Devon's bed in the middle of the night. A loud bell went off in my head when he mentioned the Tonya Harding Syndrome.

An athlete so jealous she physically harmed a rival. Named after the skater Tonya Harding's attack on Nancy Kerrigan at the Olympics years ago. The woman who just plowed into me thought I had something of hers. Did the murderer kill out of jealous rage? I couldn't stay with these thoughts. Every other part of me focused on Devon and pure pleasure. I let myself drown in the moment and didn't think anymore until I left long after midnight.

* * *

I took a cab home, showered off my guilt and confusion, and climbed quietly into bed. I fell asleep immediately. At some point, Daniel rolled over. He threw his arm around me in his sleep. My body went rigid. I stayed totally still, praying he wouldn't start half-asleep sex, which he'd been known to do occasionally.

If you're both half asleep, it's kind of like mildly drunk sex, which isn't necessarily bad (if you're willing and protected, just to be clear). But I was completely awake. Thank God he flopped around and rolled back over to his side. I lay there obsessing about who was the bigger slut, me or Daniel. Tonya Harding came in there for a minute before I fell back to sleep.

* * *

My meditation tape the next morning really pissed me off. A dark-haired adonis in a flowing white shirt with a deep, sexy voice sits on a beach.

Here are seven affirmations for a magical day—guaranteed to turn on the happiness button in your brain. I'm sure that's not the only button his voice is supposed to turn on. And it can't be all that hard to sit on a beach in Hawaii and have a magical day. I yelled at a faceless voice.

Try being a woman in a loveless marriage in NYC who's trying to be a good mom while stalking a killer. Then, see if your happy button works.

* * *

Fencing is the best way to get out aggression and tighten your butt at the same time. Marta, the Russian instructor, handed out protective face masks. Within minutes, sweat poured from my face, down my T-shirt, and into my metallic vest. I lunged and retreated over and over. In the first round with a partner, I could barely see and stabbed myself in the foot with the rubber-tipped foil. The metaphor for my life. Marta actually giggled, which got me so annoyed I scored a hit.

I showered quickly and changed back into decent jeans and a chic Lululemon sweatshirt I'd borrowed from Rebecca. This outfit, with a pair of white leather sneakers, would get me in the door of the Jean Le Claire Salon. I'd managed to nab an appointment at the same time as Marlena Shenko.

Chapter Eighteen

I walked along Madison to the Jean LeClaire Salon salon. My feet felt like lead. I had no idea how to get out of the one thousand dollar haircut. What if they asked for payment *upfront*? I used the name Buffy Chester when I made the reservation. It seemed funny at the time. Cornelia assured me Buffy Clifford never went to this salon. I changed the last name, but someone else from Spence could be there. Marlena was not part of the Spence crowd.

"My name is Buffy," I murmured as I climbed the flight of stairs into Madison Avenue's high society. I felt a dash of arrogance despite my rumbling stomach. I thought I saw Kristen Bell being ushered into a curtained area. Or maybe it was Brie Larson. I gave my name to one of the two models at the front desk. Not an ounce of body fat between them. They both wore white high-collared blouses, open practically to the belly, with wide-legged black bolero pants. Other staffers wore simple black sheaths, while the stylists wore white coats, like doctors.

They gave me a bottle of Fiji water, in case I'd gotten dehydrated climbing the stairs. As usual, everyone here was two sizes smaller than me and wore an array of platform sneakers. Black high topped slip-ons had Balenciaga written all over them. Easy enough to check the cost. $1400. White leather Prada. A cheap $720. This was fun. I almost forgot why I was there. Then Marlena Shenko walked in.

Her gold-streaked auburn hair looked perfect, as if she'd just come from a salon, which made me wonder why in the world she was here. Maybe these people were really insecure underneath their perfection. I casually got up, took a Vanity Fair off the magazine pile, and sat in an empty chair next to her. She took some papers out of a briefcase and studied them. I flipped through a few pages of *Vanity Fair.*

"You look familiar," I said. Marlena eyed me warily, as if I were trying to pick her up. "Have we ever met?" I asked. She shook her head. I gave her a patronizing Buffy Clifford smile.

"I think my photographic memory just located you," I said. "I went to an open house two weeks ago. Awful situation, really. A woman was killed. But I think I saw you leaving as I came in. I rarely forget faces."

"You were there?" Marlena looked stunned. Her voice was deep and had more than a hint of a Russian accent.

"Oh, yes," I said, with the kind of annoyed arrogance Buffy transmitted. "Of course, leaving when you did, you'd have missed the police. The victim was the ex-wife of a well-known plastic surgeon." Marlena looked smug. I lowered my voice. "I heard the doctor and his ex had a big fight, right there in that apartment just before she was killed. He was looking at the place with his fiancée. But I also heard he's a real ladies' man."

Marlena's mouth became rigid. She sucked in her already tight cheeks. "People shouldn't gossip." She shook her head, tossing her perfect hair. "But men can't be trusted. Anyone who thinks they can is a fool."

So much for Marlena being in the first blush of love with Greg.

"I know what you mean," I said. "My husband *works late* a lot." I put air quotes around the words. "Between you and me, he's not such a hot commodity. Not like that surgeon! " I sighed dramatically. "But there's always some woman looking for anything with pants."

Marlena put down the brief she'd been holding. I had her attention.

"So, what are your reasons for staying in your marriage?" she asked. "Money?" She sounded younger and almost sad.

"Of course. Why not? With the prenup I had to sign, there's no payoff in leaving." I looked at her carefully as I delivered my prepared line. "I can't leave until there's a lot of real estate that's been accrued after the marriage. I'm working on that." A spark appeared in Marlena's eyes. I pointed at her four-carat diamond. "But here I'm going on about my far from blissful marriage, and you're engaged—probably to a wonderful man." She changed the subject abruptly. As I'd hoped she would.

"Real estate is the best way to make money in this city," she said. "I'm involved in a situation. Apartments that might be a great investment for you."

"Really. Where would they be? The new Regal Towers on 3rd Avenue?" *I should get an Oscar for this.*

"Oh no," Marlena sniffed in distaste. "Far more distinctive. A large mansion never before divided."

"Oh my." I put my hand to my mouth in astonishment at my good fortune. "It sounds perfect. Alfred likes what no one else has. I can't wait to see the place."

"The apartments are not ready for viewing yet, but I'll give you my card." She took out a gold card case and handed me an elegant, hand-embossed card.

"So you're a lawyer. I'll definitely call you. When do you think the apartments will be ready?" I waited for what seemed like a long while.

"Not till next year," she finally said. "But we will be showing plans and taking deposits in the next few months. They are worth waiting for."

I tried to look impressed. " I am *very* interested." I gazed again at her ring. "Congratulations again on your engagement." Marlena's beautiful sculpted face turned hard.

"Deals are more reliable than men. That's why you need the biggest ring you can get. You keep the ring, even if the man turns out to be a loser." We both looked at my pathetic Mexican silver wedding band. Damn, I should have gotten costume rings to wear.

"My husband doesn't like me to wear my rings since I lost one," I quickly explained. "I have them in a vault at home." Marlena nearly rolled her eyes at my little woman role.

I wondered how many rings she'd pocketed before moving on. Greg was a loser in her mind already. She was not a naive woman. Maybe when she needed cash, she got engaged. That rock on her hand had to be fifty thousand dollars. Was she a citizen? Was she here on a work visa? She might be getting married for citizenship. Suddenly, she seemed older than thirty-five.

"Mrs. Chester, Roxanne will see you now." One of the model types with straight blonde hair and four-inch heels gestured to me. Uh-oh. I couldn't decide if I should run or see what Roxanne envisioned for me.

"It's good meeting you," I said. Marlena and I shook hands. Her grip was like a man's. "Are you a tennis player, by any chance?" I asked.

"I do one hundred push-ups every morning, benchpress one hundred pounds," she said. "Triathlons when I have less work. Never tennis." Her face looked as if she had smelled a dead fish. This was one powerful woman. She had the strength to have killed Karen—and the height, with her perpetual heels, to have covered the security camera at 962 Park Avenue. And she had a motive if Karen opposed her real estate plans. Karen clearly had a lot of power over the Harringtons, especially if she had used the tape with her daughter in it as blackmail.

I walked into the Salon and met Roxanne, the stylist, who looked like Audrey Hepburn crossed with a singer from a Goth band. Pixie-white hair, a dash of purple lipstick. A white coat over a silver jumpsuit. She terrified me, even though she was not Jean Le Claire. Women paid two thousand for the privilege of sitting in the owner's chair. I quickly looked at my phone and then slapped my hand over my mouth. "I'm so sorry, I have to leave."

I backed away, bumping into her colorist stand with its garish mixtures of colors. Everything looked like poison to me. "I just got a text from my daughter's school. Sick." I pointed to my stomach and ran out of the room—right into Marlena, who was heading into the curtained big-spenders area.

"School problem. Always something," I said, running out the door. I took a breath when I got to the sidewalk. Angela, from my Cut-N-Curl place where a haircut was seventy-five dollars, would roar when I tell her this story. And I'd found out a few important facts. Marlena was not gung-ho about marrying Greg. The apartment conversion at Harrington was in the works. And Marlena would get very rich. If she had to hock engagement rings, she must need money. She was an athlete; she would have been able to throw the rock at me. But there had not been even a flicker of recognition on her face just now when we spoke. Whoever threw the rock knew very well who I was.

* * *

I hadn't lied. I did have to get to Huntley. Last year, I was ordered onto the Halloween party committee by Cornelia to near-disastrous results. Cornelia this year insisted that since I'd written a screenplay and Daniel wrote cookbooks, I should become involved in The Huntley Book Fair. A very prestigious event. My body tensed as I entered the building, passing through the airtight security.

Cornelis waited for me in front of the smaller of Huntley's two auditoriums.

"This time, I hope you can stifle comments about over-privileged kids and stop looking daggers at everyone's diamonds. It's about reading, not bank accounts."

"Did you say hello? Did I miss that?" I took a cleansing breath. "I don't look daggers. I just melt the diamond settings with my X-ray vision. It's painless." Cornelia gave me a disappointing daughter look.

"Maybe this is not a good fit for you," she said archly.

"Now you're catching on. Huntley is not a good fit for me, but you know why we're here. Daniel's mother pays, Chloe loves it, I tag along," I replied wearily. "And you, in your benevolence, give me info about the folks over here to help find Karen's killer. You're my Deep Throat." Cornelia rolled her eyes. She opened the door, and I followed.

The auditorium was crowded. We found seats in the back. Everyone wanted to be part of this. There was a status to The Book Fair that I now understood was about the celebrity authors they managed to bring in. This year, it was a financial pundit, Rick Manton, from the conservative network, who'd served time for insider trading and wrote a book about how badly he had been treated. There was a young woman who had a million followers on her fashion blog. And they had landed the top-selling romance writer in the country, Carey Richards, probably the richest writer in the world, thanks to the old truism that sex sells. The snooty Huntley moms were especially excited about this steamy romance writer. What were the messages here, exactly? Do whatever it takes to make money, if you're a man. Women should focus on fashion—or sex.

The money raised did not go to some charity or NGO building libraries in Africa or sending books to underserved public school kids. It was plowed right back into Huntley, which already had a fifty million dollar endowment, not to mention tuition from each child of $70,000 a year.

"Will the meeting come to order?" called Julia Bloom, daughter of the financial king who had donated eight million to Huntley the previous year, thus purchasing the honor of being chairwoman this year. I tuned out as they went through the various committees. Cornelia elbowed me to stand when they announced the volunteer committee. I was trying to forget I'd been pushed to join. Then Fawn Billingsley, Buffy's protégée, read the list of the celebrity authors. Everyone applauded loudly when she finished. Except me. I raised my hand. Cornelia mouthed the word "No" and slid away into an empty seat nearby.

"Yes, Melanie. Did you have a question?" Fawn asked, barely moving her rigid lips.

"These authors are well known, but I wonder about the Manton guy. Wouldn't the author of *Girl Boss*, or Melinda Gates, bring more of the kind of educational message we're looking for here? Or J. K. Rowling? She wrote *Very Good Lives*." I looked around the room. Some heads were nodding, but most everyone stared rigidly ahead. I forged on. "Maybe we can't get J. K. Rowling, but come on. Rick Manton?!" There's Susan Spencer. She wrote about actions to help the world."

Fawn went 'tsk tsk' then spoke. "These authors are signed up and vetted, Melanie. The committee approved them. As usual, you were not there. Too busy, I assume."

"And some of us have sons," a woman's voice called out from the crowd. "They need role models too, you know." She had a point; all my suggestions had been female authors.

"You're so right. But do you want this guy, Manton?" I looked directly at the mother who spoke. Long wavy hair, tiny waist. "Isn't there a better male role model out there? Steve Harvey's relatable. Or the guy who wrote *Emotional Intelligence*? " The crowd started to murmur. One person left. Someone called out, "You probably want a true crime writer." Who said that? I couldn't identify the voice.

Up jumped Joan Charles, assistant principal, and damage control specialist. She took the mike with a tense smile.

"Please come to my office to address any concerns about authors. I'm sure if anyone has an author who is appropriate for our school, we can accommodate them. I know Ms Deming, you have other concerns right now, as do all of our busy parents."

Stripped naked in public. That nightmare was here again. I cringed, feeling more like an outsider than ever. Cornelia turned away. I sat down quickly, then tiptoed out of the room. I went to one of the beautifully appointed private bathrooms and cried. Why couldn't I keep my mouth shut? I didn't give a damn about the Book Fair. Chloe didn't care about the book fair, either. She thought I was cool.

My marriage was in shambles. I didn't know who the murderer was. Devon was leaving tomorrow. I'd been targeted by that rock, attacked by a runner, and warned by the police. Why did I present myself as a target again by opening my mouth? I didn't even have my usual bag with a stash of ignatia or California poppy with me—only a small, chic fanny pack, also a loan from Rebecca, to complete my outfit. I splashed some water on my face.

When the going gets tough, I go running. I left the school and headed for the park.

* * *

Fresh air makes me high. Not everyone's drug, but a good one if you can get addicted. I shook off the humiliation dumped on me by Fawn—how could someone with a name like that have the nerve to humiliate anyone. Within minutes, I was near the reservoir but on the main paved road. Since cars are not allowed in the park, you can run to the northern end at 110th Street. This is the wilder, less manicured edge of the park, bordering Harlem. Bikes whizzed by me. I passed the empty public swimming pool, where the road made a long, steep descent and picked up speed. Then, just as you think you're home free, the road rises steeply. Huge boulders rose up around me, with glacial deposits of granite and mica shining in the sun. My pace slowed up the hill.

It was the middle of the week and early in the afternoon. The Northern end of the park was empty. I felt a wave of panic. No one knew I was here. This wasn't my usual route. This wasn't a smart move. What was wrong with me? I tried to move faster, but fear and the steep hill held me back.

Suddenly, I heard heavy breathing behind me. It quickly became louder till it sounded like a roar. Again, I tried to speed up, but the hill was too steep. I felt the brush of something, someone's arm again. I screamed, "No!" and made a wide circle, running fast down the hill toward an exit to the street. My heart felt like it would explode.

"Mrs Deming, I'm sorry!" I heard a voice call out. *What the hell?* I stopped and looked. Running toward me, his arms wildly flapping, was Shane from Marc's office. "I didn't mean to startle you. Just meant to say hello. Are you all right?"

Other than almost having my heart beat out of my chest?

"Not really," I said. "Why were you running so close to me? Runners don't do that."

"Oh, I'm so sorry," he said quietly, but somehow I didn't think he was. " Thank goodness you're all right." Then he looked crestfallen. " I hope you won't hold this against me. We're hoping you come back."

Really. It didn't seem that way. Marc was not happy at the mansion." I looked at Shane incredulously. Could this really be a huge coincidence, him almost colliding with me? My meditation tape came to mind. *Say yes to the day.* I went along with the apartment pretense.

"Actually, I keep dreaming about the apartment Marc showed me on Riverside Drive," I said. "But how's the Harrington mansion sale coming? The plan to convert moving ahead?"

Shane looked around as if Marc might actually be in the park. He was dying to talk. "They might come down on Riverside. If you're interested, you should definitely make an offer."

"I will surely speak to my husband." Never. "But the Harrington?"

Shane's eyes darted around. "Things are slightly chaotic with Harrington. The buyer keeps wavering, even though the zoning is practically guaranteed. He wants the construction to start before he puts in all the money. I mean, that can be done. Marc is understandably stressed."

Shane put his hands on his hips and jerked his head high. "The buyer signed a contract. It's time to schedule the closing. It's past time."

"Really? It seems so soon," I said, my face a perfect study in confusion. " Had a contract been signed before Karen was killed? It seems pretty fast if she just got the listing."

Shane looked at me curiously. " The agency gets the construction started and gets the money back at the closing. But," he said, pausing to look around again. "This is off the record; the architect has had to pay off a lot of people to get these zoning changes. He wants *his* money repaid now. And construction costs go higher every day. The pressure on Marc is unbearable. I'm doing what I can to help the poor man." I could just imagine.

A few joggers and dog walkers came past us. Every single person, man or woman, stared at Shane. He was luscious. It was strange that his great looks and body didn't turn me on at all. I think it was his subservient manner towards Marc, even when Marc wasn't present, that took away from his sex appeal.

"Shane, would you like an iced latte or something?" I asked. "I'm walking over to Broadway."

"Sure," he said, though he seemed puzzled by my abrupt friendliness. I had more questions.

We fell into step and walked west on 110th Street to Columbus Avenue.

"Is this architect who got the zoning changes famous? Would I know him?" Let's see if Shane would spill some more.

"Not famous yet, but highly admired in academic circles. Maybe you know the name. Hugh Clark?" Great, a name.

"I've never heard of him, but I don't know many architects. Academics don't have lots of extra money lying around as far as I know," I continued. "No wonder he wants to be paid back."

Shane sucked in his cheeks and exhaled loudly. "He's not poor. Spends his summers in the Hamptons, I hear. He's just freaking neurotic. Calls all the time, demanding to know where's his money, when is the closing happening? Drives us all crazy."

"It must be a nightmare." I tried to sound sympathetic. "By the way, Shane, where does he teach?" I waited.

"On Long Island, I think. C.W. Post, maybe?"

I was not impressed. It was part of the state university system. But I could look up Dr.Hugh Clark. He might spill information, if he was waiting for money. We found a Starbucks. I got Shane the iced latte. An herbal tea for me.

"Is Marc looking for another buyer?"

Shane slurped his latte like a kid with a milkshake. "Oh, no. Marc always gets his closing. These are just bumps in the road, totally to be expected, Marc says. Once, a buyer died two days before a closing. We postponed by a week, but Marc got the widow to stick to the contract." Shane beamed, like Marc had cured cancer. There was no bar too low for Marc Olmsted to duck under.

I never asked Shane if this was his regular running route or why he'd jogged so close to me.

Chapter Nineteen

The next morning, I had the apartment to myself. Herbs and a shake (twenty-four grams of protein), and I was fueled. A quick search for Hugh Clark Architect revealed he wrote the commentary for a coffee table book about landmarked New York City mansions. I got a phone number at C.W. Post, the Long Island University campus, where he was an adjunct professor, the lowest of teaching jobs. I called and left a message that I needed his expertise about landmarked mansions for an article in a major magazine.

At the gym, it was pushups and weight lifting, as ordered by my fencing teacher. *Without arm strength, you will never win a match,* she'd said. I was in the midst of this excruciating workout when my phone buzzed. The number was Clark's. I dropped the weights.

"This is Dr. Hugh Clark." The voice was imitating Peter Sellers, the Pink Panther.

"Yes. Thanks for returning my call."

There was a moment's silence. "I am *always* available to correct misconceptions about the glorious mansions of New York," he said haughtily.

" Can you speak now, or should I come to your office?"

"I am very busy," he said with a sigh. "I can only give you a few minutes. My students need me, and I'm on a deadline with my publisher." I'd place a large bet there was no publisher. *Watch your attitude, Melanie.*

"I totally understand how a man of your stature has little time. Can you begin with the misconceptions the public has about the mansions of New York City?" I snagged a piece of paper and a pen from the bored young gym receptionist dressed in a Spandex one-piece with a red and black zigzag pattern.

"So, you need a brief tutorial." He cleared his throat. I sat down in the quiet alcove off the lobby. I pressed record on my phone and hoped my battery would last.

"Landmarking in New York City began in 1965. The first landmarked building was the Wyckoff House, a three-hundred-year-old beauty in Brooklyn. The law was passed to protect these fragile landmarks that remind us of an older, better time." I tapped my foot. I had to move this along.

"Real estate agents don't think all of these old houses are worth protecting. They say they were often cheap buildings used for SROs and brothels. Five in a room kind of thing." Susie's rant was coming in useful.

He gave a loud, long-suffering sigh. "Real estate agents are like car salesmen, interested only in money. Agents are not artists, not like I am, an architect, who studied tirelessly, for years, only to be underpaid for his expertise." *Underpaid.* That sounded bitter. *Focus.*

"We persist to bring beauty to ugly environments and raise the level of the neighborhood." He droned on. "This ignorant person has never seen an intact Gilded Age mansion from the inside. Few have. Most of the mansions are gone, purchased by schools and torn apart to be classrooms where children draw on the walls. Painful to think about. Though I suppose it is preferable to seeing the buildings torn down."

"But doesn't landmarking prevent the desecration of these mansions?" I knew the answer, but I wanted him on recording.

"You are naive," he scoffed. "Landmarking is for the outside. And even that can be changed with the right architects and lawyers. If you know your way around the Landmark Preservation Commission, know the right people, and have enough money, anything can be done." So much for preserving the elegant past.

"You sound like a pretty powerful man." I tried to channel sexy Rebecca, young ingenue entranced with an older man. I almost gagged. "Have you ever been inside these Gilded Age mansions?"

"Of course. I've seen them all. Many, thankfully, have become museums.

Though some museums, like the National Design Museum now occupying the Carnegie mansion, have still erased as much interior detail as they could, leaving only the grand staircases. The Warburg House on Fifth Avenue, from 1908, was donated to be a museum years ago. There is not a shred of history left, except perhaps the elevator doors." His voice dripped disapproval.

"I'm so impressed by your incredible store of knowledge." I could almost see Clark smile smugly. "I'm curious: has anyone ever converted a mansion into multiple apartments? What would be involved if you wanted to do that?" He didn't hesitate.

"It has been done. I will only say no one turns down fifty thousand dollars to speed the process along. But, creating multiple apartments usually requires changes to the exterior. Outdoor space and terraces need to be divided and added on. Everyone wants outdoor space these days. Some want solariums on their terrace. They want modern windows. Air conditioning can be an issue. The neighbors tend to complain and go to community board meetings. Woody Allen fought the Whitney School when they dynamited to create a gymnasium, right next to his townhouse. The school won. That's where money and experts like myself come in."

Hugh Clark was the one who'd laid out the money to get the zoning changed for the Harrington Mansion, according to Shane.

"So fascinating. Are you familiar with the Harrington Mansion?"

There was a long silence. "Yes, very familiar."

I dangerously pushed on. "I heard rumors that foreign money wanted to buy it, maybe split it up." I held my breath.

"You should ignore rumors." His voice lost some of its snooty tone. "Where did you hear that?"

"I have no idea. I've been researching this article for a long time. It was just said in passing. I don't recall any name. But would that be a problem? Sounds like it's done all the time?" I was just clueless. Maybe there was an acting career in my future. Clark was clearly involved and nervous.

"Yes. As I said before, these mansions are made into schools. Whatever the buyer wants, I suppose. I must get off now. I have many students waiting."

"If there's ever a moment when your schedule opens up, I'd be grateful for a tour of one of these elegant antiques." I was glad I recorded the call, and my phone battery held out.

"I will get back to you. Perhaps dinner." Was I imagining it, or had his voice turned seductive? Yuck. I'd have to bring Devon or Rebecca. But Devon was leaving tomorrow, again. My stomach dropped. We hung up.

Dr. Hugh Clark, professor of architecture, was like a Gilded Age mansion. From the outside, he appeared to be an elegant, expensively made antique. But on the inside, he was a tacky high rise with thin sheetrock for walls. One good punch, and he'd crumble.

* * *

Rebecca called the next morning.

"Jackie Doyle wants you to come for lunch today. She's ready to spill about Greg Sheldon. Meet me there at twelve."

"Can't you just tell me what she has to say? Or how about a phone call?" Who needed another boring lunch with another rich woman?

"Are you forgetting you got me locked in that awful room in that mansion and almost sold into slavery? You have to come, you owe me. Anyway, she won't talk to just me. You're the hotshot reporter with a column. You need this information. And it will take your mind off Devon leaving. You know how you get."

Hotshot reporter. I liked the way that sounded. I needed respect to be seen as someone of value. Daniel was so cold and distant. It drains a person, being around someone every day who disapproves. Rebecca was right. I needed this interview.

"Okay, what's Jackie's address?"

"You'll love this. It's the Beresford. Central Park West and 81st Apartment 14 S.

"Her husband must be an A-list guy."

"You don't follow Bruce Doyle? He's the star of a hot cable show, *Studs*. Gorgeous and totally unfaithful."

"But she'll get the ten million-dollar apartment when they split. See you at noon."

* * *

What's the chance of your doing an evening run tonight? I have a late flight,
Devon texted.
  Unlikely.
  How about a nature field trip? Or trip to the moon?
  I think we did that already.
  Once is not enough. Museum of Natural History field trip. I may have news.
  1:30. Downstairs entrance 77ᵗʰ. Good news?
  It is. See you then.

* * *

The best thing about lunching with Joyce was going to the Beresford and
looking at Central Park and the Natural History gardens. Built in 1929, it's
one of the classiest addresses in Manhattan. Apartments cost as much as
thirty million or as "little" as three mil for a studio. Glenn Close, Meyer
Lansky (mob boss), John McEnroe, Diana Ross, and Jerry Seinfeld are a few
of the many famous residents past and present.
  East Side doormen in starched uniforms stand at attention like they're
guarding Buckingham Palace. In my rundown lobby with mud green peeling
paint, the doormen wear white shirts and dark pants, like a bowling team.
The Beresford is closer to East Side culture. The two doormen, stationed at
a deep mahogany circular counter, wore uniforms with caps, but no white
gloves. They smiled and said to go on up, probably because Bruce Doyle
threw around a lot of cash.
  On the 14ᵗʰ floor, the hall was wallpapered in tasteful muted stripes. There
was a hushed atmosphere created by all the money that had gone into the
thick carpet and solid walls. Joyce's apartment was at the end, a corner unit
facing east and south, pricey light and views.
  "Melanie, so good to see you. Glad you could make it."

We lightly hugged. Jackie was beautiful in an artistic, not model way, with wavy, deep brown hair, big hazel eyes in a longish face, dark red lipstick, and lots of mascara. Thin but not gaunt, she wore a flowered skirt mid-calf length with a blouse and a vest. Short boots. It was a casual and arty Soho-boutique look. Feeling dowdy and middle-aged immediately, I was glad there was a mirror in the entrance so I could confirm that I hadn't actually aged ten years, though my maroon sweater and black jeans were indeed drab and dull compared to Joyce and the ever-radiant Rebecca.

"Shall we eat right away? Want some Pellegrino?" Jackie poured me a glass while I looked around at the jaw-dropping view of Central Park and the Museum of Natural History. Worth ten mil. A large living room looked out at it all. The room had overstuffed striped couches and big, comfortable-looking light green diamond-print chairs. Throw pillows were everywhere. A statue, black onyx with womanly curves and a faceless point for a head presided over one corner. A large, splashy abstract painting, possibly a Rauschenberg, hung over the sofa. The walls themselves seemed to radiate, with a paint that had an incredible sheen to it and pristine trim along the ceilings and doors—a far cry from the smudged, bubbling layers of paint on the walls of my apartment. The message from the décor here was, *We don't care how much money we have, but we care that* you *care.* Maybe I should get the name of her decorator, just in case.

"We can eat over here," said Jackie. "I thought you'd enjoy the view." A narrow farm table had been set at one end of the living room. "We're having salads from Zabar's. Rebecca reminded me you're gluten-free. I am, too. We all are here, though I have my suspicions about Bruce when he's on a set. You know… the things we can't control!" Was she still talking about food? I smiled demurely and glanced at Rebecca, who was trying not to guffaw.

Jackie went on. "Everything's GF, so no worries. There are such wonderful GF breads these days in restaurants, too. Such a relief."

I almost chuckled. I doubted Jackie ate much bread or pasta at all. And the only restaurant I ever got to was a Greek-owned diner where greasy stir-fried veggies were as healthy as they got. It also sounded like she had just admitted her husband screwed around on sets, and she'd given up that fight. The thing she can't control.

We sat down and drank sparkling water and chatted about the weather, her husband's two Netflix shows, the design business she'd just started, her two kids, and what she thought of their private school, Dalton. And then she brought up why I was there.

"You're trying to find out what happened to Karen. I want to help."

Joyce put down a forkful of the vegetarian chicken salad she'd gotten for both of us. She assumed because I was GF that, I was also vegan—a common mistake. In fact, I consume large amounts of goats' milk products and would have preferred real organic chicken salad, but my complicated food choices are not that interesting and just make me sound unbalanced. People tend to want other people to be one way or the other, not a complicated mashup. So I had to eat a gross fake chicken salad.

I got my head out of my stomach and saw Joyce and Rebecca looked confused, waiting for me to say something. Joyce's big hazel eyes were filled with so much caring that I almost grabbed her hand. I reminded myself that she had been an actress before she'd had kids and Bruce's career took over.

"I can use any help you can give. You know Greg Sheldon pretty well?"

"As well as anyone 'knows' their plastic surgeon." She put air quotes around 'knows'. My impatience took over. I didn't like vegetarian chicken salad, and I didn't want to be late to meet Devon.

"My impression was you were one of the women who'd had intimate relations with him," I said casually, breaking a piece of highly seeded GF bread in half. They load GF bread with seeds to make up for its lack of density. It doesn't work. Rebecca looked down, playing with her tuna salad. Joyce's voice when she responded was a tad annoyed.

"I didn't want to talk about that since it's over, and if you think I'm trying to get back at him, you're wrong. I was only 'intimate' with him after he and Karen split," she said. The air quotes thing again.

She was a lot of work, just as I'd thought she would be. I tried to conjure up sympathy for someone who lived so grandly while being married to a guy who slept with starlets. I found a sliver of compassion.

"Jackie, it doesn't matter to me when you were intimate, or what you did with him or where. I just want to find out what you know that might help to crack this case." I threw in the *Law and Order* jargon, since she was in the business.

Rebecca's grin was visible behind a glass of wine.

"I know Greg's assistant, Deedee, very well," Jackie finally said.

"That's nice. And?"

"She told me something very disturbing."

"And what would that be?

"The day of Karen's murder?" Her voice went up. I nodded.

"She said Greg went to view the apartment at 962 Park Avenue." I nodded impatiently.

"I was there. We all saw him." I said curtly.

Jackie shook her head. "No. I mean, Deedee was very upset. She heard Greg Sheldon tell the police he came back to the office to do paperwork. But Deedee swore to me he didn't come back. When the police called the office to speak to him, she forwarded their call to his cell phone. Greg made her promise she would never tell the police she hadn't seen him. He reminded her that their office has a back door, and he could have used that. He told Deedee he waited for Marlena after the open house, because they had things to talk about. They went for coffee. Deedee asked him why he'd told the police he came back to work, instead of just telling them he'd gone for coffee with Marlena. Greg said it made for a better alibi. That the cops wouldn't believe Marlena if she said she was with him. So instead, Deedee had to lie to the police. She's very nervous about going to jail." Joyce paused and looked out the window. She turned to me.

"Marlena came to Greg's office last week. Deedee asked Marlena about having coffee with Greg after the showing. She said Marlena just stared at her and didn't answer. Deedee thinks Marlena never saw Greg after the murder. Deedee thinks their engagement is off, too. Marlena's not the type to stand by her man. Especially since Greg has no money and his wife has been murdered." *And she already has the ring to hock.*

"Jackie," I said slowly, trying to appear patient. "Why haven't you gone to the police with this information?" Rebecca smiled slyly.

Jackie folded her hands on the floral-trimmed tablecloth. She looked around, realized no one else was there, and turned back to me. "My name cannot be linked to Sheldon's in any way. This would put me in the middle, between Greg and Deedee. She could be lying, you know. She's loved Greg hopelessly for years. Nobody has told the police what they really know. Why should I? My husband is a very public figure. The press would love this."

But I was the press. And I couldn't quote her or Deedee unless they agreed, which they wouldn't. I could now be in trouble with the cops if Sheldon turned out to be the killer. "Rebecca, what do you think?" I asked.

Rebecca looked at the view, then turned to Jackie. "Sheldon's a creep to make Deedee lie for him. I guess of the two possible choices for an alibi; he chose the woman who couldn't afford to walk away. But I don't get why Deedee told you all this if she has such a crush on Sheldon. You've been 'intimate' with him too. Like a bunch of others. Is this some kind of sisterhood?"

Jackie shrugged her thin shoulders under the white peasant blouse and green vest." Beats the hell out of me," she said, dropping the fancy lady routine. "Maybe you're onto something. Maybe she wanted to get me in trouble in my marriage. Make me talk to the cops instead of her."

Instead, you've brought the mess to me, I thought.

"Well, it's hearsay, anyway," I said. " I'll have to talk to Deedee. Might have been quicker just to have lunch with her." Jackie looked shocked. " That was partially a joke."

"Please don't tell her I told you about Greg's alibi problem," Joyce said.

"I would never name a source. Are you worried about your close relationship?"

Joyce laughed. "Absolutely. I need Deedee to schedule my Restylane and Botox appointments when I need them. The awards season is coming up. Why do you think we're 'friends'?" Air quotes again. Joyce was tougher than I'd thought.

"What's your gut feeling about this? Do you think Greg killed Karen?"

Joyce walked into her beautiful blue-and-white kitchen and came back with a platter of cookies. "These are homemade and all GF. A house specialty.

Walnuts, raisins, and cinnamon. Only made with maple syrup. And I've got caffeine-free green tea." I felt like a creep for pushing her into confessing her affair. But I knew a bribe when I saw one. I took a cookie. It was delicious. If I could be bought, it was definitely with these.

"I know Greg needed money. He asked me. I gave him a few thousand," she said. "He couldn't afford to support two households. Karen was going to court to get more alimony. He doesn't seem like the killer type, but under extreme stress, maybe there's a first time for everyone...I guess?"

I looked at the three of us sitting at the table. Each one of us was in the sort of marriage we'd never expected to have, breaking vows we hadn't intended to break, with men who'd changed over the course of time. A first time for everyone could apply to each of us, too. But none of us had committed murder. I thanked her for lunch. Rebecca stayed to get more gossip, and I hurried to meet Devon.

Chapter Twenty

"A movie in the middle of the afternoon is sinful and dangerous," I hissed. We walked through the wide exhibition halls in the Museum of Natural History. What if I ran into a Huntley parent? At least the lighting was dim. Preserving stuffed animals meant low light.

"Sinful would be coming back to my apartment," Devon said. "If I believed in sin as a way to view the world, which I don't. It's just a movie, not a hotel. No one has even heard of The *Jungle in your Backyard* unless they're dying to watch grasshoppers go at it. We have good chemistry in public places."

My chemistry was heated up already just standing next to him.

"We've got a whole hour," I said, linking my arm through his like we were just old friends. We walked past Mammals of North America. Beavers had made a remarkable comeback so now they were being trapped and killed again. The message—do well, and you get hunted. When I got closer, I got to a killer; my life could be in danger.

I related Joyce's story about Deedee that Greg's alibi was bogus. "What about you talking to Deedee?" I asked. "Deedee said she lied for Greg. She might spill something useful. She sounds scared."

"I could go there before I leave, get a little Botox."

"Great idea."

He rolled his eyes.

"Just talk to her." I squeezed his arm. " You won't be the first man to stop in and ask."

"Can you call John at the precinct? They might have something new on Sheldon. Maybe they're reconsidering his alibi."

162

Devon took out his phone. We stood in a corner near the theater, close together. He got John on the first try. While they went through the usual banter about the Yankees, I noticed a sign for the Planetarium advertising a show about black holes. Sounded like my marriage.

"Right. Got it, suspicious but she's positive. Willing to take a lie detector test for him. Anything else?" Devon listened and put an arm around me. "Okay, thanks. Let me know." He put his phone away and kissed me ardently in the alcove, away from foot traffic.

"Are we celebrating? Is the case solved?" I said, stepping back, panting. "This is way too public."

Devon caressed my cheek, destroying my resolve. Maybe nothing else mattered but his fingers finding their way down my neck. Those warm blue-gray eyes made him irresistible to me.

"I've been thinking about your mouth since you left the other night," he said. "Give me a break." I shook my head.

"First thing is Karen's murder. What's up?". He acted like a soldier going off to war, instead of getting on a plane to go eat at good restaurants and visit cultural icons.

He dropped his arm from my shoulders. "John said the cops have tried to reach Sheldon for two days. He's away on business, according to Deedee. Chilton told Sheldon not to go anywhere. Deedee swears she can't reach him. So yes, the police are suspicious."

I grinned, feeling ridiculously happy that Sheldon was under investigation. Devon made me happy, too. "Maybe if he's running, that means he did it. I wouldn't mind seeing him locked up." Devon kissed me again, and I pressed against him. My tense muscles turned to jelly.

We entered the cavernous IMAX theater, grandly embellished from another era, built right inside the Museum of Natural History. It was one of my favorite places in New York. Nature on a big screen, with no city noise. It was always a quiet miracle.

"Sit anywhere," advised the young usher with long, multicolored woven braids. There were four other patrons in a theater that could seat four hundred . I stood in the aisle.

"As much as I want to lounge in this theater and make out, which is clearly your plan, you're leaving for Africa tonight. This is your only time to get info from Deedee. You should go now."

"Deedee can wait." Devon pulled me into a remote seat, out of view of the usher. Who wouldn't give in? We did what teenagers do at the movies. He was right; the electricity between us was even more insane here. The desperate kisses and groping took me back to being sixteen when this was the only safe place I could be with a boyfriend. But it's a hell of a lot easier to make out in a movie theater when you're sixteen. I jumped up.

"Ow," I yelped.

"Are you all right, miss?" The dreadlocked usher suddenly pointed a flashlight at us. I turned a shade of red that wasn't normal.

"Yes, fine. Just a muscle spasm." The usher shook her head and walked back away.

" That's it," I hissed. "We'll get arrested if we rip each other's clothes off. Deedee is waiting."

He sat back with a self-satisfied grin. "It could be great publicity, getting arrested at IMAX at the Museum of Natural History. You'd get thousands more followers." A little glee bubbled up at the idea of all those Likes, but I glared at Devon. He stood up.

"All right. I'm going. But consider an after-dinner run." He left to walk through the park. Without me. Susie's spies could be out jogging.

I found my way to the Hall of Gems and Minerals and walked straight to the six-foot-high geodes of sparkling turquoise and amethyst. As my eyes adjusted to the dark light, I saw two shapes against a wall. It was Gabbie, the other West Side mom from Huntley. Not with her daughter, but standing close to a well-built weight lifter type. Too close to be a friend. Ha, I wasn't the only one meeting a guy for an afternoon squeeze. She glanced up and saw me. I smiled but quickly walked out.

I went down to the basement exit and left by the side door. I hurried across the street to the park and ran the rest of the way to pick up at Huntley.

* * *

"You're crazy. I hope you know that. You've gone off the deep end." Daniel announced as he stacked dishes in the sink. We'd had a calm dinner together if you counted silence as calm.

"Which deep end do you have in mind?" I had no hint this battle was imminent.

"Come on, Melanie. You cause trouble everywhere. Cops show up here. You cross-examine parents at work. That poor guy, Sheldon. He's a grieving widower, for God's sake, and you storm into his office?"

"I don't know who's feeding you information, but a grieving widower he's not. An arrogant bastard who stole money from his kids' trust funds is who he really is. He might even have killed his wife. How would you know?" Daniel looked a little shocked at this info, but he didn't let a dose of truth stop him.

"I don't know who killed that woman, but that's not the point." His voice went up when his patience with me went down. "You go view apartments. Are you moving out?" He walked away from the sink and rummaged in the freezer drawer, presumably for ice cream.

I wondered if he knew all the places I'd seen.

"You really think I'm looking for an apartment? You know why I went there. It wasn't to buy." My eyes opened wide at the sight of Daniel's stomach as he bent over the open freezer. Where was his Santa Claus belly? I moved to his face. I could almost spot his cheekbones. He'd lost a lot of weight. I'd definitely not been paying attention.

"You've lost weight," I announced. It sounded like I was accusing him of hiding something. He must have lost weight to impress someone. I actually felt a twinge of attraction for my husband.

"So, you finally notice something other than your column and screenplays." Daniel closed the freezer, giving up on the ice cream. Something huge was going on if Daniel was dieting. When people diet, they get angry. "I heard that Greg Sheldon is missing now. Did you have anything to do with that?" he demanded.

My mouth dropped open.

"Are you joking? You think I've kidnapped him to get a free facelift? You're the one who's off the deep end here. I'm not a crook or a cop. I'm a reporter." I would have shouted this, but I was afraid I'd wake Chloe. I could just take out the ice cream and feed him with a spoon. That would end the argument. I tried love.

"You know, you look great." I put my arms around his neck. "It's definitely a turn-on."

He pulled away and took my hands down from his neck.

"I don't know who you are anymore," he snapped.

I stared at him, hurt. "I don't know who you are either." This was a make-it-or-break-it moment.

He winced and stepped back.

"I didn't marry a writer who plays detective," Daniel hissed. "You're an intelligent woman, Melanie. You could have gotten an MFA. You could have worked your way up at the magazine with Belinda. You might have been a style editor by now."

That was a low blow. I looked around for one of his incredibly heavy pots to swing at him.

"Let me get this straight," I said. "Writing a column and screenplays is dumb and crazy, but being a style editor at *Food Lovers* is the height of genius? That's nuts. *You* used to be fun and interesting. You applauded me when I first got into screenwriting. We went to a writing group together, remember? When we first dated, we talked about how I wanted out of the magazine game." I felt a wave of sadness about the closeness we'd had, followed by a tsunami of anger.

"I could write the next *In Cold Blood,* and you'd tell me it's trash," I said bitterly. "But you'd be right there at the awards ceremony, cashing in on the publicity."

"I'm going out," he said through gritted teeth. He stormed away, leaving behind, somewhere in that freezer, a pint of Haagen-Dazs Chocolate Peanut Butter. Twenty-four grams of fat. That was how I knew for sure he was meeting Nadine.

"Meeting anyone I know?" I called. He didn't answer. He just gave me a look that said our problems were all my fault. Daniel slammed the front door. I collapsed on the couch in the living room.

Had I changed so much for the worse? In my gut, I knew I was becoming the person I was meant to be. I was shocked sometimes at the risks I took and my intense drive to find Karen's killer and write the story.

Can you talk? Devon texted.

Yeah. Daniel just stormed out. Within seconds, my phone rang.

Devon's voice burst with excitement. "Big news. John called from the precinct. They got a tip. Greg Sheldon was in the Beacon Hotel for the last few days. The police found him there unconscious, overdosed on OxyContin and alcohol. They don't know if he's going to make it, or what his brain will be like if he does."

"Do the police think it was a suicide attempt? Was there a note?"

"Nobody is saying anything. I'll keep working on it."

"I feel awful for his kids. His seventeen-year-old daughter Jennifer already has an eating disorder and maybe more," I said. "Do you think this means he killed Karen? He didn't seem like a guy who'd overdose from excessive guilt, even if he had committed the murder. I bet it was about money."

"You may be right. It might be an accidental overdose. Sheldon partied at the hotel with women. Drugs go with that scene," Devon added.

"God, he's even more degenerate than I imagined. His in-office rich lady sex wasn't enough? Buffy Clifford and her ilk won't want to be identified with hotel parties. He could lose business over this."

"That's if he makes it," said Devon. "You sound a little naive for someone who's been at two murder scenes, and been up close with more than one suspect I had nothing to say. He continued.

"I spoke to Deedee. She swore that Greg was right there in the office directly after the open house. She cried quite dramatically. 'How could anyone think he would hurt Karen when he worshiped her?' she said. Sheldon's a saint in Deedee's eyes."

"I did hear you say Daniel walked out," Devon went on in a soft, husky voice. "I'm here. I could be there if you want on my way to the airport." A drive-by felt worse.

"And then you're gone, and I'm out there alone. Daniel started a fight.

Crime writing is bad. I'm bad. He's with Nadine right now, having orgasms, talking about her buttercream frosting. She'll be happy to remind him how awful I am. Which would be really tacky of her after I saved her life."

"Very ungrateful. " He chuckled but stopped quickly. "What can I do?"

"Let's work, get back to the screenplay." We divided up the newest scenes.

I took the hair salon with Marlena, where I realized she was strong enough enough to kill Karen. Devon would write about Sheldon's hotel exploits. I'd take the office visit. It was a relief to brainstorm and not think about Daniel.

"Can we eliminate Susie Carlbach as a suspect?" Devon asked.

"It's hard to believe even an agent would commit murder at her own open house. But she could have let the killer in. Are her motives of jealousy and wanting the Harrington listing strong enough to be an accessory to Karen's murder? "

"Could be."

"Marc Olmsted, using Shane, Greg Sheldon, and Marlena, all have stronger motives. Marlena is involved in the deal-making with Harrington was alone at the open house at all. "And what about Peggy Fitzgerald? I don't know what her motive could be. But I think she pushed me down in the street, and according to Patty Baylor, she re-entered through the back door at the open house." I thought for a moment. "Whatever was in Karen's briefcase has to be the key. What was in it?

"Be careful, Melanie." Devon's tone was serious. "You talked to a lot of people, angered some. Sheldon may have had information, and the killer got to him, making it look like an accident. Whoever killed Karen murdered the handyman at 962 Park. This person, or persons, has already killed two people. And now maybe Greg. Don't meet anyone else alone. Agreed?"

"Yes, of course," I agreed, just so we wouldn't argue. I got off the phone and fell into bed, exhausted.

Chapter Twenty-One

When I woke up around one AM, Daniel was not in bed. I tiptoed down the hall and found him asleep on the couch. I slept badly after that, with frightening dreams. A high-heeled woman in a flowered dress pursued me, brandishing a sword in a 5K race. I bolted upright in bed. OMG

There actually *was* a 5K race after school today, organized by Huntley. I had forgotten.

* * *

"So, Mom, you're running in the park after school, remember?" Chloe's angelic eyes glanced almost shyly at me as we went down the stairs to the bus. I needed to get back on board and in her life.

"Of course. I even had a dream about it. We're going to run together, right?" It was another fundraiser, this time to send kids to Puerto Rico to help do repair work after the hurricane. Of course, they'd stay in a big hotel. So, it was an excuse to party during spring break. But Chloe dreamed about being a high school girl sent on a humanitarian mission. I had to run.

"No, Mom, the parents run together, and we kids run together. The high school kids will beat everyone, anyway. See you at the end."

She got on the bus. I ran up and down the stairs to the fourth floor five times. A good fourteen hundred-step warmup for the race later and a way to stall till Daniel left the kitchen. I didn't want to talk about last night. Maybe he'd be going out for breakfast. Sometimes he did a sneak review at the Four

Seasons Hotel cafe, where a big breakfast could set you back one hundred and fifty dollars for one person. All covered by *Food Lovers*.

Damn, there he was, cooking away. A sirloin steak had been delivered on ice from some ranch out west. He cooked the steak alongside many eggs. My stomach threatened to explode. I held my nose and took out my reliable goat yogurt (6 grams of fat, 8 grams of protein, one hundred and fifty calories), grabbed a handful of walnuts, and scurried out of the kitchen. Daniel whistled as he cooked. This was a first.

"Can't stand the enticing aroma of a great steak?" he yelled after me. I resisted the bait, throwing my breakfast in a bag and opening the front door.

"You can run, but you can't hide," Daniel called after me.

"You were the one who ran out last night. Why don't you try running this afternoon at the Huntley 5K," I yelled. And slammed the door. I loved having the last word. Even if it meant eating breakfast on a bench in the women's changing room at the gym.

* * *

I finished the yogurt. The CD of the girls with Eric Harrington at the mansion was in my bag, a constant source of guilt. I hadn't even viewed it since the day at the Mansion. I had twenty minutes till fencing class. What could I do about Eric Harrington giving drinks, and who knows what else, to underage girls? I didn't want to get the girls in trouble. They'd all be called in to testify.

Suddenly I had a strong impulse to call Detective Levano who was based in the nearby west side precinct. I knew him from the murder last year in the local playground where I had worked. He was somewhat of a friend. I called his cell phone from the alcove at the gym.

"Levano here."

"It's Melanie Deming. How are you?"

"It's been a slow day until now. Where are you trapped?"

I forced a laugh. "Nowhere at the moment. Except in my head."

"So why call me? Isn't that your shrink's territory?"

170

I tried a girlish giggle that failed. "My shrink always had the same answer—stay out of trouble. So you're it." He didn't hang up. "Here's the problem. What if a person has evidence of girls being served alcohol who are underage with a much older male and inside this person's house and drinking with him. What happens if the police get this evidence?"

"Assuming the evidence is clear, we bring him in. "

"Yes. What about the girls?"

"The girls are not arrested, but they would be asked to identify the male, maybe testify."

"The parents are notified?"

"Yes, we have to," Levano said. I sighed loudly

"You're holding onto evidence of a crime but don't want to turn it in," Levano said.

I was not going there. "This is hypothetical," I said. "Someone told me there was possible video footage."

"Melanie, I have a strong feeling there is no *someone*. But tell this *person* that they're holding onto evidence of a crime. And we all know it's likely gone beyond underage drinking. It should be stopped. Gotta go." He hung up.

I'd thought the same thing. That it must have gone further than drinking.

* * *

At 2:30, I was in Central Park for the fundraiser 5 K. The moms from Huntley were decked out in running gear and sneakers exploding with color: orange, fuschia, lime green, bright purple. Sneakers coordinated with leggings, some in rainbows of merging colors, low-cut running bras, tight tank tops, jackets from Patagonia, or the trendy *On* brand, three hundred and fifty dollars and up. The weather was mild. Many mothers brought their babysitters to hold their jackets and pick up their kids at the end.

I spotted Cornelia in conservative robin's-egg blue; Buffy, Bia, and Fawn pranced around together, their ponytails tied with scrunchies that matched their neon sneakers. Sandra Crane wore loose-fitting Nike gear, the least sexy outfit in view. I'd upped my game and found a T-shirt on sale from Oiselle, a West Coast running brand. Of course, I covered it with a sweatshirt, which would end up around my waist.

There was a lot of bunching up at the start, no order at all. A few dads, with not a trace of body fat, joined the women.

"Shocked you made it," Cornelia mumbled. We hadn't spoken since the Book Fair meeting.

"Of course. Sending private school kids to Puerto Rico over spring break is such a worthy cause," I said. She laughed. I felt warmer toward her even though she was Daniel's confidant.

Over the loudspeaker, a voice announced. "Welcome to the first Huntley 5K, running for a great cause. Send our juniors and seniors to Puerto Rico to aid hurricane victims. Have a great run. And now let's go! The same booming man's voice started counting down, "Ten, nine, eight, seven, six..."

I stayed close to the front. Cornelia was jostled away. Suddenly, Buffy Clifford was next to me on my right. There was a loud bang, and the voice on the speaker bellowed, "Go!" I started running slowly because there was such a bottleneck. Someone behind me didn't want to wait big time. I felt a deliberate shove on my back, pushing me off balance.

"Hey, cut that out," I shouted, trying to turn and see who it was. The next thing I knew, a foot pushed in and around my calf, leaning hard. The damn hand on my back shoved me; my foot left the ground. I toppled hard to my right with no control at all over my body. I slammed against Buffy, who like a domino fell into Bia, who then fell onto Fawn. The Disney Bambis were down and under me. Disaster.

Buffy shrieked so everyone could hear, "What have you done?!"

"Someone tripped me," I yelled just as loud. I jumped up quickly to get my weight off the trio, relieved I could stand. I looked around, but with so many parents moving past, it was impossible to tell who had done it. No one bothered to stop. I offered Buffy a hand.

"You must be kidding," she scoffed. "I was the captain of my college track team."

"Help, my ankle!" It was Fawn. "It's broken. My ankle is broken. Help someone help." She kept yelling, "Help, help!"

The three of them glared at me. "You did this on purpose," Bia snarled.

"I was pushed! You think I'd want to fall on you? I'll call 911," I yelped. But at that moment, the school nurse rushed in. Buffy gave up pretending to care about Fawn and started running. I took off after Buffy.

"Eat my dust," she yelled. I ran full out, catching up to her. We breathed down each other's necks until my side hurt along with my calf. I refused to let her finish before me. Who pushed me? What was the point? It had to be someone who fit in with the crowd. My anger kept me running hard.

We crossed the finish line at the same time. As it turned out, Peggy Fitzgerald beat everyone by a full seven minutes. I walked around till I got my breath. I hadn't done badly, considering I was tripped, shoved, and accused of deliberately injuring Fawn. Technically, Bia fell on her, but they'd never let me forget this. Fawn might sue me. But I ran three miles in twenty-eight minutes, even with the delay. Peggy had done it in twenty-one.

Who tripped me? The leg wrapped around mine was too much to be an accident, and the shove from behind was the deal clincher. I perused the parents at the finish line while I waited for Chloe. I didn't recognize any of the men, though a tall guy vaguely reminded me of someone. I said hello to Gabby and Babs Bernstein. I took some pictures. Then I saw Marc Olmsted, in way too revealing spandex bike shorts and a yellow T-shirt, cross the finish line. What was he doing here? I waited till he cooled off and strolled over casually.

"I didn't know you were a runner," I said when I got close enough. "And here you are running for this Huntley fundraiser." He actually flinched at the sight of me.

"I'm not bad. Get out every day. I got a late start today," he said as if this explained his finish time, which was ten minutes after mine. He walked away from me. Maybe he pushed me and then waited to start. I quickly pursued him.

"You have strong connections to Huntley. You knew about the parent meeting the other week, too." He looked at me as if I had open sores. But I also felt something else coming from him. He was nervous.

"I know many of the parents from Huntley," he said stiffly. "They have great faith in Olmsted as their agency." He rudely turned away from me. "Gloria, how nice to see you!" He ran off to greet a thin, attractive blonde who must have been an upper-school parent; I'd never seen her. The tall, unattractive, gawky man had disappeared. It could have been Marc who'd tripped me.

I stood on the edge of the dwindling group while I waited for Chloe.

"Mrs. Deming," a voice hissed. I turned and saw Karen and Greg Sheldon's daughter, Jennifer, standing just behind a tree, wearing running shorts and a long sleeve lightweight hooded shirt. She gestured to me. I hadn't seen her since the day on Madison Avenue when she ran away from me with that older guy. I strolled over.

"I don't want anyone to see me talking to you." If possible, she looked thinner than when I'd seen her outside the diner on Madison. "But I don't know who else to talk to. My dad's still in the hospital, and my grandparents are useless."

My heart broke for her. "How can I help you?"

A tear slid down her cheek. "I think my mom was killed because of me. It's all my fault." Her grief overflowed, and tears streamed down her cheeks."She found a CD that had me in it at the Harrington mansion. It was at a party with Eric, their grandson. I know she used it to get the listing. They must have had her killed. Don't you see? It's my fault." She hiccuped, and her thin body shook.

I hadn't looked at the CD since we'd found it. And we rushed through it then. Why hadn't I recognized her? I should have looked at it again. If you don't know what you're looking at and it's a shock and a crime, it takes several viewings to really see what's there. Now I knew one of the girls was Jennifer. I put my arm around her shoulders and walked her further away from prying eyes.

"Jennifer, you're not to blame at all. Don't do this to yourself. Even if the Harringtons somehow caused your mom's death, which I doubt, it's still not your fault. People who murder are evil and crazy, and you didn't make them that way. And why would they kill her anyway? They were going to get the

174

money they wanted."

She stopped the sobbing and looked up. Her large brown eyes held so much pain, it almost knocked me over. "You don't think they had her killed?" I shook my head vehemently.

"No, I don't. There are many others who had more to gain financially and who needed the money more than the Harringtons." I didn't say what I actually felt, like a thud in my stomach, that it was just possible the Harringtons' reputation might be worth murder. Jennifer didn't need that burden. "There are real estate agents and people who want to buy the mansion and develop it. They need money and control of this project." Also, her father, Greg Sheldon, needed money. Could I ask her about her father? And was there sex at the party with Eric Harrington? If I wanted her to feel safe around me, I'd keep quiet about those questions.

She looked up at me. "You're supposed to solve murders. I guess I can believe you."

" You did the right thing by coming to see me. I know about the CD. That's all I can say, but you did nothing wrong. The police don't think you were guilty of anything. Stop torturing yourself. You have so much to deal with now with your mother gone and your dad hopefully getting some help. Your grandparents, I bet, love you. Let them. And get some sleep."

Her frail body seemed to relax. " Mom was so worried about money."

"That must have been hard for you all. But it was not under your control and not your responsibility. Your parents had problems that had nothing to do with you. You couldn't solve those. It's hard to accept it, but that's the truth." It had taken years for me to believe this.

"They fought all the time. "She sighed, and her lip trembled again. Thanks, Mrs Deming."

"If you need me, you can call any time. Be good to yourself." I gave her my number again. She scurried away. *And stay away from older guys*. I thought. Hopefully, she was not anywhere near Eric Harrington. Now that I knew she was in the CD, I had to tread very carefully with it. For her safety, and for mine. Is that why she got the listing?

* * *

I found Chloe, and we walked home. My leg ached, and now my heart ached for Jennifer. I had a million thoughts ricocheting around my brain. All parents running in the race needed a computerized ID to enter. But many parents invited outsiders, like Marc Olmsted, to join and help raise money. So, the official list might not have all the actual runners. Damn, I wished I had looked behind me instead of just at Buffy. I texted Cornelia.

I was pushed over at start of race. Did you see?

I barely got out of that mob scene alive. Don't get paranoid.

I landed on Buffy and her two stooges. Fawn says I broke her ankle.

It can't make your relationship with those three any worse than it is.

They may sue. Did anyone look suspicious or like an intruder?

I forgot to bring my spyglass. Forget it, it was an accident.

Did you hear about Greg Sheldon? What can you tell me?

Not in a text.

My phone buzzed. Devon was calling from the airport. I didn't pick up.

Chapter Twenty-Two

Chloe ran to her room, slammed her door. Her own phone buzzing. I looked at my phone. Sandra Crane had sent condolences and a picture. Oh God. There was my rear poking up from the pile of Bambis. Not my best angle. I got an ice pack for my leg, fell onto the couch, and had a major self-pity attack. Devon again. Bad timing.

"What's up?" I asked. The bitchy tone was instantly a mistake.

There was silence."What's wrong?" he finally asked.

I told him about the mess at the 5K race. And about Jennifer Sheldon and the CD.

Devon cleared his throat nervously.

"Let's work with three different endings. Greg Sheldon, addicted husband needing money. Olmsted, Shane, or Susie clutching the listing over Karen's dead body. Buyers of the mansion. Three different directions and motives,"

Devon's voice got louder and more adamant. " I know you'll think I'm a male chauvinist, but stop now. Whoever's following you will back off. No more interviews, no more confronting people. Just stop, stay home, write. When the cops make an arrest, we'll have our ending."

It was annoying, but I had no choice. "Agreed. But we have to add a jealous woman or man to the possible endings. Peggy Fitzgerald, though I don't know her motive. Other women and men who were used sexually by Karen or Greg. " I stopped, feeling sick. "And now it could be someone the Harringstons hired. If Karen used the CD to blackmail them."

I could write about other crimes on the Upper West Side. That would distract the killer. The tension drained away. Exhaustion took over. "I'm too wiped out to follow leads anyway. Why did you call?"

"That went a little too smoothly. Not sure I believe you." He waited, and I said nothing. Joe told me the police found a note from Greg. It said he could never make Marlena happy, but she did the right thing by breaking up with him. He wouldn't stand in her way. Real soap opera stuff. The cops are not convinced he wrote the note, which is interesting." Devon had to shout over announcements in the background. "Which doesn't mean you cross-examine every woman he slept with to ask if she wrote the note and drugged him. Let the cops do their job."

"Sure, sure," I said. But I didn't trust the police.

"I've got to go. Just hunker down and write. I'll miss you.," he yelled.

"Same here." We hung up. I couldn't stay mad at him. Devon had a way of making me feel taken care of without being stifled. Was this love? I wasn't sure I'd ever been with a man where every feeling of mine was accepted. Every problem talked about. I felt a shiver. More dangerous, marriage-destroying comparisons. But then I wasn't married to Devon. Marriage changes people. Look at what happened to Daniel. Look who I'd become.

* * *

"Tea at the Park Lane," Cornelia ordered. "That's the only way I can tolerate talking about Greg Sheldon. After that unflattering race disaster picture, I recommend a dress. Counteract the bad press. Meet me there at 1:30."

I hated the Park Lane. If you didn't wear pastel and sleeveless, you stuck out like a weed in Martha Stewart's garden. I dragged out an old calf-length floral dress with a black background and put a blazer over it. Annie Hall West side.

I took out the CD of the party at the mansion and somehow googled enough directions to get a snapshot of the girls without Eric Harrington. Sure enough, blending in with the other teenagers, was Jennifer Sheldon, I saved the photo to my phone.

We sat at a prime table, with a pink tablecloth to the floor and a floral centerpiece. Around us was an acre of pink, with massive cloth napkins folded like swans. Amanda Schwartzkopf, in a fitted sleeveless daisy-covered chemise, stopped at our table.

"Hello, ladies. Nice to see you, Cornelia." She smiled at Cornelia and gave me what could only be seen as a disgusted look. She smiled again at Cornelia. "Have a lovely tea." She walked away. I'd been snubbed badly.

"What was that?" I asked.

"Don't you know? Buffy told everyone you deliberately fell on them, which is why she didn't win."

"Damn her. Buffy knows I was pushed. She would never have beaten Peggy Fitzgerald anyway. Peggy lives to compete and destroys anyone who gets in her way." I didn't tell Cornelia I was knocked down the other night again. And warned to 'stay away from what wasn't mine.' I didn't need a lecture about running at night. I went on.

"Buffy's blaming me so she doesn't look like a loser, which she is. But who pushed *me* over?"

Cornelia shook her head at me. "You live in the Huntley world. Even if you don't care about other people's opinions, think about Chloe."

" The Bambis just happened to be shoved up next to me. Chloe knows that." Cornelia smiled a smidgen at the Bambis.

"Can we talk about Greg Sheldon?" I asked weakly. Now I worried that Chloe was a target at school.

Cornelia shook her head and took a sip of tea. "You're letting your libido run your life. You'll have to give Devon up."

Another punch in the stomach. Cornelia really was in rare form. "I don't know what you're implying," I said. She raised her eyebrows and sipped her tea. "You think writing and investigating is about Devon? It's not." My head felt like it would explode all over the pink tablecloths.

"Anyway, we're way off topic." My fists clenched under the table. "I came to this outmoded bastion of New York society to ask if Greg Sheldon is an addict. Porn? Women in hotels? You know something, I'm sure." I should have had tea with Joyce. At least I'd get GF cookies with no icy looks. I tried to lift my caffeine-free, lukewarm peppermint tea, but my hand trembled. I had to get out of here.

Cornelia gave me her signature this-is-a-waste-of-my-time look.

"I'm going on record as having warned you to pay attention to Daniel and stop the murder-Devon obsession. My conscience is clear." She stretched her neck like a swan and gazed around the garden of tables at her pastel peers. "Yes, Greg had parties at hotels. I heard from a woman who attended that there were plenty of drugs. And don't ask me who she is, because I won't tell you." Cornelia unfolded and refolded her napkin on her silk abstract floral sleeveless shift with her Chanel sweater draped over her chair.

"Mothers from Huntley may have even participated too. Women will still flock to him for Botox treatments. And for more, as you know."

"So he's an addict? Would he write a suicide note? Was he getting money from patients to pay for his addictions?" I fired these questions at her. "He could have been high when he killed Karen."

Cornelia waved to an older, white-haired woman sitting at a nearby table with a strikingly elegant older man whose picture was in the paper, the new conductor at Lincoln Center.

"You have a strong imagination, Melanie," she said dismissively. "Good thing you're a writer. I think Sheldon was in rehab a few years ago. Those things rarely work, as we have seen. A suicide note? Why not? He wanted attention by any means. He used money to impress Marlena. When he ran out of cash, she rejected him, which is the rumor. He thought this dramatic gesture would get her back. Stupid man." Cornelia studied psychology for a year at Vassar and screwed her professor. She thought she had laser vision about the mind and why people did what they did.

"Karen wasn't tough enough," Cornelia continued. I don't know if Greg killed her. That's for the police to find out." She looked at me pointedly. "It's time for you to clean your own house, wouldn't you say?"

I put my elbows on the table, a faux pas, and placed my forehead in my hand.

"Seriously?" I said, looking up. "You don't even clean yours. People do that for you. Is Daniel talking to you about our problems? He sounds like you. Or you sound like him."

"I'm flattered. He's such a sweet man. He is truly worried about Chloe—

and about you, too. Remember I told you to keep your husband happy, then do what you want." She took a small bite of pineapple.

I ignored her 1950s rhetoric. "At the open house, did you see Greg before I got there?"

She thought for a minute, casting smiles at women around us. "I think I did. He looked disheveled."

"I never saw him. He must have gotten out before I got there," I said.

"You were late, as usual." She shrugged.

My leg jiggled uncontrollably. "Since Greg was there before I arrived, did he have time to kill Karen and get out before Patty Baylor got to the bathroom?"

She lifted her cup of tea. "Probably, but it's a police matter, not yours or mine."

I took out my phone.

"Look at a picture of some girls at a party? I can't say where it was held, but these kids are underage and drinking.

"You know I don't want to be involved in your sleuthing business." I stood up to leave. Cornelia waved me to sit back down.

"All right. I don't believe this is just about protecting innocent teenagers, but. let me see the picture."

I sat down, took out my phone. Cornelia's mouth dropped open.

"Oh God. Look what they're wearing. Barely a slip and showing everything." I rolled my eyes. "That one is Karen Sheldon's daughter, Jennifer, as you know. This other one is Brooke Wanamaker. Her father's the head of a large entertainment company. Like IMAX or something." Cornelia looked at me over her two thousand dollar Cartier gold frame glasses. " If you're going to make a case that Karen was killed because she knew about these photos and you don't tell the police, it means that you could be next. You do understand the seriousness of what happens here?"

"I don't plan to go after anybody. Even I'm not that crazy, " I said.

"You should go to the police. Or give me the photo. The whole photo. I'll take care of it." My mouth dropped open.

"Isn't that taking police work into your own hands? "

"I have my ways," she murmured.

"I might take you up on your offer. But not yet. You don't want to be the next victim. Tom wouldn't be happy. " She shook her head at me as if I was a lost cause.

I felt nauseous at the idea of a mother not protecting her daughter so she could get a listing.

But I didn't go to the police to protect myself either. That was a mistake.

* * *

Chloe seemed her chatty self on our walk home from school. I was in knots.

"Chloe, would you tell me if anyone at school made you feel bad?"

She stopped, folded her arms, and looked disapproving. Ten going on thirteen.

"Mom, are you talking to Dad? He asked me the same thing. Nobody makes me feel bad about anything. There are mean kids in every grade. I don't listen to them."

My kid was wiser and tougher than me. "That's very smart, but are kids asking you about the race when I got pushed into Mrs. Clifford and her friends?"

"You mean like when Kevin said, 'Your mom cheated.' That was just stupid. You're not a cheater, and you didn't care about winning that dumb race. Right?" I saw the slightest fear and worry in her face. I felt like murdering Buffy for spreading vicious rumors.

"Yes, exactly right. Cheating is bad. Even if I wanted to win, I wouldn't cheat. It's not winning then. And tripping myself would be a bad plan. How could I win that way?" Chloe broke into a big smile.

"I gave Kevin a punch in his arm," she said proudly. I held back a laugh.

" Well, that likely felt great, but don't fight anyone. You'll get in trouble. Tell a teacher or tell me. I'll talk to Ms. Charles."

She sighed. "Oh, no, Mom, don't talk to her. Samantha and me, and our friends know what really happened. We think it's like TV. You'll find out who did it, and then everyone will know Kevin and his friends are jerks."

Whoa. Chloe's faith in me was a tidal wave, drawing me back into water way over my head. I wanted to tell her finding the killer would never clear me with Buffy's clique. But she was right. Some parents might see me as a hero if I solved Karen's murder. Forget my promise to Devon to sit back and wait. Forget Cornelia and Daniel. If I was going to have Chloe's trust in me restored and clear my name at Huntley, I had to keep going to find the killer.

I gave her a hug. " I'll race you to the house." We took off down the block. Chloe won.

I called Rebecca later. "Can you make a quick trip to 962 Park tomorrow morning to work your magic with Super Rjek? "

"Okay," she sighed. " But after this, I start charging. And no more locked rooms, or my fee doubles."

"I'll bring my twelve-piece pick set. Guaranteed to break us into the safe at the Bellagio."

"I'm not all that sexy early in the morning," she added.

"You're Marilyn Monroe compared to me. Meet you at the crosstown bus at 9:30."

* * *

Rebecca beamed her thousand-watt smile on Anthony Rjek. His face lit up, but his eyes became suspicious.

"If you're here, you want something."

"You are brilliant. I hope your Board Pres knows that," she cooed. He melted.

"We just need five minutes," I rushed in. My heart pounded, standing in the lobby. Anyone could walk in and see us. "To measure the height of the security camera in the basement. The one that was covered when your handyman was killed."

"The police wanted to know the same thing." He shrugged. "It's not going to bring Hernando back."

"We can't do that, but we can find who did it," I said.

"All right. Just five minutes." He chatted happily with Rebecca while I tagged along to the basement.

We looked up at the camera. It was pretty high. I had a fold-up yardstick of six feet. The camera was at least eight and a half, maybe nine feet high.

Someone tall. Olmsted, Shane, Marlena, in heels, who might be six feet. Or someone hired. "How tall are you, Anthony?"

"I'm six feet. Let me get a cloth." He came back with a large rag. It took three tries and even then it didn't cover the lens completely. "They had to stand on something," he said. He went and got an empty bucket. When he stood on that, it took two tries to get it covered.

"Would this bucket be out in the open, where anyone could find it?" I asked.

"Sometimes. Or it's in a closet."

"Thanks, Anthony. Definitely, one of them had to be tall. Hernando must have spotted them. Would you agree more than one assailant? Anthony nodded.

"Hernando was strong. One person could not overpower him." The three of us stood silently, picturing the murder. The super looked near tears. *Change the subject.*

"Any news about the apartment being sold?"

He looked down at the ground. Rebecca jumped in.

"Oh, I wish I could afford to buy that grand apartment and live here," she cooed. "Having someone like you to call on would be a dream." I thought he'd have an orgasm on the spot. Her lips pouted. "Can you tell us anything more?"

He would have jumped off the roof for her. "A contractor has been in to take measurements, with that Susie agent. I think something has been signed."

So Susie had a signed contract, and the closing could be soon. We thanked Rjek profusely and left.

"You really ought to think about acting," I said to Rebecca. "The role of the sexy secretary or hooker married to the old rich guy is made for you."

"Nice. Not Shakespeare?"

"Not enough money in Shakespeare." I shook my head. "Whatever was in

that briefcase was valuable enough for someone to kill for a second time."
My phone rang.

I picked up and was surprised by the caller. "Sure. Tomorrow is fine. I'll
be there. You don't want to tell me now? Okay. Tomorrow."

We reached Lexington Avenue, busy and noisy where you could get a
subway and find stores.

"That was Patty Baylor," I said. "She has something she wants to tell me,
but not today and not on the phone."

"Was she the one who found Karen's body and wears expensive running
clothes but doesn't run?" Rebecca asked. "That's a thing, you know. Like
owning a fancy juicer but not juicing." Suddenly, she was riveted by a jogger
running past. Broad shoulders, no shirt, and sweat glistening off his pecs.
She sighed and turned back toward me.

" Melanie, didn't you just tell Devon you'd back off and write?"

I nodded. "But I'm close to something.

Don't do anything stupid." Rebecca looked at me sternly. "I don't have
time to follow you around."

"Talking to Patty Baylor out in the open can't be dangerous."

Rebecca's pink lips trembled. "I'm a terrible friend. What's wrong?" I
asked.

"Paul's mumbling about changing jobs. Oregon or some other remote
outpost. He's been texting with a female doctor out there." Rebecca's eyes
teared up.

"So it's not about a job; it's a woman. A new flirtation, or is it an affair?"

She waved a hand to stop me. "I don't care if he's flirting online. That's
within our rules. But moving? Oregon's a retirement place or for hikers.
He'll never really do anything. He's just trying to shake me up. But
it's working. I'm having nightmares about massive trees and kids in
Birkenstocks." A sly smile appeared. " But I met a hot prospect at a poetry
reading. We're doing lunch, and who knows what else. Gorgeous, young.
We can read poetry to each other before, during, and after sex. My idea of
heaven." I laughed.

"Thank God your idea of heaven is right here in New York. Please don't leave." I clutched at her arm like a kid. "I can't take Devon twelve thousand miles away and you, living in Oregon. Maybe we can find a hot new receptionist for Paul." We hugged and went our separate ways.

Chapter Twenty-Three

Devon texted he'd arrived in Adelaide, Australia. Adelaide is the furthest city from NYC in the world. Belinda, who's both Devon and Daniel's editor at Food and Culture Lovers, Inc, changed Devon's assignment at the last minute. Belinda is also Daniel's good buddy. Adelaide has no food or culture of any interest. It fulfilled one criteria—it's far away from me. Next time, she'd send him to the cannibal tribes in New Guinea.

I wrote a column for the Wild Westsider.

News from the *Park Avenue Murder*

There are further complications in the murder of Karen Sheldon, killed during a Park Avenue Open House. Dr. Greg Sheldon, her soon-to-be ex-husband, was found unconscious at the Beacon Hotel by the police, who received an anonymous tip two weeks after the murder. The police have labeled it an accidental drug overdose. Close friends reported Sheldon was depressed because of his ex-wife's death, which has been ruled a murder. The police have not made any arrests as of today. Greg Sheldon remains hospitalized. There has been no comment from his fiance, Marlena Shenko. Although there have been unconfirmed rumors that the engagement is off.

I wrote nothing about screwing his patients. Or the suicide note. Or money. Putting in Marlena at all was dangerous. I could be attacked, or worse. Harold, my editor, disagreed, of course.

"If they sue you, they sue the paper. We get more publicity. You say he had a drug problem. I know an insider at the hospital who will swear Sheldon came in for drug problems. She'll say anything for me." He stressed "anything," so I would know what a stud he was, even though his hair was greasy and his beard always speckled with food. His B.O. was staggering.

"Show me your insurance policy," I countered.

"That cop at the precinct gave information to your boyfriend, Devon. I think that's enough corroboration. Let Sheldon sue me. We'll get thousands more readers. Be brave. Tell your readers he left a note. Put that in."

"He's not my boy—" Harold hung up. If Harold, who had the social sensitivity of a slug, picked up romantic vibes between Devon and me, everyone must have. Harold had given me bad advice before. Meanwhile, my account of Greg Sheldon made him sound like a morose widower, despondent about his murdered ex-wife. He'd likely get even more women now. I added that the police were still investigating the circumstances around his overdose, that there were others using drugs at the party as well.

I included parts of my interview with Sheldon at his office. Because my usual column was called *Afterward,* the interview made sense. What was the impact of Karen's murder on him and the family? The description of his barren office and his untroubled good looks, and the quote, *"As I told the detective, Karen and I had an amicable separation, ..."* sounded as cold and phony as it had then. I hoped it aroused suspicion with the readers. My phone rang.

"This is Hugh Clark. I'm looking for Melanie Deming." My BP went up for a moment. I didn't like the architect and his phony, pompous accent.

"Yes, we spoke a few days ago. You're the architect."

Clark continued. "I have had a brief opening occur in my day." As if this were a miracle. I doubted he had much of a schedule. He cleared his throat a little nervously. "Would you care to join me for lunch and then a brief tour of the Harrington Mansion, now unoccupied and available for viewing? For your article."

Lunch sounded awful, but a tour sounded perfect. I'd get to see the upstairs. Maybe I could channel Rebecca's pouts to pry the names of the buyers from him and how he'd gotten the zoning changed. A shiver ran through me. Rebecca and Devon's voices screamed at me to stay home, or at least not go alone.

I ignored those voices. The pompous architect was too good an opportunity to pass up.

"How lovely of you to think of me." My attempt at matching his fake British accent came out as Helen Mirren with a New York twang. "I'm afraid lunch is not possible today, but I can meet you at two p.m. at the mansion."

"That is too bad. I know a small French restaurant on the East side, within walking distance of Harrington."

I was not sitting knee to knee with him in a dark bistro.

"Well, then, we can just do this another time," I countered. " if lunch is that important. But not today."

He quickly recovered. "Oh, no. Your article and my expertise are far more important than lunch. Two p.m. is fine. There is a side entrance to the right of the mansion. You'll see a path. I'll meet you there. I have a key to the gated backyard. Quite impressive."

I agreed and got off the call. My stomach was queasy. It was already nearly noon. I knew I should call Rebecca and tell her about this rendezvous, but she had mentioned pointedly she was working that afternoon. Devon was asleep on the other side of the globe. Cornelia wouldn't care. Or I'd get a lecture about Daniel. There was only one name left on my short list of people who had an interest, and that was Harold, my editor at the *Wild Westsider*, the home of my column.

"Of course you go," he bellowed. "What's your problem? And take pictures. I'll include some. Not sure how this figures in the murder. But Sheldon's ex-fiancée is the lawyer for the deal. Karen Sheldon was the agent for the mansion's sale. You can make this work. Maybe you'll get lucky, and something dangerous will happen." Harold snorted with laughter.

"That's not funny, even for an editor, and I've worked for some of the worst. If you don't hear back from me by four, you better call the police."

"Absolutely. I'll come myself and identify your remains." He laughed uproariously again. I threw the phone at the couch.

I took DHEA for energy, rhodiola for focus, and ginkgo biloba because I felt a headache coming on. Also B-100. I threw some California poppy in my bag for fear, while ignoring the tightness in my chest. I couldn't call my old therapist. I hadn't seen her in months, and she'd tell me to make an appointment. I put on my black jeans, a silky white T-shirt, and white sneakers.

I race-walked around the reservoir, veering out of the park at 86th on the East side near the Metropolitan Museum. I walked past Buffy's townhouse, resisting the impulse to throw a pebble at one of her massive windows. Chloe would be so happy when I figured out who killed Karen and my name restored at good ol Huntley.

I swore to Devon I'd never meet anyone alone, but I had to do this for Chloe's sake. I wasn't a very good wife. But I could be a great mom and do what I'd set out to do. Chloe got out of school at four PM. I could easily make it to Huntley for pickup after meeting with Clark.

* * *

Architect Hugh Clark was on time at the side entrance. He was quite tall and had the air of a startled, bearded scarecrow in a three-piece suit. Big glasses perched on a large pointed nose. The suit looked more expensive than I expected for a professor at a 3rd-tier college. I guessed he was in his late forties. No smile, no hello. I had the urge to leave but didn't.

"I'm Melanie Deming," I said. "Is this still a good time for you?"

"Yes, of course." He got more social. "I'm surprised at your age. I expected you might be one of those millennials. This is far better. For an article about the Gold Coast mansions here in New York, it's right that you should be a mature woman of the world. You'll have a greater respect for these elegant grande dames and all that has been lost."

What the hell? A "mature woman of the world." I was on the tail end of millennials. My dislike for this guy tripled. He must have a thing for young girls. I flashed on the party video. He might know about the party scene here. His eyes looked around vaguely. Was it drugs or early Alzheimer's? Then I smelled wine. He'd gone to lunch without me. He might even be a little drunk. I noted his weak, watery eyes behind thick glasses.

"Well, let's get started. We'll go in through the garden." He opened an ornate iron gate, wrought with lions and birds. A brick path through hedges opened into the walled backyard. Diamond paving stones, planted gardens, two seating areas, the outdoor kitchen—I'd seen all this before. I took out my phone to get a photo.

"No pictures, please," Clark put his hand up to block the shot. What the hell? "Nothing except professional photos are allowed. We want only the most spectacular pictures taken."

I nodded and put away my phone, but it seemed strange. He seemed to calm down. "How elegant and unexpected! And in midtown, no less. We could be in Greenwich, or Southampton." I gushed.

Hugh dismissed me with a wave of his hand. "Much more elegant, please. The gentry of the early 1900s spared no expense. Of course, the mansion has been updated and redone over the years."

We entered the house, as I had done before, through the large but unimpressive kitchen. Clark walked quickly past it. Then we were in the vast expanse of black and white marble, the three-storied entryway with the wide staircase.

"As you can see, first impressions were paramount. The staircase had to say that a family of importance lived here." I nodded. "Shall we go upstairs to the bedrooms?" He put his hand on the small of my back and guided me up the stairs. I quickly darted ahead of him. I didn't know what this guy had in mind.

"So, how many bedrooms does the mansion have?" I took out a pad and pen and began taking notes in earnest.

He got the idea. "Ten. Here is the double master on this floor and two more bedrooms." The bedroom was enormous with wide open double doors, " On the third floor are three more large bedroom suites. All with sumptuous dressing areas and baths. And three smaller suites on the fourth floor. Of course, there is a two-bedroom servants' apartment downstairs. It is relatively small, for one of these homes. There were some that had twenty bedrooms and more. Those, sadly, are no longer single-family residences."

"But you mentioned this, too, could be divided. That it was possible. Do you think that might happen?"

Clark didn't answer. His phone kept buzzing with texts. He wandered out to the wide landing outside the bedroom as he read them.

My mind suddenly clicked. I had seen Clark before. At the gallery with the awful poet and climate-change art. One of the three pompous academics trying to impress each other.

"I saw you at an art gallery and poetry reading a few weeks ago," I said when he returned. "You were with friends. We agreed the art was laughable."

Clark continued to look at his phone. "Really. I don't remember that. It was a waste of my time. I only went because...." He stopped himself. Because what?

"Let's proceed," he said.

We toured the bedrooms, enormous salons with old furniture, deep-set windows with faded cushioned window seats, and dusty curtains everywhere. No one had lived here for a very long time. I'd bet this white elephant had been on the market for years. Clark droned on about Samuel Harrington, slaving away over the plans one hundred and twenty years ago. He kept getting texts. I walked out to the landing and still heard him whisper something. Did I actually hear him say, "Yes, she's here"?

My stomach clenched. Who was he talking to? Who was it who wanted to know if I was here with him? Could it be Marc Olmsted? The thought of Marc and creepy Clark discussing me was suddenly terrifying. Something told me to go back downstairs. I did, casually at first and then more quickly. *Stop*, I finally said. At the the bottom of the stairs, I felt silly. His wife probably just asked how the interview was going. I really had to stop this disaster thinking.

Then I heard him say in an annoyed voice, "I'm taking care of her, don't worry." What did that mean? When a bad guy on TV said, 'I'll take care of him,' it meant only one thing. The front door was twenty feet away and totally exposed. He might still be on the phone. My brain said *the time to leave is now.*

Chapter Twenty-Four

"Ms. Deming, where are you going? I have to accompany you around the house, and I haven't yet shown you the terraces," Clark called out, sounding irritated and panicky. I flattened against the bottom of the staircase.

No way was I going out on a terrace with him. I'd say I had a family emergency. I lifted a foot to leave the sheltered space next to the staircase and waved goodbye as I left through the front door. Clark's clomping footsteps were loud; he walked slowly down the stairs. I peeked quickly up the railing and saw him holding something shiny. Could it be a gun? No, it must be his big iPhone. It was black and shiny. Was it his phone or a gun? Was he a boring architect, or a goddamned killer?

What had I been thinking, coming here alone to meet this guy? But there'd been no hint of anything sinister about him. Maybe he was bragging to someone that he was getting great publicity by talking to a journalist. Taking care of me might mean he'd give me money to sweeten my review. Money was better than knocking me off.

Suddenly, it hit me: The gallery wasn't even the first time I'd seen him. He was definitely the man I saw with Marlena and the Russian buyer as they left the mansion. He probably spent his own money bribing city officials to get the zoning changed. This was not a rich guy. Not getting his own money returned with millions more through the development of this mansion was a solid motive for murdering Karen. Assuming Karen wouldn't go along with his plans. Whatever was in that briefcase was the answer. Coming here alone was one of my less brilliant ideas. I peeked again. Looked a lot more like a gun than a phone.

Terror sharpened my vision. I made it to the fireplace next to the stairs without being seen. I grabbed an antique poker with a sharp point and looked frantically for a place to hide. I didn't dare make a dash for the front door now. He was almost down the stairs.

Gun or phone. My gut said it was a gun. I'd only seen one up close for a minute last year. I was no expert and I wasn't thinking straight. I wished I was wrong, but I couldn't take a chance. I thought I was setting Clark up to give me information, but he found out who I was. Someone coached him on the phone. So unfair. I couldn't lunge and parry against a gun, or outrun a bullet like Wonder Woman. It was too risky to try and disarm Hugh Clark. Why the hell weren't there better gun control laws in this country? Devon would kill me for coming here alone. Daniel would have grounds for divorce. If I got out of here alive. If I died he wouldn't have to bother. He'd be relieved.

A storage area disguised with ornate molding was under the circular staircase in the center of the grand gallery. I remembered Shane describing it. Frantically, with sweating fingers, I looked for a hidden lever. There had to be one. Clark's footsteps meant he was now in the entryway at the bottom of the stairs. At the last moment, the ornate door swung open just enough for me to push against it and squeeze inside. Aha, another good reason for my fanatical eating habits, I could squeeze through a small space. I blessed every container of goat yogurt.

It was pitch black. I couldn't see my hand. Water bugs. Oh God, I jammed my hand in my mouth to stop the scream that wanted to come out. I hated water bugs. Something I bet was creeping up my leg this minute. *Stop. Shut up.*

Clark was an architect and an expert on this house. He probably knew about the secret storage area. He could shoot bullets through the door. He'd get me before the water bugs did, anyway.

Clark called out in his fake English whiny voice.

"Ms Deming, where have you gone? Have we had a misunderstanding?" *You have a gun, I thought. No misunderstanding that.*

194

"I have a story I need to tell someone. You're the only one I trust." I barely stopped myself from loud guffaws. Seriously, did he think I'd fall for that?

Become entirely still. Where'd that voice come from? *Only breathe through your nose. The only thing moving is the air coming in and out of your body.* It was the gorgeous guy, on the beach in Hawaii, from the meditation app. Finally, he'd come through at the right time. Becoming entirely still truly was the best advice right now. *Your breathing is becoming slower and slower. So less air is coming in and out.* Good idea, considering there wasn't much extra oxygen in this space, intended for a few buckets and mops.

Notice if you're feeling any particular mood right now. How about extreme terror?

Breathe. Was Hugh Clark the tall guy I'd seen at the race? He pushed me, I was sure. *Breathe.*

I should have recognized Clark's voice on the phone. I heard him at the gallery. So stupid I'd walked right into this. My hands shook so badly I was terrified I'd bang the fireplace poker against the wall. *Stop shaking. Breathe.* I held the poker like my life depended on it and somehow pried a few fingers open to also hold my phone. I wrote a text to Cornelia, Rebecca, Chilton, Devon, and even Levano. *Help. Trapped at Harrington mansion with killer.*

Clark's loud voice startled me. He must be nearby. I nearly dropped the poker. I clicked Record on my phone. If I was going to die in this closet, maybe they'd find my phone. Maybe he'd say something that could convict him. At least I told Harold I was meeting Clark here.

"Do you have any idea what it's like to know you're entitled to a gracious home for the rest of your life and your son's life, and then suddenly there's nothing? No one would stand for that," Clark lamented with huge gobs of self-pity. "The shock when I found out my insane wife blew through her trust funds—every goddamn penny. Our home in the Hamptons, gone. All on an online scheme with some hunk? "

What was he talking about? So he killed Karen to get money. Was he about to confess? I hated to tell him, but if this was his murder defense, it wouldn't fly. If you were allowed to kill a business partner because you couldn't live in idle splendor, or your spouse had blown the family fortune on some hotty, there'd be no one left on the planet, or at least on Park Avenue.

Who was his wife—a rich woman with a son. In the Hamptons. No, it couldn't be. The last names didn't match. But then it all made sense. The skinny, insanely competitive runner. The auction where she threw money at ugly jewels. How many endangered diamond animals did Peggy Fitzgerald have? I nearly called out, "She can sell off her jewels." Hugh Clark kept confessing. He liked to lecture.

" So, I came up with a conversion plan. Perfectly legal, right up my alley. Convert this monstrosity to six apartments. Make one hundred and fifty million dollars, not forty million. Everyone was happy. We had the buyer. And then that bitch decided she wanted half the profits. She had a report about serious structural cracks in the basement. I never saw any. But she said it was true. It was covered over years ago, she said. She said she had the old report. It meant hundreds of thousands more to renovate. The buyer might get cold feet. No one likes structural damage. She threatened us. The evidence could make the mansion unsellable and seriously delay construction. " He laughed in disgust.

"Why the hell would she threaten like that? She was crazy." *She wasn't the only one.* The old, long-ago-buried report must have been in the briefcase.

Hugh Clark's near deafening frantic voice, bounced off the ceiling and uncarpeted marble. He went on with his rant. "And the one hundred and eighty million would be lost. We had to get the document. She wouldn't give me the briefcase, so we had to kill her. Anyone could see that. She had no right to go against what we'd all agreed upon."

This defense also wouldn't hold up, I'm afraid. We didn't agree on a business arrangement, Your Honor, ergo she had to die. "

"If the Harringtons couldn't sell to someone who would convert, and she'd only get forty-five million even, we'd all get a piece of nothing." I prayed my phone was recording.

To me, it still sounded pretty good. Even one-fortieth of forty million would be one million. I could make do with that. But it wasn't enough to keep his son in polo ponies. I sweated gallons from the heat in the closet, and his maniacal voice was getting closer. What if he just started shooting?

Daniel and Cornelia were right. Here I was again. Only this time, in a closet the size of a box, and there was a gun. At least I was far away from home. If I died, it would just be me.

I heard the squeak of a rubber sole, a sneaker. Then, "Hughie, where are you?" A woman's shrill voice pierced the silence and echoed around the entryway.

"I'm in the entryway, near the kitchen, looking for that stupid woman who thinks she's a reporter." Really. Insult me first, and then shoot me? Now I was angry.

"What are you doing there? She could run out the back door." the woman yelled.

"She wouldn't dare."

"Darling, you don't have to do this. I'll do it." Whose voice was that? Peggy's? She didn't seem like the "darling" type. For a brief second, I thought it sounded like Deedee, from Sheldon's office, someone flirtatious. But the voice took on an angrier, whiny tone.

"Hughie, you've been cheating on me with that awful woman. Don't you know she just wants your part of the money?"

"I don't know what you're talking about. I don't want anyone but you. You know that. No one else."

Someone began sobbing. I couldn't tell if it was a man or a woman.

"Really? You love me that much?" It was quiet for a few moments. I swear I heard kissing and groaning and a chair being pushed, then moaning and crying out. Oh, God, they were doing it either on that couch foyer couch or on a kitchen counter. I thought I heard metal banging. And with a gun. I wondered if I should make a run for it, while they were locked together. I touched the door, but they were about as quick as a couple of rabbits.

"What?" I heard Clark's startled voice again. "Give me back that gun, you bitch!"

"I'll shoot her. You're too soft. I saw you with that Sheldon woman. It took two of us. Scrawny dame you couldn't just do it in the end." The same voice but not whiny now. So there was a gun. I felt pleased with myself that I could spot a gun from far away. And then I knew for sure I was crazy. Most important, I had a confession from a woman that they'd killed Karen.

"Don't wave the gun around," Clark said. "We need to find this Deming woman. She knows everything now."

"Don't worry. She can't escape from here. There are plenty of bullets; I loaded it myself. And I know where she is."

I started shaking so hard I almost didn't feel my phone vibrate with an incoming text. Detective Chilton. *Stay put.* Really, where was I about to go?

"We're nearly there," the woman went on. "We're going to be rich."

I heard more footsteps tapping on the floor, running? Maybe May-Ling in her heels, come to rescue me? Then, the loudest noise I'd ever heard. I thought a bullet had gone through the door of my hideaway under the staircase. I waited for pain, but there was none. No bullet. Someone was screaming in pain. Then I heard a new voice. A second woman's voice, not the detective.

"The two of you, just lie down on the floor. Calm down, you're not going to die. It's barely a leg scratch."

I had to get out of here. This new voice lectured Clark, and the whiny-voiced woman, who I assumed was Peggy. Hopefully, the second woman had shot them both, or else it was the three of them against me. I didn't like those odds. I had a minute while she berated them. I pushed open the door an inch. I saw no one. I slipped out and kept to the far wall as I moved toward the front door. I could still hear the woman's voice.

"What a mess you've made," she said. "It should have been so easy to dump the contents of the briefcase into a bag. But you went and took it. And then left it in the basement. Like a scared kid. And then the handyman had to be silenced. I broke my own rule. Never work with amateurs."

There was silence for a moment, then the second woman's voice again. " I'll take the gun. I know where that silly woman must be. If you move, I'll shoot you too."

I assumed she had two guns now. This could be an anti-gun commercial.

My legs shook. I couldn't walk. Thank God I had on my fashion statement white sneakers, which were both silent and stable. No one should ever wear anything but sneakers in New York.

I watched with dread as a high-heeled and slim-suited woman came out of the kitchen. She strode straight to my closet hiding area. Could I make it out the door and time it for the exact moment she looked in the closet? I was still holding the sharp-tipped poker from the fireplace. Fencing builds all the muscles in the shoulder around the rotator cuff, as well as the wrist and grip. I hadn't known that till it happened. Suddenly I was hoisting fifteen-pound weights with less agony. And I opened jars Daniel couldn't open.

What if I threw the poker like a javelin? Would my shoulder and wrist be strong enough to make the poker travel thirty feet across the room and still have the thrust to injure her? I doubted that. It would only provide a distraction for a few seconds. If I were a Marine, I'd know stuff like this. I should have joined the Marines. I'd wasted my life.

Pull yourself together.Mourn your wasted life some other time.

I held the poker toward its center. I could handle it; it was way lighter than fifteen pounds. My mind said run; too risky to try to throw across such a big distance and get out before a bullet hit me. I darted to the front door, jumped through it, and heard a blast. A bullet hit the wall where I had stood moments before. My legs buckled. Move! I screamed at my legs. Another bullet smashed the glass around the door. She was coming for me. I could hear the heels running across the tiled entryway. My rage and adrenaline roared up and into action, pushing me down the steps to the sidewalk. I flattened myself against the building behind a huge urn holding a withered evergreen. She burst out the door. Now!

I lifted the poker, aimed, and threw it at her side with my newly chiseled, admittedly quivering biceps. Her horrible scream filled the quiet street. I saw the triathlete, Marlena, fall on the steps. I hoped I hadn't killed her. Such a gorgeous, talented woman, whose priorities had just gone berserk.

Cars screeched to a stop, police vehicles, and one unmarked. Out of the unmarked car jumped Chilton and another man in street clothes, both with guns drawn. They ran up the walk to the steps with four uniformed cops.

Chapter Twenty-Five

"What the hell is going on here?" Chilton bellowed. "Call the medics. Is she dead? What the f...is this? A spear?"

"No, Lieutenant, it's a fireplace poker," said one of his officers.

"Jesus, I'm in the middle of some kids' Clue game. The butler must have done it." The officers chuckled. "Get in there and fan out. See where that goddamned reporter is and whether she's been shot." I stepped out of the shadow of the planter.

"Nope. Still alive."

Chilton stared at me like he'd seen a ghost. It almost made the last hour worth it.

"Send your men to the kitchen and the back exit," I ordered. " The two who committed the murder are still there, I hope. I don't think they're armed. Marlena took their gun and shot one of them in the leg,"

"Okay, get moving. The kitchen and back exit." Chilton yelled at the men still on the sidewalk. They ran around the side of the house, guns drawn.

"It wasn't the butler. It was the architect. Marlena was in charge," I said, my voice a high-pitched squeak, a sound I didn't recognize. "Hugh Clark with help from his girlfriend. Guess I win the game." I started to shake. My mouth kept moving, as if words would calm me, as if the terror of what I had just done and what could have happened would disappear. "It's more like Monopoly, really. Agents, lawyers, and architects go to jail, do not pass go."

Breathing was getting harder. "I did it. I threw the spear at her," I whispered. I held myself by my arms and rubbed to get some circulation going. Everything had gone numb. "Is she dead?"

"She's alive so far," said Chilton. "And you're not dead. I suppose that's good. Though you look pretty pale. Are you going to pass out? Was she after you with the gun?" I nodded yes. My eyes widened, and my mouth dropped open. This was all too much. I slumped against the stair railing. Now, I was hallucinating. A man walked up to Chilton. But it couldn't be the same man I knew.

"Are you all right?" The man was suddenly right next to me. Holding my elbow. His voice was deep and assured, not timid. His face as Brad-Pitt perfect as ever.

"Shane?" I'd gone completely insane. "Are you Shane?" He laughed.

"Actually, my name's Bob Martin. I'm a detective."

"You—you're an undercover cop?"

He laughed. "Pretty good, huh? Acting classes. We've been watching Olmsted for a while. Suspected real estate fraud."

I was so astounded by Shane's complete transformation into a red-blooded gun-carrying cop, I forgot how terrified I was. I forgot to be nauseous when I saw the medics stopping the blood that oozed from the wound in Marlena's side. Her eyes were closed, but she mumbled in Russian. I hadn't killed her.

"Did you deliberately follow me in the park?" I asked Shane, now Bob Martin.

"Protecting you, I'd say. Dangerous running alone in that area. You'd already had a warning."

"So what happened today? How come you didn't follow me here? It might have been a good idea," I sniped.

"Guess we slipped up. Thought you'd given up sleuthing."

"Couldn't, " my voice squeaked again. "It's my job to write about crimes. Hugh Clark invited me to tour the mansion. But he had a different agenda." More tremors hit me, but there was no place to collapse. I grabbed the railing.

"I brought you the guilty parties on a silver platter, same as last time." I looked at Chilton with as much disdain as I could manufacture. "Hugh Clark and another woman who might be his wife, I hope, are still on the kitchen floor. I'm not sure which one of these three actually choked Karen. Marlena knew the whole plan. They were all in on this together, to make sure this place was divided into enough apartments to get one hundred and eighty million. Apparently, Karen wanted a bigger cut, or she wouldn't subdivide."

Chilton interrupted me. "We knew about the conversion plan. We just didn't have enough to connect them to Karen Sheldon's murder. Until today." He paused. "I don't need to tell you what we found out, but since you put your life on the line." He shook his head. " I'll let you in."

Was I supposed to thank him? No way. He went on. "We finished going through the elevator videotapes, compared who came in, who went out, and how it matched up with attendance at the open house. Susie Carlbach stalled us, made excuses that she didn't have a complete list of attendees, or she couldn't give it to us. She wouldn't look at the tapes with us. Kept stalling. Until today, when we threatened to arrest her for obstructing justice."

About time. I could have died here.

"Turns out the husband of the couple who were in contract to buy the apartment were in the elevator coming in, but not leaving. It was Clark. We had no way of knowing who he was because of Susie Carlbach. She didn't want to lose the sale. She only agreed to watch the tapes today. And then I got your text. I would have loved to lock her up, but she came with her lawyer. We may still charge her with obstructing justice."

"Too bad you didn't find out sooner. I could have done without playing war games. " The shakes wouldn't stop. Bob Martin gave me his jacket. Nice guy.

"Typical of Susie not wanting to nail a killer if it meant losing a commission," I continued. This was so horrifying I couldn't even laugh. I went on.

"Hugh Clark and a woman, who you'll find in the kitchen, recited a confession. I think I have it on my phone. So Hugh Clark is the missing man from the elevator?" Chilton just nodded. I babbled on. "Clark said Karen had to go, that she was against the condo plan. And he needed money. Something about his wife spending the trust."

"That would be Peggy Fitzgerald, who apparently has a spending problem. She's Clark's wife," May-Ling said. She walked up from the squad cars. The street was blocked with police cars. I suddenly thought of the two of them having sex in that awful kitchen, which made my stomach turn over. Then, I caught a glimpse of Marlena's bloody wound as she was loaded onto a stretcher with an IV hooked up. I needed a bathroom this minute.

"What did you do to my husband? I told you to stay the hell away." Peggy Fitzgerald, in running gear as usual but panting, ran up to me and screamed in my face.

"Peggy?" I was incredulous. "You're not inside with your husband?"

She looked at me with hatred. "Of course not. I just heard that he came here. I've been worried about him. He's been obsessed with this place. And with you." She glared at me. "Then I saw there was money missing."

"Obsessed with me? I never met him before today."

Peggy's face drained of what little color it had. "I don't believe you. He talked to some woman all the time."

"Why would you think it was me? Is it fifty thousand that's missing?"

"You deliberately looked for him at the gallery, didn't you?" My bewildered look was her answer.

Peggy's panting got worse, and fast. She was having a panic attack and would faint in a minute. I tried to put an arm around her, but she pushed me aside. I turned to Chilton. "There's a woman in there, and I guess it's not Peggy." So, who was inside with Clark?

"I've got to use the bathroom." I beseeched Chilton and Bob Martin. They both shook their heads.

"What about that planter outside?" Chilton said, chuckling. I wished I had another poker on hand.

"Now. In a bathroom inside. I know where it is." I had no idea where the bathroom was, but Olmsted had said there was a powder room.

"Bob, go with her and watch her." So the hunk formerly known as Shane escorted me into the mansion. We found the bathroom across from the massive curved staircase, just as a stretcher carrying Hugh Clark rolled out. Handcuffed and hobbling behind him, muttering "Stupid, stupid, stupid," was Patty Baylor. Patty Baylor. First one at the murder scene at the open house. Hysterical Patty Baylor. It was all an act.

Peggy Fitzgerald, Hugh Clark's wife, saw Patty. These two women glared at each other with boiling rage, reminding me of two pit bulls. Without thinking, I asked Patty, "Why?" Patty narrowed her eyes and lunged at me. I ducked.

Peggy Fitzgerald gasped, seeing her husband on a stretcher. She followed him and yelled. "What did you do now, Hugh?" Then Peggy turned around and yelled at me and Patty Bayloe. "Patty stalked me, copied me, destroyed my life. I've never even talked to her. I told Hugh. He said don't bother with Patty. Hugh said it was you who called him. Wanted to sleep with him." She pointed at me. "But now I see he lied. I have to call our lawyer." She turned and ran out the doors of the mansion.

Patty Baylor turned to me. Her blazing wide stare was frightening.

"Peggy's never worked a day in her life, and look at what she has, the skinny bitch. I hate these people born with money. I deserve her life, Hugh, and a pony for my son. You'll see. We'll get our share. The courts will be sympathetic." Her chin jutted up in the air. She marched out almost proudly. Patty Baylor's pathetic Robin Hood reasoning almost sounded sane until I saw her crazy eyes and remembered she was ready to kill me. She and Hugh and probably Marlena killed two innocent people, and they would have killed me without thinking twice.

What a sad, sick pair they made. My guess was they both had a part in killing Karen. Hugh Clark arrived at the open house by elevator. Probably, he told Karen he needed to talk about zoning. And in the privacy of the bathroom, killed her. Then, left through the back door with the briefcase. He stupidly stashed the briefcase in the basement without taking out the contents. Truly a panicked amateur mistake. Patty locked the door. Marlena was right. These two were bad news. If the papers about the cracks in the foundation were in the briefcase, why not leave the whole briefcase at the murder scene and take the contents? Hernando was dead. Two murders now on their heads.

I wondered if Peggy Fitzgerald would be forced to continue with the purchase of 962 Park Avenue or forfeit her $800,000 dollar down payment? Her whole life was in shambles. In the end, money hadn't helped her marriage. And it surely wouldn't help her son to have two crazy parents.

I made it to the bathroom just in time, retching until there was nothing left. When I came out, there were swarms of police and technicians.

Maybe I was wrong about who strangled Karen. Marlena could have done it, but my guess was she provided the plan and a distraction at the Open House. Obviously, she was capable of murder. She almost killed me.

"Feeling better?" Bob Martin asked in a smug voice.

"Not at all. This much greed and violence makes me sick."

"You get used to it. Dealing with depravity is part of the job." I wondered how far he'd had to go with Marc and his impersonation of a slavish gay man. Maybe he was bisexual, which would explain why men and women found him attractive. I had another question.

"Where do Peggy and Hugh actually live?"

"You'll love this," said Bob, sounding almost like Shane again. "They just moved into a cheap rental, all the way on First Avenue. Left a family hotel apartment at the Carlyle, since they couldn't make the rent. They used stock to buy the Park Avenue place, but it turned out the stocks had lost half their value."

So it was all show and bluster. Desperation spurred Hugh to insane actions. Marlena must have been desperate as well. Patty Bayloe wanted everything she thought Peggy had.

Which one killed poor Hernando in the basement at 962 Park? That I'd leave up to the cops to find out. One of this monstrous trio would surely rat on another when they were questioned separately.

Outside, the only evidence of Marlena was a small pool of blood on the brick walkway. And, of course, the shattered window where the bullet struck.

"I've just had a near-death experience," I announced. "Not my first, but this time with a gun. I need to go home." Chilton eyed me suspiciously.

"I'll take her home and come back," Bob said. "You'll come to the precinct later today to give a statement, right?" I didn't know why he was helping me, but I'd take it.

"I'll send you the tape I have now." I took out my phone and sent them both the MP3 of Hugh's confession. This satisfied Chilton.

"Thanks. You're a good guy," I said to Bob on the way back to my apartment. Shane wasn't such a bad kid, either." He was silent.

I looked at my watch. It was 3:30. One and a half hours since I'd met Hugh Clark. My phone buzzed. It was Rebecca.

Where the hell r u? I called the police.

Alive. With the police now.

I'm having a heart attack, texted Rebecca.

Breathe deeply. And cough. Postpones heart attacks. Come to the apartment. Or I'll be at the 19th precinct later if you want. I'm ok.

Be at your place in fifteen.

Then came Cornelia: *I assume that text was your sort of joke.*

No actually. Can you pick up Chloe? I'll stop by later to get her.

And from Devon: *"Are you alive?"*

You missed it again, I texted him. *There was a gun this time.*

Jesus, Melanie. Relieved you're ok but what the hell? We had a deal.

Why did I tell him about the gun?

You're right. Going to precinct.

Chapter Twenty-Six

Rebecca came with me to the 19th precinct on East 67th. They oversee the wealthiest in a rich city. Bob Martin met us in the waiting room. Rebecca nearly panted once she picked up the decidedly straight vibes now coming from the former Shane.

A female officer led us to a green linoleum-tiled room. There was only a small, high window with bars. A stenographer took notes. They also took a video, and all I could think of was I'm not wearing makeup. I told Chilton, Martin, and May-Ling about Clark's invitation to show me the mansion and then in detail what happened at the last of the Gold Coast palaces. I repeated Patty Baylor's confession as she stupidly said the court would understand why they killed Karen and Hernando. How unfair life was. Everyone snickered.

"Patty Baylor?" Rebecca whispered when I finished. "You never mentioned her. Isn't she the Lululemon but never works out?"

" She seemed unimportant. The one who started screaming when she found Karen's body. It was all an act." Rebecca put her hand on my still trembling arm."Patty wanted to meet me again. Good thing I never met her, or she would have tried to kill me."

Shane checked a computer. "Marlena has been charged with embezzlement before, but it's on appeal. A former boyfriend accused her of theft."

"I bet it was an engagement ring," I said.

"How did you know?" The puzzled look on Chilton's face gave me the kind of satisfaction a mentalist must get when he confounds his audience. Was it worth it to almost be killed so I could feel smarter than the cops for a minute? I thought of Daniel, and my stomach lurched like I was on a boat in a hurricane.

"The back door being locked made me think there might be two people involved in the murder," I said. " Now we know there were two, or possibly three. " My phone rang. It was Devon. "I'm gonna take this. My writing partner." It seemed like everyone looked up at the ceiling, smirking.

"Hi. Can we talk after I'm done? Okay. I'll put you on speaker. Okay, Detective?"

"Just for a question, not an answer. No press coverage yet." Chilton said.

"Hi all. Great job, guys," Devon's voice boomed from Australia. " I have one question about Greg Sheldon and his overdose. I wonder if Marlena was responsible."

"Chilton speaking. We hear you. We aren't able to comment. She's in custody and you know from Melanie what happened."

"Not yet, actually. Glad she's alive and well. Speak later, Melanie." And he clicked off. "All right. Let's get on with this. No more interruptions," Chilton continued.

" Susie didn't give us a complete list of who was at the open house until today. We knew Peggy Fitzgerald was there. Turned out Peggy wrote down her husband's name. We didn't know who we were looking at in the videos. Many people came into the elevator during the open house. We only concentrated on those who got off on the eighth floor." *That was a mistake.*

"Clark came without Peggy, but he didn't get off on the eighth floor. He got off on the seventh floor. We had no idea who he was until today. It was just before the open house. A few people got off the elevator on seven. He was camouflaged by them."

I started talking, imagining the scene."So then he walked up one flight and came in, likely through the back door, which Patty opened. Susie had not arrived yet; only her assistant was there. Clark found Karen Sheldon. He and Patty Baylor used a wire to choke her." I felt like throwing up." It's still a shock to me that Susie Orbach refused to watch the tapes or give you a complete list until today. These two whackos planned to kill me." My

208

leg started shaking. I clamped my hands on it. Rebecca put a hand on my shoulder.

"Did Peggy Fitzgerald have any comments?" I muttered.

May-Ling nodded. "She never saw him. He texted he was going to miss it. She's already gotten herself a lawyer. She swears she had no idea he was there."

The pieces were fitting together. "Judging by how Peggy Fitzgerald acted at the mansion today, I'd say she told the truth. So Clark was in the back bathroom with Karen and Patty. Clark took the briefcase and left."

I continued. "Then Patty locked herself in the bathroom with Karen's body and waited ten minutes before she emerged. Giving Clark time to get out of the building." I looked around the table. "How did he get down to the basement without being filmed?"

Chilton's mouth was tense. "He walked down the back staircase. Turned out they didn't have cameras there. They were saving money. They said the doormen were enough security. We spoke to the Board members, "There will be cameras installed in the back stairwell."

"When Clark stashed the briefcase how was he not seen on the camera in the basement?" I looked at Chilton.

He sighed. "He got lucky. The building has nothing on tape for that period of the morning, the day of the murder. The super said that the camera had shut down on and off for days. He put a call in to get it fixed, but the company was backed up.

"But still, it was a stupid move. He could have just brought a briefcase with him and stashed the contents in his briefcase. Then, left from the stairs at the lobby. Marlena was right. She called them amateurs. Hernando would still be alive," I said.

Chilton nodded. "My life is easier because criminals make mistakes. And harder because Park Avenue residents think their buildings are impenetrable with all their doormen. And they're cheap. Their cameras need a serious upgrade." He looked at a computer on the table. "I don't think Clark or Baylor has any priors. Just Marlena."

Bob broke in. "After Clark left he texted Peggy Fitzgerald that she should make an offer. I thought you'd like that." He grinned at me.

"How disgusting," I let out a whoosh of air. "He kills Karen in the bathroom with his girlfriend and plans to live there with his wife?"

Rebecca spoke up. "These are crazy people, Melanie."

Bob filled in more gaps. "I'd guess Marlena was trying for a big payoff here, so she could disappear and live in South America. She's going to claim she was threatened by the Russians who hired her. Bring them the deal or else." He shook his head. "This case could drag on for years."

That was upsetting. "So what will happen to the mansion? Can it be sold? Will Olmsted still have the listing?"

Bob Martin spoke with the expertise of a former Olmsted employee. "Olmsted can't sell now to the Russian buyer. The Harringtons will likely take it to another agency. And with this much bad publicity, the zoning board may refuse to allow any changes at all."

I felt a wave of relief. " Have you listened to the tape? Karen had evidence of structural damage in the foundation, covered up over the years. She threatened to expose the damage. Now everyone will know. That should lower the price the Harringtons can get, and cut down on changes the city will allow." Then I remembered Chloe and the race.

"It was Hugh Clark who knocked me over at the Huntley race," I said. "I'm sure of it. I saw him at an art gallery opening a few weeks ago. But after today, I realized he was at the race. White spindly legs in big shorts. He pushed me over. My daughter will be thrilled that my name can be cleared. And she won't have to deal with bullies."

"You risked your life for your daughter?" asked Chilton. I couldn't tell if he was impressed or disgusted. "You've got some powerful guardian angel. "

I shivered like it was below freezing in there. "I guess. Guns are terrifying. My daughter gave me the boost I needed to stay with the investigation. I had to stop the teasing at school about her mom."

Chilton and Martin looked bewildered. "Long story. Good ending. But I'd better get the gossip started now to clear my name." I took out my phone to text.

Bob put up his hand. "Not until we release the information about the arrests.

Everything stays here." Chilton gave me an evil smile.

"Melanie, don't you need to call your husband and let him know where you are?" Chilton wanted Daniel to keep me out of crime scenes in New York City.

Rebecca jumped in. "We're done here, right? Melanie can tell him when she gets home. She needs to rest. And this is personal, really not police business." She gave Bob Martin and May-Ling a dazzling smile. "It's been a pleasure to see how you guys work, keeping us safe. Thanks a million." She pulled on my arm. "It's time to go."

Chapter Twenty-Seven

The police announced the arrests of Hugh, Patty, and Marlena the next day. My story appeared hours later. *I'm the Unexpected Hero in Arrest of Park Avenue Mom Killers.*

"Harold, that's wrong. I got myself trapped. I'm not a hero. I just got lucky again," I argued futilely. Harold interrupted me with a booming voice.

"The Wild Westsider is having its biggest day ever. Great headlines get readers. Don't argue with genius and the voice of experience."

We did have over fifty thousand readers, so maybe he was right, though I'd never tell him. The *Times* even picked up my story and gave me a byline in an article on the front page of the Metro section. *New York* magazine interviewed me. The terrifying part (worse than a bullet exploding inches away) was the calls from TV shows. I found a manager to handle that. We agreed to wait until the screenplay was ready to be sold. Our agent, Suzanne Fleisher, was wheeling and dealing. I had nightmares about being in front of an audience and drool falling from my mouth.

The gym got over a hundred inquiries about fencing classes again. But there would be no new members. It was too hot in our outdated gym.

Devon was still away. We'd ferociously sent rewrites back and forth. I submitted the screenplay, *Park Avenue Murder* to Suzanne a week ago. Suzanne called a few days later to say we needed to have a meeting.

I'd first met Suzanne at a cocktail party more than a year ago, the same night I'd met Devon. She still wore her platinum/gray hair in a sharp pageboy cut at the chin. Today, she also wore a Cheshire Cat smile.

"There are several places interested. A big production company that sells to Netflix, among other stations, wants to bring you out to LA. They want to see how you'd do on a tour to promote a TV movie. Why don't you read this out loud." She handed me two pages of copy.

A white-gloved Park Avenue building and an invite to a packed Open House was the last place I expected to find a dead body. Forty impeccably dressed and loaded buyers checked out the thirty-foot-long living room and eight hundred-square-foot terrace. When I found the strangled body of a beautiful real estate agent and fellow mom in the servants' quarters, my first reaction was to run to the nearest bathroom. Being a crime reporter and hating blood is a problem. The perfect elite of Park Avenue annoyed about this delay in their lucrative lives, were questioned. Karen Sheldon's athletic, beautifully groomed body still lay on the bathroom floor, when I learned the victim had just gotten an exclusive right to sell one of the last Gold Coast mansions in Manhattan for $45 million.

I looked up. Suzanne wasn't smiling. Not good. I kept reading through descriptions of apartments and suspects and then the violent and dramatic end of the story.

The architect for a secret project to subdivide the mansion and sell to Russian oligarchs invited me for a tour. Going alone was a dumb move. When the mild-looking architect drew a gun, I was doomed. I grabbed a fireplace poker before I desperately slithered into a secret closet.

When I finished, Suzanne lowered her turquoise-framed reading glasses.

"Well," she cleared her throat, "Not to worry." I hadn't been till now. "The publisher will get you help with your delivery. Writers are not actors. No one expects them to be."

"You're not building my confidence, Suzanne."

Suzanne ignored me. "There's a lot of interest from more than one production house. If you agree to do a tour, we'll set you up with all the bidders. If they think you're marketable, along with your story, I'll have a nice bidding war going. The price that Netflix will cough up could increase enormously. Maybe double it. Which would double what Little Brown will pay for the book rights. It's all up to you." She looked at me menacingly. She did not want to lose fifteen percent of a lot of money. But how much?

"So, can I tell them you're ready to fly to LA any time? You'll have to have coaching, clearly." Her holier-than-thou tone made me want to choke her.

"Double what amount?" Not choking her just yet. "I have to call Devon. I can't make any decisions without him; both our names are on there. How much are we talking about?"

Suzanne put her glasses back on and smiled slowly at me over the top of the shimmering frames. "High six figures. If you wow them, definitely seven figures. And then there might be Netflix. You could buy a condo."

I gulped. "Not after this. I'm never going to another open house." I breathed deeply. How long would I have to be away?"

"Two weeks, maybe less. The publisher will put you up in a nice hotel suite, maybe on the beach. Send a car. The bidding production companies will talk to you about your story, interview you. They want to know what you're like. What you eat. Why do you study fencing? What does your husband think of all this? They'll ask personal questions. The juicier the answers, the higher the amount." Suzanne's eyes watered, moved by the possibility of so much money.

"Do they want Devon also?" She shook her head.

"He's not the hero. He didn't almost get killed. He didn't find the body or know the woman. He's the second name on the script. Not that he couldn't be there to talk about the script with the TV writers. I'm sure we could get him a hotel room."

She looked at me knowingly, as if to say she knew my status with Devon was not just co-writer. What she knew or thought didn't matter to me; rumors and gossip were good for her business. For me, going to L.A. was a dream come true. But dealing with Daniel would be a nightmare, if not the final battle in our marriage. And what would Chloe think?

I hoped Daniel could be swayed by the money. He'd barely said a word to me once he learned about the gun and spear fight at the OK Corral, otherwise known as the Harrington Mansion. Only a terse, "Now you've done it." I didn't ask what he meant.

What Chloe thought mattered more. I remembered something Rebecca said.

"Men don't suffer this guilt BS the way women self-flagellate. *I work to support my family, but I feel so guilty because I'm not home*, stuff.

"I have to check my schedule," I told Suzanne.

"I'll need to know by close of today to have bargaining power." Her stern look advised me not to blow this.

* * *

"Can I come with you? Can we FaceTime? How long will you be away?" Chloe's little face was scrunched up. We crossed the park.

"No, it wouldn't work this time. I would love to have you there, but I'll be too busy. We can FaceTime as often as you want, though. And it will be two weeks, maybe less."

Chloe knew a little of what had happened at the mansion. She didn't want me to leave her now. I got silent. I could say no to the trip. We walked past the Great Lawn, with skyscrapers shimmering in the distance.

"I'll see if I can do this by teleconferencing," I said, squeezing her hand. "I know this isn't a great time for me to be away."

Chloe swung my hand back and forth wildly. "Oh, Mom! You don't understand. How about...I get to do as many sleepovers as I want with Samantha when you're away. And we go to Disney World on my birthday?"

I burst into laughter. "You have a great future as a negotiator. You've got a deal."

I gave her little shoulders a hug. "As long as Dad agrees."

"Oh, Dad will say yes. No problem."

Chloe's confidence was contagious. I texted Suzanne.

Green light. I'll go. Bargain away.

Immediately, terror swooped in through my stomach and up to my heart and head, nearly forcing me to fall onto a bench. Now I had to face Los Angeles with my old baggage of not being clever enough, gorgeous enough, tough enough. Chloe would do better taking meetings than me. She always thought ten steps ahead and spoke up. Was this because I hadn't made her feel safe?

I pictured Rebecca slapping her head, or mine. *Cut it out. Your kid knows what she needs. And asks for it. That's healthy. Just because you can't, doesn't make it bad.*

Chloe wanted sleepovers. Maybe I did, too.

There was still unfinished business because I had the repulsive CD with the girls at the mansion. Karen might, in fact, have used what she knew about the Harrington grandson giving parties to get the exclusive listing to sell. But the Harrington family wasn't guilty of murder. I still had a problem. If I gave the video to the cops, that would risk exposure for young girls. I didn't care about protecting the parents. I only knew one person who could get this settled discreetly.

* * *

"Cornelia, I need to talk to you. Not on the phone."

"Melanie, if you ever learn anything from me, which I'm beginning to doubt, it will be telephone manners. How are you, etc? The Chinese do this beautifully in their tea ceremonies. Negotiations after. The Russians drink vodka."

"Do you want a bottle of Grey Goose? I can afford it, I think. Once the contracts are signed."

Major sigh. "You will never learn. I wave the white flag. Come over in an hour. I hope this is important enough for me to reschedule a pedicure with Roxanne."

"It is."

* * *

"Come in, Ms. Deming. Nice to see you."

"Hello, Thelma. Good to see you, too." I stepped into the apartment from the private landing. Cornelia's was the only apartment on the floor of this

216

Park Avenue exclusive building. Nothing sold for less than ten million. Hers would go for twenty-five mil. The wide carpeted staircase in the large entryway led to four bedrooms and then outside to a solarium and wrap-around terrace.

Thelma, the head housekeeper for many years, was in a white uniform. She led me into the library. Cornelia was on the phone.

She waved me to a seat in a velvet armchair. I took out the video.

"So that's what this is about," Cornelia said as she got off the phone. She took off her Dolce and Gabbana reading glasses. She had many pairs. These were deep purple.

"Something has to be done. Going to the police, which was your solution, is not going to help. The girls will get in trouble and what's the point? Eric Harrington didn't kill Karen. But he does get underage girls drunk, and there was probably sex involved, though it's not on the video. It has to be stopped. And you can do it."

Cornelia gazed at the hundreds of books in the library; none read, just ordered by her decorator.

"I know the grandfather, Nelson Harrington since my father played cribbage with him. I don't want my father to be involved. He has too much already with my mother's health." She looked through a large leather bound book, She picked up the phone.

"Nelson, yes, it's Cornelia. How *are* you? And how is Greta?"

Cornelia mouthed I'll call you later. I left the video with her.

* * *

Cornelia accomplished miracles on several fronts. Eric Harrington was sent to work with a distant uncle in Australia, where, as she said, "They will punish physically if anything happens to their daughters. So he will keep his pants zipped. And he has no mansion to use for partying. His budget has been cut back."

"I love the way you work, Cornelia. The rich and powerful get things done so well when they decide to do good."

She cleared her throat. "I think you're implying rich people are not always on the side of the law or charity, but I don't have time to argue. Do you want to hear the rest?"

"Of course. And I wasn't talking about you. You know that."

"Don't pander to me, Melanie. It won't work. The second part is that the Harrington Mansion is being sold to the Croft School. They had made a lower offer than the Russians. The papers will be signed this week. No brokers will be involved. It will be a private sale,"

My heart soared. Tears filled my eyes. The Croft School was a not-for-profit school and foundation for children with severe learning disabilities.

"I bow before your abilities, Queen Cornelia. You have a heart of gold. Eighteen carat, of course." Tears fell. "Thank you. I appreciate what you've done. Now I can sleep better."

"Well, it would be good if that was with Daniel, don't you think?"

Of course, she had to get in a dig.

Since my near-death encounter at the mansion, Daniel was out most evenings. When I did wake up, he was asleep on the couch.

Chapter Twenty-Eight

The Garden of Eden Restaurant in Santa Monica, one block off the beach, was exactly that. Glass doors opened to a terrace bursting with flowers. The ocean sparkled of course, just visible through the always open doors. I didn't see how anyone could get work done with this perpetual summer. I pretended to study the scripted answers to forty questions sitting in front of me. The publisher's PR department gave me the script. Sound completely unrehearsed, they said. Also clever, funny, and relatable (a very big word in PR), all while promoting the movie. Impossible even for Meryl Streep, who I heard lived right nearby in a canyon somewhere.

Don't memorize these answers, they said. But how else could I get through these meetings? My best idea was to hire an actress to play me, do the interviews. Someone sexy yet approachable, like Kyra Sedgwick or Julia Roberts.

Or anyone walking down the street, for that matter. This was L.A. Everyone was an actress or a model. Suddenly, a thirty-something in shorts and a T-shirt, and wedge sneakers, highlighted gold hair tumbling down her back, strode by. I jumped up and ran outside.

"Are you an actress?" I asked. " I need someone to play me in interviews about my screenplay. Are you available this week?"

Her very pretty face smiled. "Of course. Usually, people go through my agent, but here's my card. My rate is five hundred dollars a day. Upfront. Just email me a script." She sashayed down the block. Sophia Henley.

I trotted back inside, feeling relieved for a second. My agent would definitely nix the idea. She didn't understand that LA. was a bad place to be alone when you were inclined to feel insecure about clothes, weight, stomach, legs, nails, hair, a tan, laugh lines, frown lines, perkiness, warmth—pretty much everything about the way I looked and sounded.

So I was living my dream while at the same time trying to stomp out loud voices that said go home, you can't do this, who do you think you are? There were four companies interested in our *Killer on Park Avenue* screenplay. The money could be very big if even two made offers and they bid against each other. I had appointments with all four production companies and already two wanted me back a second time. I spoke to Chloe every day. She wanted to know every detail, including what I wore to each meeting, party, and interview. She bragged about me to her friends.

"Mom, guess what? Everyone at school says you're a hero. You can stay out there. But not too long. Or I come too."

"I'd love that. Venice Beach is a great place, with lots of fun shopping and performers, right on the sand. This time is mostly work, though. And I'm only a hero because you believed in me, Chloe. I couldn't have done it without you." She rated my outfits on her computer.

Daniel was another story.

"You don't care about this family," he raged. "First, you put yourself in that mansion as a target. Now you leave Chloe for weeks. I want a separation. One of us will have to move out."

My heart crumbled. "Is this really just about my being gone for two weeks? Let's go to a counselor when I get back. We owe Chloe that, don't you think? And all our years together."

Daniel breathed heavily into the phone. He sounded like a fire-breathing dragon, or a dying rhino. "I'll consider a counselor to help us separate, for Chloe's sake. But I'm moving out when you get back. You see how it feels." And he slammed down the phone.

I allowed myself to cry for a few minutes. I was shocked he said he'd move out. The apartment had been with his family for fifty years. He really wanted away from me. Or he wanted to sleep with Nadine every night. Nadine likely convinced him to divorce me so he'd get a chunk of money. Nadine always looked for the money. Daniel had deliberately ruined my California dream big time.

My head throbbed. I couldn't afford to think about this now. I had a job to do here, and I was going to do it. The hell with him. He'd never been happy about my success even though this time, the money could be big enough to change our lives. Split two ways, it would not stretch forever. I'd have to find another story and another screenplay.

I put on the annoying gorgeous guru tape who promised happiness if I just said yes to everything.

Daniel was the brave one. He was doing me a favor. Happiness in love was out there, an oasis waiting for me I'd never been brave enough to reach for. My vision was messed up with fear. According to the gorgeous guru, Daniel was giving me the hard shove I needed toward a colossally wonderful life.

It was all too unknown. How could I be sure. The one thing I knew at this moment was to put a full stop on any thoughts about my marriage and commit to this moment in Los Angeles. I had to be super confident, fascinating and girl-next- door sexy in front of these studio types.

Los Angeles studio executives' style ranged from Italian suits to Larry David casual. The male writers did the grungy, several days growth, T-shirt, and jeans. How clean depended on rank. The women execs all had perfect hair and nails, whether they wore skinny jeans with boots and tailored shirts or suits. The publisher paid for my clothes so I would look like them. My hair was enhanced with highlights; my nails were longer than usual and dark red. Suddenly I sported leggings with silk blouses, long chains, thigh-length sweaters—Joyce artist look. One suit with red and pink silk blouses. The mom was gone.

I barely recognized myself heading out to these interviews.

"You have to be realer than real," said Lisa, my hired coach, stylist, and escort, as we role-played the interviews. "Your story is great, but it has to *sound* great. Be *in* the story as you tell it." Easy for her to say. I did stop saying 'umm' every other word. And biting my nails. I was still a nervous wreck, gulping California poppy and passionflower.

Devon was on an assignment, flying somewhere in the Pacific. He'd "try to get there" was all he'd been able to promise. I'd been here five days, and

I had no idea how I came across, whether they would make large offers because they saw me as a valuable audience-building asset. Or withdraw their interest in disgust. One of the studio types, with a tan that looked painted on, said I'd come across more sympathetic if I'd been wounded at the mansion. He suggested putting my arm in a sling. I nearly walked out.

All around me in The Garden of Eden, was the low hum of deals being made and gossip being exchanged. I was alive and healthy. Chloe was a blessing. The sun was always shining. We had almost sold a screenplay. It was a done deal, except for the final number. And I helped to find, and hopefully convict, killers. I was staying at a great hotel, all expenses paid. And I was sitting on the patio of a trendy restaurant, looking at a crazy rainbow of begonias. *Stay in this moment only.*

Rebecca called. She was bubbly. I didn't tell her about Daniel. She was too happy.

"Things are great. Paul dropped the Oregon idea, or his new buxom professor dropped him. Either way, we're staying. The poet is as good in bed as I thought he would be. I chatted on the phone with Detective Bob Martin. Don't know if he's straight or bi, but I don't care." Rebecca's stories made me laugh.

"You're incorrigible and fabulous. Have fun."

"You too. Even if Devon's not there, there are lots of hot guys in LA."

"Right. If I was you." I hung up and took another cleansing breath of ocean breeze. I turned back to the damn script that wasn't really a script.

"So, you actually study. How impressive."

I knew that voice. It made my stomach clench, my heart race. and I felt flushed all over my body. I looked up and saw a tanned, blue-eyed man with come hither lips in well-cut chinos and a form-fitting T-shirt that showed his muscular arms.

"Somebody has to make the money around here," I said with a laugh. "Other people get to take vacations and eat in exotic locations and call that work."

Devon grinned and sat down—way too close, considering this was a popular place, catering to the health-conscious movie crowd. Raw and vegan everything, from Almost Meat steak tartare to raw cold pizza (as bad as it sounded). Any close contact here was like taking out a billboard on the freeway.

I drank in Devon's warm, compassionate face. Then his expression hardened, and he brought his lips close to my ear. "If you ever pull that kind of near-death stunt again without me, I'm out." The cloud passed, and he broke into his heart-melting grin. "And besides, I can't justify taking any money if you take all the risks. You make me look bad." He put his arm casually next to mine on the armrest, so only we knew we were burning up being this close together.

"I'm serious, though, about not taking half the money this time," he said earnestly. "You're the hot commodity, you took the risks, you're the story. I'll take a guest writer fee." I nodded in agreement.

"I thought a different cut, like sixty-forty? I mean, I have a daughter to support. " I felt like every greedy person I'd ever made fun of. "It should be enough for both of us if I sell myself right." I quickly added. But Devon smiled broadly and put his hand on my arm.

"I'm already sold," he said softly."seventy-five, twenty-five will do just fine." He didn't care about the money. He cared about me.

He covered my hand with his. Tears threatened, but my heart opened. Maybe it was inevitable. The gods put Devon in my path. Daniel was ready to leave me and make Chloe a two-home child. And what I had with Devon had all along felt so right. Maybe he was the oasis I needed, but I'd barely allowed myself to consider him anything but a temporary mirage. A wonderful man like Devon had flown halfway around the world to be here right now with me. No mirage, no fantasy.

In another minute, I wouldn't be able to resist him, here at this table surrounded by pots of begonias and bougainvillea and Hollywood marketing types.

"Can we get out of here?" he asked as he locked his fingers in mine, and his lips came tantalizingly close.

"I thought you'd never ask," I murmured, panting.

And we did.

About the Author

Nancy Good is the best-selling author of the How to Love a Difficult Man series, which has been published in 12 languages. She has appeared on Oprah, CNN, Geraldo and across the United States and England. Nancy is a lifelong Upper West Side resident of NYC who loves biking in Central Park and along the Hudson River, jumping on ferries to bike the boroughs, and hiking and cross-country skiing in the Catskills and the Berkshires. As a pianist and singer, she has performed over fifty times with choirs in Carnegie Hall as well as in concert halls around the world.

AUTHOR WEBSITE:
  nancygood.com

Also by Nancy Good

How to Love a Difficult Man (St Martin's Press)

Slay Your Own Dragons (St Martin's Press)

How to Live with the Difficult Man You Love (St Martin's Press)

Meditations for Loving a Difficult Man (Adams Press)

Killer Calories (Level Best Books)